emerge 18

ABOUT *emerge*

In its eighteenth year, *emerge* is an annual publication produced by students, alumni, faculty, and industry guests of the Writer's Studio. Students are assigned to teams and, over a four-month period, work with the publisher, editors, designers, our printer, and local booksellers to produce, market, and sell this anthology.

ABOUT THE WRITER'S STUDIO

The Writer's Studio is an award-winning creative writing program at Simon Fraser University that provides writers with mentorship, instruction, and hands-on book publishing experience. Over the course of a year, students work alongside a community of writers with a mentor, developing their writing through regular manuscript workshops and readings. Many of our alumni have become successful authors, and have gone on to careers in the publishing industry.

The Writer's Studio 2018 mentors:
Hiromi Goto—*Speculative Fiction and Writing for Young Adults*
Kevin Chong—*Fiction*
Betsy Warland—*Poetry and Lyric Prose*
JJ Lee—*Narrative Non-Fiction*

The Writer's Studio Online 2017–2018 mentors:
Eileen Cook—*Speculative Fiction and Writing for Young Adults*
Jen Sookfong Lee—*Fiction*
Jordan Abel—*Poetry and Lyric Prose*
Claudia Cornwall—*Narrative Non-Fiction*
Stella Harvey—*Fiction and Personal Narrative*

sfu.ca/write

emerge 18

THE WRITER'S STUDIO ANTHOLOGY

Carleigh Baker
Foreword

Simon Fraser University, Vancouver, B.C.

Cover Design: Solo Corps Creative
Cover Illustration: Kitty Widjaja
Typesetting and Interior Design: Solo Corps Creative
Printing: Friesens Corporation

Printed in Canada

LIBRARY AND ARCHIVES CANADA CATALOGUING IN PUBLICATION

emerge 18: The Writer's Studio anthology /
Foreword by Carleigh Baker

ISSN 1925-8267
ISBN 978-1-77287-048-0 (paperback)
ISBN 978-1-77287-049-7 (ebook)

A cataloging record for this publication is available from Library and Archives Canada.

Creative Writing | SFU Continuing Studies
Simon Fraser University
515 West Hastings Street
Vancouver, B.C., Canada, V6B 5K3
sfu.ca/write

SFU Publications
1300 West Mall Centre
8888 University Drive
Burnaby, B.C., Canada, V5A 1S6

To Wayde Compton:
Director (2012–2018) and
mentor (2006–2009)
of the Writer's Studio

You invited us to speak from the margins,
to workshop with compassion, and
to write with open hearts and minds.
You will always be part of the TWS community.

"The universe is made up of stories, not atoms."

—Muriel Rukeyser

Contents

Carleigh Baker xiii Foreword

NON-FICTION

Julie Gordon 3 Learning to Listen
Ann Wilson 7 Becoming
Vicki McLeod 12 Long Night, with Flowers
Paula Wellings 16 Two Fish in a Tank
Joanna Baxter 19 Wrecked
Carolyne Montgomery 24 Tsusiat Falls
Maura Wong 27 OMG!
Emi Sasagawa 31 Selfish Love
Nicole Jess 36 Pedestal
Evie Gold 41 A Determining Train Ride
Marian Dodds 46 The Man in the Cinnamon Suit
Stewart Dickson 51 The Story That Never Ends
Sriram Iyer 56 The Busyness of Unemployment
Averill Groeneveld-Meijer 60 Circus
Tamara Jong 65 The Will
Nadia Ashley 68 "Say Goodbye to Daddy"
Maureen Duteau 72 Old Hands
Georgia Swayze 77 Daddy Issues
Joseph Onodi 82 The Bicycle

FICTION

Lynn J. Salmon 89 Loss of the *Sea Dragon*
Dayna Mahannah 94 This Girl Jane
Gillian Tregidgo 99 Seagull

Debbie Bateman	104	Your Body Was Made for This
Jonathan M. Bessette	108	Freud to Frisco
Felix Wong	112	Chinese Funerals Are Weird
Shane Leydon	117	Three Flags
Kate Flannery	121	The Rat
Matt Brandenburg	125	Bone Chandelier
Avalon Bourne	128	The Other Woman
Isabel Spiegel	133	Refuge
DeeDee LeGrand-Hart	135	White Lion
Dianne Carruthers	140	Schadenfreude
Griffin Tedeschini	145	Sticktown
Ann Svendsen	150	The Man Who Came Through the Window
Karla Kosowan	154	The Lady in the Cake
Spencer Lucas Oakes	158	Team Building
Kathleen Kerwin	163	San Domenico
Erica Hiroko	168	Two pieces

POETRY

Tamar Rubin	175	Tablet Fragments
Sareh Donaher	180	Five poems
Deborah Harford	185	Five poems
Rowen EB	190	Three poems
April Lewis	195	Knotting Memory
Alex Duncan	197	A Relationship in Three Parts
Brad Akeroyd	202	Two poems
Sabyasachi Nag	207	Three poems
Katie McGarry	212	Three poems
Sarah Mostaghel	217	Five poems
Megan Frazer	222	Mended
Lorne Daniel	227	Three poems
Razielle Aigen	232	Mountains
Erin Brown-John	237	Matthew

SPECULATIVE AND YOUNG ADULT FICTION

Brook Warner Jensen 245 Baking with Betsy
Benjamin Thiede 250 Stay Out of the Tall Grass
D. R. Spicer 255 Application Reboot
Wendy Naava Smolash 259 The Institute
Spencer Miller 264 Forever in Warfare My Heart Is
Yuki Abovearth 269 Chariot
Lula García 274 Patos
Kimber Anderson 279 Mystery of the Jack of Diamonds
Zahida Rahemtulla 284 Julio's House
Miraya Engelage 287 The Crescent
Elise Thiessen 292 Green Eyes
Samara Malkin 297 Porcelain
K. J. Kwon 300 The Bully
Koreen Heaver 304 Grounded
Lorraine Erickson 308 The Night
Rory Andrew Stevens 312 Fission
317 *Contributors*
336 *Production credits*
337 *Acknowledgments*
338 *Artist's statement*

Foreword

Writing is medicine. It's also painful as hell, which makes writing the Buckley's of creativity. Feel the burn, and eventually, feel better.

Here is your glamorous metaphor to begin this foreword—writing as expectorant. Gross, but let me tell you, these authors know what I'm talking about. They have just survived a concentrated dose of the writerly process that civilians imagine to be magical and glamorous, but is actually anything but. These authors have become masters of the slack-jawed stare, the pants-free revision, and the Cheeto-encrusted sob, sacred techniques you will never see on any cheery online "Tips for Writers" list. They've taken fifteen trips to the fridge for snacks, and they now know the secret to success. Not good snacks, though they certainly help. The secret is going back. Back to the page. Over and over and over again, until the story or poem is finished. This is the only thing that separates the dabblers from the writers. Finishing.

I feel a little awkward presiding over this collection of work like some kind of expert. The writers are the experts here. They are holding court in new worlds, and grappling with imagination. In Koreen Heaver's "Grounded," Emma creates a healing meal from the earth, but its ingredients are foreign and unrecognizable. This dialogue between the familiar and the strange encourages readers to reconsider our own perceptions of reality. Members of the non-fiction cohort have crafted memory into compelling stories. An excerpt from Joseph Onodi 's "Indian Summer" captures the freedom of a child's first bicycle, a victory made more poignant amidst the stark poverty that colonial power has left in its wake. And the poets, they've been busy. In Sabyasachi Nag's "Strangers," a chance encounter finds two women seeking solace in the river, grieving the loss of wild nasturtiums. A moment in time cracked open to reveal staggering intimacy, through the precise use of language. These works and others have been carefully selected and honed to entertain and teach, to build bridges and widen perception.

Since my time at the Studio in 2012, I've always considered the program to be like the mafia—but the friendly kind. There are no shakedowns. No one ends up sleeping with the fishes. But what I did find is a *famiglia* who understands the sacrifices I've made to get here and is ready to celebrate my victories and throw shade at my critics. Discreetly, natch. Community is also medicine.

To the authors, I'm not going to lie: this gig doesn't get any easier. But please keep speaking your truth, always. Welcome to the *famiglia*. And for those of you about to read, buckle up. These are stories and poems crafted with sprawling imagination and fearless honesty. Holy crap, writing is hard. And sharing your writing is terrifying. The fine humans represented between these pages have spent a year doing just that. For some it was new, and for others, a refresher. But for all of them, respect is due. Give them your eyes and your hearts.

—*Carleigh Baker*, Coast Salish territories, 2018

Non-fiction

Julie Gordon

Learning to Listen

AN EXCERPT

I turn off the island highway onto the unpaved logging road that heads west toward Zeballos, a tiny fishing village at the mouth of the inlet that shares the same name. I have been driving for almost six hours now and although this last stretch of the drive is only 40 km, it feels the longest. I hadn't anticipated the giant potholes, exaggerated after a long rainy season. Eventually, the road becomes Macquinna Drive, Zeballos's main street, and winds its way through town to the base of the inlet. When I arrive, the sun has faded and the streets are empty, a heavy mist hangs in the air, and it seems as though this part of the world is forgotten or somehow suspended in time.

In the morning I wake early and head to the dock to meet Victoria Wells. Victoria belongs to the Ehattaseht First Nation. She is a language activist and learner who has made it her life's work to revitalize her language as well as that of the neighbouring Nuchatlaht Tribe. The two communities share much in common: they have an overlapping territory, a common history, and many shared traditions. They also speak similar dialects of the same language, and those languages can therefore be archived as one. I am here on behalf of a client—First Nations Foundation—that funds the language archiving project, to observe and record Victoria's progress.

Victoria has a striking beauty that seems to derive from her grace—bronze skin over wide cheekbones, straight black hair streaked with grey stretching down her back, and deep-set, clear eyes. She tells me to call her Vicki as I climb into her little aluminum boat, and soon we are underway, heading for Espinoza Inlet and the village of Oclucje.

Oclucje is a traditional village site of the Nuchatlaht people, and it's also the official reservation. It houses about twenty of the two hundred or so members year round. Others live off-reserve in Zeballos, Campbell River, or further afield. We are heading there to meet Alban Michael, who, at eighty-two, is the oldest living member of his Nation. He is also the only remaining one to speak his language fluently, and that makes him critical to Victoria's archiving work.

The boat ride reveals what is perhaps the most pristine coastal environment I have ever witnessed. Its wild beauty takes my breath away. Giant conifers tower over a rugged coastline. Deserted white sand beaches and endless fjords and inlets define the shore. The ocean is calm and clear; diamonds sparkle on its surface in the early light. Aside from the steady drone of the motor, the only sound comes from birds, the plaintive cries of gulls overhead, a high-pitched *chip chip* of a passing eagle, and an occasional squawk when a heron takes flight.

We arrive at a lush and verdant enclave dotted with a dozen or so homes. Alban's is a short walk up from the shore. Waiting for us in the open doorway, he greets us with a wide grin that changes the direction of the weathered cross-hatching on his face. Alban lives alone now—his wife Rose passed away a couple of years ago—and I get the impression that he welcomes visits from Vicki and the language volunteers. It gives him a chance to speak the words of a language he loves but no longer uses day to day.

We head upstairs to the kitchen, where Julie Smith, one of Vicki's volunteers, is waiting with a pot of strong, hot tea. Vicki has brought lunch and I help her lay it out on the table. Cold cuts, buns, lettuce, apples, store-bought cookies—these offerings are a gesture of appreciation for Alban's time, and as I unpack them I silently wish I had thought to bring something as well. While we eat, we make small talk. "How was the boat ride?" "About time that rain let up." "They really need to pave that Zeballos road." Alban speaks only in Nuchatlaht. Vicki and Julie switch between their language and English, translating for me from time to time. When I speak, Alban watches me shyly from the corner of his eye.

After lunch Vicki cleans up while Julie sets up the recording equipment. She places a microphone on a stand in front of Alban. Across the table from him she opens a laptop, connects the mike and computer with a small box that she tells me is an audio interface, and then sits down facing Alban.

Thinking that this is the moment I have come for, I get out my camera and take a few pictures while they set up. I am expecting Alban and Julie to simulate the language-recording process while I observe and document it. Instead, Alban begins to speak in a soft, low tone. His pale eyes stay focused straight ahead; his voice is steady and clear, his tone serious. Julie stops fiddling with the recording equipment and, together with Vicki, sits back in her chair to listen intently. Following their lead, I set my camera down and wait.

Alban speaks in Nuchatlaht for a very, very long time. I try not to glance at the kitchen clock, but after about twenty minutes, I start to get restless. With the lunch and small talk, we are already well beyond the time I had allotted for the visit, and we have still not begun to record the process. I am not staying in Zeballos overnight and I need to make it to Alert Bay. I don't like driving in the dark and am not looking forward to navigating that road again, but I know it would be disrespectful to interrupt, so I try to listen too. Eventually, I start to relax. Alban's voice is calming and the sound of his language has a hypnotic quality. I soon find myself immersed in the moment, and although I can't understand anything he's saying, it becomes a meditation of sorts.

Finally, Alban stops talking and nods his head forward subtly to indicate he's done. The room fills with silence, and Vicki puts her hand on top of his and squeezes lightly before she turns to me. "I think he has just told you his life's story." She translates as best she can what Alban has spoken about. Vicki is not fluent, so she repeats his story in fragments.

She tells me he talked of his childhood here, of what life was like before colonization, and how his family lived in a traditional way. He also spoke about how life changed afterwards. He talked about being taken away to residential school in Tofino, what it was like there, and how happy he was to return home. And he spoke with gratitude about his ancestors, especially his mother, who spoke only in Nuchatlaht with him when he returned. "This," Vicki explains, "is why he retained his language while many did not."

Vicki's tone is one of astonishment and her eyes are moist. It's clear that she is deeply moved by what has just happened. I also see that she was not expecting it any more than I was. "I think he has been waiting for this," she says. "I think he has wanted someone to listen to this story for a very long time."

We wrap the day up with a brief simulation of the language-archiving process so I can make notes and take pictures, but the exercise now feels more like a formality than the main reason for my being here. Julie speaks a series of simple English words off a list—mother, house, kitchen—and Alban repeats each one into the microphone in Nuchatlaht so they can be uploaded into the digital archive. These recordings will help a future generation of Nuchatlaht people communicate in their own language. But they don't tell Alban's whole story, the story he shared with us and that we did not record that day.

When I leave Zeballos that evening, it's nearly sunset. I drive the potholed gravel road while the light fades and the sky turns to the deepest blue. As I drive, I go over the events of the day and think about everything that happened. Mostly, I think about the gift that Alban has shared with me. And I think about how my own impatience nearly got in the way of being able to give back the only things I had to offer: my time and my desire to listen.

Ann Wilson

Becoming

AN EXCERPT

The house breathed a deep shuddering breath.

[Haaa...aaahh...mmmmmm]

She stretched and creaked against the sharp east wind. She liked herself better when she was a granary. Her windows were open. Swallows made nests under her roof. Mice and racoons raised their families here too. Now, with this family who'd put in windows and locked the doors, hammered tin sheets on the outside and painted her white, she felt she had to hold her breath, and hold her belly in.

The deer in the pasture looked up and curled their ears in the direction of the creaking. [Hmm] The house sat starkly in the moonlight as usual. Nothing to worry about. The dog was sleeping. They bent their heads down again to the clumps of sweet sedge.

The house knew Rose was awake too. She saw the child at the upstairs bedroom window, listening to the song the big spruce trees were making with the east wind.

[Haaaaaaaaaaaaaaaaaawhooooooooooshhhhhhh]

The owl in the tall cedar tree near the house turned her head and blinked her large yellow eyes at the child. She saw the girl imagining, flying, flying with the wind through the branches in the deep whispering roar.

"The child is learning to see in the dark too," said the owl to the house. "Who is this little one becoming?"

"I wonder too," the house answered, the sound of worry in her voice.

"The girl prefers to be outside with us," the owl said.

"Yes, I know," the house sighed. "There is much that is in the dark inside."

"Now she will dream," said the owl. She watched the girl climb back into her bed. The dog slipped under the covers too.

Rose was nine, maybe ten years old, when she noticed she had grown a shadow.

"Huuuh!"

She felt it inch larger each time her mother found something wrong with her. Her mother was angry with her when Rose was there and angry when she was not. Rose thought it was because she was just not right as a girl. She laughed too loud. She wrestled with her brother. She asked too many questions and didn't listen to her mother. She refused to give up her rubber boots and she always forgot to sit with her knees together.

"Phhluuuuh."

But more and more, Rose thought she was wrong because she was … herself.

"Maybe if I was invisible … hmmmm?"

She learned to slip silent as a ghost out the back door to the big spruce by the fence line. She swung one leg over its low branch and climbed up high to her nest on two thick limbs growing out close together. There Rose could see out and not be seen. She folded her legs in front of her and leaned into the trunk to listen to the instruction of wind and spruce branches. She stared out, seeing, seeing, wondering, wondering who she was becoming.

Rose worshipped trees, and the wind, and doves murmuring their prayers at dawn, and …

But she had not learned the wisdom of keeping these things to herself.

"RRRRRRROOOOSSSE. Get in here."

Rose ran to the house when her mother called her to set the table. Her father was in from the fields. She gathered up her shadow, sat up straight and invisible at the supper table, until she heard it …

[Haaaaaaaaaaaaaaaaaaawhooooooooooshhhhhhh]

… the hushed roar of the wind and the spruce trees just before that fresh July evening breeze entered the hot kitchen through the screen door on the porch. Rose watched it lift the black curls from her brother's damp forehead and press her father's sky-blue shirt sleeve against his leathery arm. But her father sat, unmoved, at the end of the table, holding his cup against his lips. Her mother twisted her mouth and watched her older brother earnestly sipping his coffee, copying his father. Her little sister chased a slippery sliver of peach around her bowl.

It was then, when Rose stretched her arms up and up and backward in this big love, in an impossible arc, in her body's reckless, innocent forgetfulness, that the back of her mother's hand struck Rose's open mouth.

The dampness of spit sprawled across Rose's cheek. Dishes lifted off the chrome kitchen table and crashed to the floor … it was Rose's legs … her knees bucked and thrashed against the table, desperate for escape … her mother's hands grabbed and scratched … her mother's mouth, a wordless purple gash, opened and closed.

One of Rose's legs sprang out from under the table, carried her—*crash*—through the screen door … her bare feet pounded past the cattle barns to the cool sandy lane to the woods between the corn fields … she smashed through the corn rows until she knew to stop … she breathed silent breaths at first. [Uh … uh … uh]

Here, only corn leaves and wind whispered together …

[Shhushuuhhh—shhushuuhhh—shhushuuhhh]

… brushed her neck and arms, and watched her torn mouth turn down into sorrow.

The fox stopped, one front paw lifted, curved her ears back toward the house, and sniffed the air. She looked into the cornfield with her liquid black eyes. [Oaahhhhhhh] *The child will find her way in the dark*, the fox thought and turned to walk in the shadow of the fence line toward the woods.

Rose returned as a near-darkness fell on the house. Her father had fed the cattle. Her mother had cleared the supper dishes away. Rose slipped into the house through the back door and heard the sound of the television. It held everyone captive at the end of the house. There was her father asleep in his chair, her little sister asleep against her mother's shoulder, and her brother stretched out on the floor with his head propped up on his hands.

The house finally breathed [Hoooooaahh] when she felt Rose's bare feet run up the stairs. The dog followed. The bedroom curtains shushed each other in the night breeze at the window where the child came to sit. The dog lay down across her bare feet. The house saw that Rose's shadow had grown larger.

"What will happen now?" the house whispered to the owl. "There is so much silence."

The owl knew everything. Past and future. The mother hated her daughter. It was true. It wasn't personal. The owl knew all forms of the ancient woman-hatred. It was inside and outside. It was mundane. It was catastrophic. It had swallowed the mother.

The owl knew it was in the mother when she took in her daughter's body at the supper table, when she glimpsed her daughter's barely perceptible new breasts as the child stretched against the smiling blue cartoon whale and the curly-haired stick girl holding her sand shovel and pail impossibly high, growing up, and up, above the wild orange fringes of Rose's fading sun top.

The house watched the child looking out the window into the dark. Rose breathed in the scent of rain. [Uuhmmmm] She watched the bats wheel and swoop in the dark. The owl took the child in with her large yellow eyes.

"She's growing up. She is becoming," the owl said to the house. "Now she knows how to move through the dark and find her way back."

Vicki McLeod

Long Night, with Flowers

I lie wide awake, bones aching on the hard floor, steady heart beating. I am in a sleeping nest made of blankets and pillows. Sheltered between the bed and the chest of drawers, both towering overhead, I stare upward and see the vague square shapes that surround me and the mute ceiling.

The ceiling fan rotates and its breeze reaches me in my tiny canyon. It is the heat that drives me out of bed. The mattress gets hot under my skin, the energy of my radiating sixty-year-old body trapped in the bed.

There is a younger part of myself that joins me on the floor, restless. She is searching for something, remembering. She fears death, this one, doesn't know she is already gone.

A still smaller aspect, a littler girl, is beckoning, urging me to make a fort with the blankets, tuck them overhead, and make a proper shelter. I follow their little shadows into the night. These two barefoot ghosts are busy.

I think over a story I am writing about a house at the corner of our street. It is a blue house, and even in midsummer, the front porch is strung with gaily coloured Christmas bulbs. The cement walkway leading up to the house is lined with planters filled with sunny flowers, but here I am stuck: *What is the name of that flower?*

I know the flower I am trying to name—I've planted some myself in a basket on our front step—but the name will not come. In front of the blue house, on either side of the wooden steps, is a riot of petunias mixed with lettuce, burgeoning squash, and geraniums.

Not geraniums.

Pot after pot of bushy tomato plants mark the edge of the property. I asked Mike, who lives in the blue house, about their robustness. He told me he gets up early in the morning and shakes the tomato plants. This must be done before 7:00 a.m., he explained adamantly, not one minute later.

Not dahlias. Not rhododendrons.

I squirm on the floor, trying to find a position that does not hurt my hip, tucking a pillow along my back, hunting in the thicket that is my brain for the name of the elusive blossom. The overhead fan turns. The younger version of self traces her freckles and moles, trying to remember what it is she has lost, while the littler one considers the engineering problems of pillows.

Not rose, obviously. Or daisy.

Mike has an old brown dog named Frappy that lies on the grass in front of the house, not too far from the crab apple tree on the corner and not too far from the porch. Sometimes he lies by the big stump of a dead cedar in the middle of the yard, as though in the shade of the vanished tree. He yips in his sleep, dreaming old-dog dreams.

It occurs to me that I may be lying on the floor like a dog for a reason that has nothing to do with hormonal heat, something I can't yet fathom. I long to fall into sleep. My slender young self is fretting. Littler Self would like to invite the dog over.

Not lobelia. Not lily.

Why can't I remember the name of the flower I know so well, or help my younger self find what it is she is so forlornly seeking? I do not understand why I am driven to lie on the hard floor in the dark. I am floundering, drowning in blankets, lost in the weeds of wakefulness.

Not chrysanthemum, although that feels close.

Hydrangea? Calendula?

My shoulder aches on the hard floor and I reach my fingers over my shoulder to knead and soothe the muscle. My fingertips encounter not smooth skin but lumps, nodules beneath the surface of the skin. They move almost imperceptibly at my touch. Younger Self sits up erectly, alert in her white nightgown. She misses nothing.

I begin to think of the plants that burst and bud beneath the earth, the tubers and corms that push away rocks with relentless roots and shoot green spikes upward out of hard dirt. They bloom like feathers out of the surface of the earth, unstoppable.

Lily-of-the-valley?

No. It's the hardier kind of plants that grow underground, in the dark. Like the places in the body where our bones grow, tied to muscle, deep in the blood and skin, held by joints and tendon. It is these bones that grow in the night. Younger Self wants me to name what has not been named. Her teenage hands press against my cheeks.

Tell me, she whispers.

At the shock of her touch, I run my brain against the void that is the place where the word for that small dense flower is meant to live. The blankness I find there is not the same as the repeated confusion I have about impatiens and begonia, both shade-loving plants, or the familiar tangle of thinking that Joan Baez is Canadian. It is prairie-born Joni Mitchell I know. Still, they both ended up in California, and when I part that thicket in my brain, there they are in beads and caftans, sitting cross-legged in a field of grass and singing protest songs together in high clear voices.

Alyssum, fuschia, foxglove, snapdragon ...

I begin to drift off and feel a tugging. My young self is pressing on in her quest; she is willing to play nest here with us on the floor for a time, but she has a puzzle that must be urgently solved. It is not flowers she wants named. She turns to Littler Self, who pats pillows in the dark, finding the softer places.

Show us the story, she commands.

Littler Self settles into the pillows, an imaginary dog at her side. She takes us to the time before words ...

She is crouched in a flowerbed, watching things, the shape of trees, bark, the texture of flower petals, the way the earth is humped around the roots of things, ants. The flowerbed runs along the front-yard fence of a large wooden house with a big outside porch. The street beyond the fence is a busy one. The garden we are visiting, though, is peaceful. And so is Little Self. We are in the time between sorrows.

In this sunny afternoon scene we can only catch a glimpse of what is to be. Little Self is sensing herself apart from soil and insect, flower and tree. The droopy heads of blood-red peonies bend low, and she can see there is an end coming to them. A petal drops. A fragment of a poem writes itself in the bark of the tree. She can't name it, but she feels it ripple across her skin. She points us to the boughs of a tree, heavy with tiny roses, foretelling that forgiveness will be required. Little Self tells us that a storm is coming our way.

I can think only of the roses blooming on the branches and wonder why there are so many, hundreds and hundreds, and why they are so small.

Peony? Never.

The nodes under my shoulder blades multiply like stolons, running underneath my skin, craving the surface. Memories threaten to burst forth, unfurling like leaves. There is a pain like blood as my skin rips apart and the leaves sprout greenly, taking wing. Little Self fades into sleep. Her work is done. My bones grow into the floor, organs dissolve into rhizomes, and the words that cannot be spoken emerge. I curl into the nest, my body made of bark. My arms are wings, made of bone and grass.

Penis

Blood

Cousin

Just thirteen.

Younger Self circles me in her white gown, stops and plants her feet. She raises her thin arms, like branches, toward the sky. The flower I cannot name is made of grief. It does not bloom at night. In the daytime I will know its yellow face. It is the one that lights the way for that which is lost.

Marigold.

Paula Wellings

Two Fish in a Tank

I consult a highly detailed spreadsheet to calculate the exact number of days: ninety-eight.[1] Ninety-eight days ago, as Hurricane Harvey raged hundreds of miles away and concerned texts arrived from far-flung family members, I found my way to an inland sea.

With windshield wipers set to chaos, I left my home that morning in The Mood. The Mood is a persistent and wrenching aspect of The Wait, which began nine months ago. The Wait is counted in months, never, ever, in days, for there are far too many of those.

It officially started after a criminal-background check, a physician's certificate of good health, a marriage and financial verification with licenses and tax returns, a review of house floor plans and smoke alarm locations, various financial and legal agreements, the completion of a family profile book, and a home visit from a social worker who said in all seriousness, "Tell me about your mother."

What I crave in this time of The Wait is a lightened heart and soft edges. To this end, I travel through the hurricane-derivative downpour in search of a small freshwater aquarium and a few genetically modified danios, popularly called GloFish. They are easy and cheery, movement against stillness. In these past months, I have stopped running (too tiring), stopped eating salad (too virtuous), and stopped working on complex projects (too fuzzy static in my brain). I have developed a new habit of deserving cake, and a fondness for chips and cheese baked in the toaster oven for two and a half minutes.

1 The Highly Detailed Spreadsheet can be found at tinyurl.com/twofishinatank

During the first trimester of The Wait, I read books such as *The Open-Hearted Way to Open Adoption* and *Birthmothers: Women Who Have Relinquished Babies for Adoption Tell Their Stories*. We believed we could become parents at any moment. It does happen. The next trimester revolved around support groups, workshops, and encouraging conversations with friends and family. Only in the third trimester did The Mood arrive in full force. I no longer mention when we are being considered as adoptive parents. It prevents the second conversation, which starts with "So?" and requires the response, "We were not chosen." Everyone tactfully withholds "Again."

With two big-box pet stores kitty-corner to each other, I expect to easily find and purchase the fish tank solution: maternal longing blunted by way of glow-in-the-dark fish. Instead I stand in a dimly lit geodesic structure called AquaDome. The sphere is filled with the sea, segmented into hundreds of chambers all linked by Habitrail plumbing and brimming with alien life. I challenge the storekeeper to disqualify me, to send me back to Petco for a lightweight acrylic tank. Instead she steps with me into the storm, and we load my car with jugs of salt water, living sand, rocks from Florida, and a sixteen-gallon glass Coralife Biocube.

My nascent Sea World requires a life support system, and the first visit to AquaDome is followed by the purchase of a heater, an improved water pump, a wave maker, a protein skimmer, an in-tank media basket, filter media, better filter media, a water testing kit, a replacement light kit with mobile app, an algae-scraping magnet, a refugarium light and chaetomorpha, an accurate heater that doesn't cook the tank while I'm on a business trip, and a second aquarium when the first springs a leak.

The sea creatures join the tank by mercurial decree, each decision vindicated by extensive research, methodical care, and retrospective logic. Clownfish and blue leg hermit crabs follow AquaDome's advice. The first corals, candy cane and *Ricordea*, conclude an hour-long conversation about clean-up crews at the other local fish store. Pipe organ, *Blastomussa*, and neon green hairy mushroom arrive from an online shop that makes helpful YouTube videos. Duncans appear, with *Pavona* and *Caulastrea* added on to make the free shipping minimum. An open brain *Trachyphyllia* is traded for the *Pavona*, who was aggressive and sad. Each day, I consider placement, lighting, and flow, and measure the success of this life support system against the lives it maintains.

Ninety-eight days is coincidentally fourteen weeks. My two lost children also swam in warm salt water. Each grew as large as a lemon but never an apple. The first time my tank crashed, I was sent home to muddle through the ending with a pamphlet. The second time an obstetrician performed a D&C and I slept through the part where the dead future child went down the drain.

The Wait turns ten months tomorrow. It will persist until a mother, and perhaps a father, choose us to be the right family to parent their child. In the meantime, I tend nine small coral, two fish, one shrimp, and a variety of snails: Trochus, Nassarius and Margarita.[2] I read discussion boards, learn biochemistry, talk to geeky strangers near and far, and continue to test the waters. The Mood wanes as the aquarium grows. I am told The Wait will be forgotten when it finally ends.

2 See them on Instagram, @twofishinatank

Joanna Baxter

Wrecked

AN EXCERPT

I was jolted awake by a walloping thump as a mass of ice-cold water soaked me from head to toe. The canvas lee cloth that kept me from rolling out and onto the teak floorboards was soaked, as well as my bedding and mattress, all flooded, permeated. I bolted upright and slammed my head on the bunk above mine, gasping in the pitch black. My crewmates were each exclaiming with shock and scrambling from deep sleep to high alert. The boat swerved, heaved, rolled, and fell; sails cracked like whips. The terrifying creak of thousands of pounds of metallic torque released with a terrifying, booming pop. I disentangled myself from my berth and struggled to stand as another wave drop-kicked us. After a few minutes of pitch-black mayhem, someone found a headlamp, shedding a white light on the new world around us. We were five off-watch mates, my three cousins and their father, my Uncle Skip, standing unsteadily, grasping at any solid holds, all of us bracing and knee-deep in seawater that sloshed and splashed up into our panicked faces.

"Is everyone all right?" asked my Uncle Skip in his deep voice, a combination of doctor, father, uncle, and skipper. We each called out in the affirmative, like an urgent roll call. My glasses were lost in the deluge, swept off their place beside my pillow, the myopia adding to my confusion. The boat thrashed around in unpredictable directions. One moment we were airborne, the next we were slammed hard to one side. Plates and cutlery smashed inside the cupboards as I tried not to bite off my tongue.

The shock of being ripped from sleep affected us all in exactly the same way, and there was a communal rush to vomit in the galley sink. The urge was so immediate that one or all missed the target altogether. Vomitus floated and swirled in the water, sloshing around us. The cabin had never felt smaller and stank of bile. All of my senses were stretched to the limits of endurance, challenged further by the ceaseless violent pitching of the boat. The miserable scene made me gag, and I took my turn too. The low whine of the bilge alarm had been sounding constantly, the pump working overtime and moaning below the floorboards. It could take hours to drain the immense volume of water that had just poured in from the open companionway. *How much water does it take to fill a forty-four-foot sailboat?*

Boots thumped above my head on deck and I heard my dad's voice, sounding very far away and yelling something about our steering. *Papa, what happened? Are you there? Is this real? Who is on watch? It's so late, you must be up there with Uncle Don—where's Don? Why is there only one voice from the cockpit?*

Uncle Skip found another headlamp and staggered through the water toward the storage locker in the aft quarter. After a few minutes he re-emerged, passing forward a six-foot steering tiller. The tiller was made of steel with powder-coated white enamel. Holes in incremental sizes were cut out of the sides to make it lighter, but it still took two of us to hold it. This was day three of our five-day race, and I had grown accustomed to the regular twenty- to thirty-foot swells that were the norm as major currents converged in this part of the Atlantic. By the way we were getting hammered, it was obvious we had lost our steering. Our boat was turned sideways against the waves, into the most vulnerable position.

I caught blurry glimpses of the cockpit through the narrow companionway. The binnacle, which houses the compass and the steering wheel, was askew, with the wheel unmoving, and on a sharp angle. With the wheel disengaged from the rudder, we were at the mercy of this huge, roiling sea. Attaching the tiller was our only hope to regain control.

Uncle Skip gripped the handrail and climbed the ladder, his body swinging like a pendulum. We waited for him to clip his safety harness to a stanchion before passing up the tiller. His face came back into view to shout, "Stay below!"

For the last two days the wind had been at our back and the sails had been trimmed like opposing wings, the large jib sail billowing out to starboard and the mainsail out as far as possible to port. To keep the boom from swinging across the cockpit, it had been fastened to a pulley system that was clipped to the railing on deck.

Somehow, the men above deck were able to secure the tiller and immediately steered us perpendicular to the waves. The relief of an up-and-down motion, as opposed to the random side-to-side pummelling thrash, was immense. However, pointing directly into the waves meant a stomach-turning ride up to the cliff's edge only to shoot down the backside to plunge into its trough. Over and over again, and yet this was at least predictable chaos, far less dangerous than the blind boxing match of being hit on the side beam.

After a few minutes in this relative calm, Uncle Skip reappeared in the hatch opening to tell us again to stay below, as if to make doubly sure we understood, and looked me right in the eye before disappearing again. I could hear him yelling back and forth with my dad. The bilge pump had finished its job and we were finally standing on a firm surface. Someone had switched on the emergency cabin lights, and in the dim sepia I watched Drew, my oldest cousin, wedge himself into the chart table to begin the distress calls. There was little for Tom, Mike, and I to do but put on our life jackets for warmth and protection and stay out of the way, busy enough with the ceaseless work of shifting and bracing ourselves.

Above the roar of the sea, Drew called over and over, "Mayday, Mayday, Mayday. This is the sailing vessel *Bellatrix*. We have lost steering and require immediate assistance."

The word *Mayday* comes from the French *venez m'aidez*. Every three minutes, Drew repeated his call. *Please come help me. Help me. Help.*

The steady cycle of roller-coaster waves became our unit of time. The rudder reverberated under us. The stern lifted up with each plunge of the bow, giving me a glimpse of my dad through the dark. I tried to keep my eyes on him. Part Jacques Cousteau, part weathered fisherman, he straddled the tiller, his head and neck craning to the horrible horizon, his whole body muscling over each wave.

A signal, barely audible, then a message came through in a scratchy blast: "*Bellatrix,* ... your Mayday call. *Bellatrix*, your Mayday call has been received. I repeat, your Mayday call has been received. This is ... We are a thirty-two-foot sailing vessel positioned at ...

"I repeat. This is ... We are a ... current vessel position at longitude ... latitude ... Do you read? Over."

I was the only girl in this clan of non-hugging boys, but I grabbed Tom's hand in the wet and the cold and squeezed it hard. He was the youngest of my cousins, seventeen years old, two years older than me. He was crying too. We lived on opposite ends of the country, but when we saw each other every few years, we were best friends. We clutched at each other grimly, knocking our knees together.

Drew quickly plotted the position of the responding ship on the water-logged chart. Smaller than us, and almost thirty-five nautical miles southwest, their boat was too small and too far to help. Mike relayed the thin news to the cockpit, and Drew resumed his broadcast. He told us between calls that he suspected we were doing very well in this race, well ahead of much of our fleet. He was trying to lift our spirits. We should have been happy, we were on a great adventure. We should have been snug in our bunks until our respective shifts. But that reality was done, over, destroyed, replaced with Drew's Mayday calls searching and pleading for help.

But help from what, exactly? None of us below deck had any idea. We knew we were midway between the start line in Boston and the finish line in Bermuda. We knew some sort of giant wave had struck us from behind, a wave big enough to almost swallow us whole. We also knew our rigging was damaged; we had heard things break. I had never heard the term "rogue wave" and could not imagine such a monster, let alone the near-impossibility of encountering one. It would not be until morning that I would learn the extent of what it had done to us, and what it had done to Don.

My dad and Uncle Skip had done their best to protect us by keeping us down below. They made sure none of us saw Don's body, not even as it was lifted off our boat and onto the large vessel that rescued us in the faint light of dawn. I remember my dad scrubbing and scrubbing the deck as our rescuers towed us to safety. The last I saw of Don was a single globule of congealed blood, there in a far corner of the cockpit. My dad had missed a spot.

Carolyne Montgomery

Tsusiat Falls

With each step, icy water sloshes between my socks and the soles of my feet. Three white stripes brand my blue suede running shoes. They are not the proper hiking boots for this trip. This is the fourth day of a seven-day hike on the West Coast Trail, the fourth day of intermittent but daily rain in the coastal rainforests of Vancouver Island. It is 1977 and I am poor. *You may be in over your head. This adventure is more than you have planned for.*

I am loaded with a sixty-pound backpack and hiking as quickly as I can in order to reach the campsite at Tsusiat Falls before it gets dark. It's mid-August. Here at the forty-ninth parallel, the sun that I cannot see for the clouds and rain will not set until after eight this evening. I have only completed the first third of this seventy-five-kilometre hike. My wet canvas pack feels a little lighter each day, but food is an issue. I have a meagre supply of raisins, oats, a plastic tube of peanut butter, some nuts, and tea remaining. Should I try to eat the grape-like berries on the salal? Water is plentiful, as the creeks are frequent and full. I extract the iodine from the vial with the glass dropper and drip the drops carefully into my water bottle. *You can't get sick.*

I am wet. When the rain stops, the water continues to assault me from the overhanging branches of the cedars and salal that are choking this trail. My yellow plastic jacket is as soaked on the inside from my sweat as it is on the outside from the rain. The flat rubber soles of my runners slip on the decaying mossy logs, the mud, and the wooden boardwalks. My feather sleeping bag is the only thing I am carrying that is still dry. I have crammed it into a nylon stuff sack and then wrapped it in two layers of green garbage bag. *If you can stay warm at night, you will be fine.*

After the bushwhacking of the first three days, the boardwalk I am now hiking on is boring and relentless. I need to concentrate so I don't lose my footing on the slimy boards, or a rotting one finally gives way. *You can't fall. Don't fall.*

I am thankful that I am no longer hauling myself up the muddy creek banks. On the previous days, I had scrambled up the steep twenty-foot slopes by gripping the broken and unstable tree roots used by other hikers. In some places, the only way out of the creek beds was by using the wooden slatted ladders that were in random states of decay. In the rainforest, things rot quickly. I tested every tread and root before transferring the weight of my burdened twenty-one-year-old body. *You should have brought a rope and gloves.*

Occasionally the forest breaks, giving glimpses of the surf of the Pacific Ocean crashing on the beaches below the trail. Flocks of shrieking sea birds, mainly large seagulls, skirl about in windswept formations. Thick banks of grey fog break off from the low clouds and roll toward the shore. The cove is choked with massive silvered driftwood logs. *You have never seen logs that are that big.*

I look longingly at the firm wet sand at the tideline, certain the hiking would be easier down there. My ability to read the wallet-sized cardboard tide table I had bought in Port Renfrew is uncertain. The guidebook is clear on the danger of being trapped and drowned on these small beaches should you get caught in a rising tide. *You are from Ontario and you only understand lakes.*

The leathery and sharply serrated leaves of the chest-height salal on either side of the boardwalk continue to slash at my face and arms as I squeak past in my noisy runners. The afternoon sun is struggling to break through the thinning grey-black clouds. I'm starting to feel warmer and happier. With each step, the light catches in the spray of the drops of water from the heels of my shoes. The clouds lift further and I peel off my coat. My navy cotton kangaroo jacket might dry a bit as I walk along. I can make out the rushing sounds of the Tsusiat Falls, my destination.

The burning of my shoulders and back means more frequent pauses and futile adjustments of the felt-lined leather straps of the pack. I still have to get down to the beach at the foot of the falls. There is one last ladder. I descend backwards, slowly, carefully, rung by rung by rung. I'm too exhausted to rescue myself if I make a mistake. *You can't make a mistake.*

I thud onto the soft dry sand, stagger over to the nearest log, and pull off my pack. The openness of the beach—no moss, ferns, or salal to slap my face—makes me laugh with relief. Five chutes of sparkling water spill noisily over the limestone cliff into a peaty pool. I have about three hours until dark. The tide is low, a steady wind blows on shore, and the surf pounds onto the beach. I strip off to my underpants and vest and lay my soaking jeans, plaid shirt, and jacket on the log. The sun dries my grimy, sweat-coated skin and my clothes steam in the heat. *You can swim in the rock pool. It is warm enough.*

I scuff off my runners and yank off my socks. My feet are white and wrinkled. *Trench foot*, I think as I wiggle my toes in the fine sand at the edge of my log. When I wring out my socks, the water is swallowed up and leaves a small dark circle on the surface of the sand. I twist each empty shoe forwards and backwards. The sunlight is reflected in the drops of pale brown-and-blue tinged water that drip from my fingers and reflect the light from the lowering sun. *You will be drier tomorrow and it will get easier.*

Maura Wong

OMG!

OMG! It's Zachary calling on Whatsapp!

My heart leaps as I grab the phone.

I put him on speaker so my husband can hear him as well, even though I am dying to hoard this conversation all to myself. I haven't spoken to my son for three weeks since he went down to New Orleans for spring break.

He is the part of me that has reincarnated, reliving college life as a lonely sophomore, thousands of miles away from his family.

"Hello! How's everyone at home?" His voice is warm but a little deeper than usual. Could it be a sore throat?

He had an exhausting week, having just finished his last mid-term exam and turned in all his problem sets. We chat about some random things before I ask him about his trip to New Orleans.

"So who did you go to New Orleans with?"

There is no hesitation this time.

"I guess I am going to tell you guys. I have a girlfriend. We have been spending time together for a while and we decided to take a trip, thinking that by the end we would either hate each other or really get along. I guess it turned out to be the latter." These lines roll out smoothly with suppressed excitement. My intuition tells me they have been rehearsed many times and finally found an opportunity to be out in the open.

I throw a glance at my husband. His eyes widen and a big grin is beginning to spread on his jovial face, before it is checked midway by the thought that maybe he should see how his wife responds first to this bombshell.

"Good to hear. That sounds cool. What's her name?" I invoke all of my inner peace from years of meditation to feign calmness.

I honestly feel slightly relieved. I have told my husband I hope Zachary will find a girlfriend soon. My husband and I met in college, and that was a big part of how we survived those four grueling years.

"Natalie. She's Korean, from southern California."

Fifteen seconds later, my husband shows me a picture of Natalie on Facebook. He found her among Zachary's Facebook friends, and he is more than excited, undoubtedly feeling smug about how fast he was able to find Natalie's picture.

Long dark hair, nice cheekbones, smiley eyes. She looks a little like Zachary's high school sweetheart.

I want to say something nice about Natalie but catch myself before doing so. It will tip Zachary off that we have immediately looked her up. We will look like the creepy helicopter parents that we hate to admit we are. Instead I ask my son what his girlfriend intends to major in. Linguistics, he replies. Finally, I find the courage to ask about her, sensing that Zachary wants to talk about her.

"So what's she like?"

"She is nice. Not the debating type." Zachary is a world-ranking debater.

I smile; that's good, yin and yang. I am a headstrong woman with a sharp tongue and I know the trouble I can give to a husband.

When I was in college a Korean American friend met his wife through matchmaking arranged by their parents, still a common practice among Koreans and Korean Americans. He told me that because he was a single child, his parents helped him pick a young woman who was neither the eldest nor a single child. This way, if they got married, they wouldn't have to take care of two sets of aging parents one day. At the time, in my early twenties, I found this overly calculating, believing in free choice and true love and nothing else matters. Now that I am in my fifties, I've begun to think about fit when it comes to my children's future partners.

"Jason was here yesterday, visiting. He said I'd better tell you guys about Natalie so you all in Hong Kong can stop wondering if I am gay."

Jason is Zachary's best friend from Hong Kong, attending university an hour away from Zach's college. They have been visiting each other so much on the weekends that my husband and Jason's dad, also high school buddies, started joking that maybe they would find themselves as in-laws with each other.

Now I remember. Zachary showed us a picture of himself and five other friends from college when he came home for Christmas. One of them was Natalie, but he didn't say anything at the time. Usually we only see his pictures with friends on Facebook or Instagram, but at Christmas, he gave us a stack of pictures.

Out of the corner of my eye I see the picture that has been on my bedside for over three decades. It was taken during the first trip my husband and I took after we started dating. As poor college students, we took the bus to Atlantic City. It was only forty-five minutes away from the university, but it felt like we were on a different planet. It was either autumn or spring and the day was overcast. The sand and water were grey, but I was wearing a yellow tank top and red shorts that brightened up the pictures we took. We walked along the boardwalk eating ice cream and hotdogs, and we hung out until sunset. Before we left the seaside we took a selfie with an automatic camera that we positioned precariously on a stump. I was in my then-boyfriend's arms and I pointed toward the setting sun. Taking a trip together was a big milestone for a college relationship then and, I guess, also now.

After the phone call Zachary sent us some pictures from his trip to New Orleans. On a solo shot, he captioned it, *This is Natalie!!* I imagined the pride in his voice as he hoped that his parents would like her and be happy for him.

Zach, we do and we are.

Two hours later, I was lying in bed trying to take all this in. Zach has a new girlfriend. Wonder when we will get to meet her. Will we have to take our family holiday trips with her at some point? I feel there are some changes I need to adapt to, but I'm unsure of what they will be. It feels foreign and natural at the same time. I chastise myself for being over-sensitive because of this empty nest thing.

Get a life! Stop worrying about the children!

This is when ageing hits home. I am acting in ways that I thought I never would. The only explanation can be age.

I wonder what Natalie's like. She seems sweet, but she calls herself angsty on her Facebook page. Two angsty kids together, they will understand each other well. I hope.

My husband and I spent a lot of our time together at college studying in the library. We were geeks. Our college lives were monotonous and simple, which made it easy to be content. We didn't worry about internships, jobs, and GPAs like Zach and his friends do now.

I really should work on getting a job again so I can take my mind off my college-bound kids. My younger son, Nick, will be gone in a year's time, then I will be left with empty rooms, loads of memories, and an unclear future. Chances are my generation of women could live well into our nineties. That means I could have just passed the halfway mark. What am I going to do with all that and nothing to centre my life around?

OMG!!!

Maybe I should sign up for a writing course.

Emi Sasagawa

Selfish Love

Loving you is the most selfish thing I've ever done.

I stood out in the corridor and looked at my watch, wondering how long before I could leave. The door ajar, I walked into a room teeming with people, a growing pile of shoes, a long line to the bathroom.

I surveyed the apartment, looking for my friend, but you caught my attention. Straight black hair, brown eyes, broad nose, thick lips. You smiled from across the room. My gaze followed your neck line, then your collar bone, a long-sleeved black dress. I inched forward, saying hello to familiar faces. You walked toward me, navigating a sea of people between us. We stopped right in front of each other.

You put your fingers through your hair and parted it to the right. Then you told me your name and asked for mine. I raised the sleeve of my shirt, showing off my tattoo. A brush of your hand against mine. Your cheeks flushed—I couldn't tell if it was me or the alcohol.

I learned we had common friends and a few shared interests. I told you about my month-long train trip up the west coast of the United States. You said you'd love to do something like that one day, and you told me about your love for music and how you had attended a performing-arts high school. I said when I was young my parents thought I might be tone deaf. I also told you about my obsession with Lego and building model cars. You asked me how often I played with them.

An hour, two hours passed. Your questions became more personal. You asked where I lived. I told you I was moving into a new apartment on Commercial. I asked if you had roommates. You told me you lived with your boyfriend. I looked around, trying to find him. You said he wasn't at the party, then you sighed and changed subjects.

I spent the night talking to you. I watched as the room around us changed. Furniture was rearranged to make more space for people. Some arrived, some left. Growlers emptied. We switched to vodka, whiskey, gin. We listened to Rhye, Drake, Fleetwood Mac. You and I were the last to leave. You walked home, and I took a cab. I didn't ask for your number; there was no point wasting my time.

The next day I learned you were interested, interested in me.

"She told her sister she has a crush on you."

"What? She's got a boyfriend."

"Sometimes that doesn't mean much."

My friend uninvitedly analyzed the situation. Maybe your relationship was falling apart. Maybe you were polyamorous. Maybe you were curious about being with a woman. I basked in the vanity of my self-love and imagined what it would be like to implode your world.

Days went by and you kept popping up in my head. First my thoughts, then my dreams. I fell in love with the potential of you. Eyes closed, I would retrace our steps, replay our conversation, relive the night I met you. Weeks passed and I saw you at a party, at a lecture, at dinner, for drinks.

I smiled at you and you winked at me. I tucked your hair behind your ear, you put your legs between mine, I breathed on the back of your neck. You turned around. I kissed you.

The first time we slept together, you went back to him. I stayed awake the whole night, my sheets drenched in the smell of you. My body tingling from your touch. I imagined you going home and explaining where you'd been. I pictured you lying on his chest, caressing his face.

Looking at the empty space next to me, I wondered what it might cost you to be here.

That night I typed and re-typed messages telling you we should put a stop to things. This was wrong. The timing was off. We would regret this. I never sent one. Instead, I charged forward, and at every touch it became harder to watch you leave.

When things between you and him ended and he left, I allowed myself to feel all of the emotions I had kept in check. The lust, the love, the sadness, the anger. They came in waves of varying sizes. Sometimes the water would barely touch my feet, other times a wave would knock me on my back. Eyes open, I wondered about the things I'd left unsaid.

We seized every opportunity to be around each other. You'd squeeze in a coffee with me between meetings, I would take the bus just to go on an evening stroll with you.

You and I stayed up most nights catching up on all the things we had yet to discover.

I learned about your relationship with him, how at the end he would disappear for nights on end, how he'd never wanted to move in together, how he had a drinking problem.

I learned about your dad, how he left, how he sank into depression, how he rejected all earthly ties and became a monk, and how he died.

At every story I was overcome by the desire to fix things, to create a world in which you didn't have to suffer. I wanted to save you. I would lie awake at night plotting the ways I could repair the broken parts. I arrogantly believed I could do better and give you more, but in my efforts to change things, to change you, I began to unsee you.

One morning an unexpected wave crashed on us. I was getting ready for work. You called your mother and put her on speaker phone. You told her about us. You spoke in Cantonese, but between words I couldn't make meaning of, I recognized the disappointment in my mother's voice when I told her I loved a woman.

I watched your world fall apart. She gave you up. I held you tighter. You accepted things as they were. But I couldn't bear what I wasn't able to control.

So, I planned a life for me, for you, for us. You became an image in my head, a combination of all the things I wanted you to be. It was easier to live in the future, to think of all the things that we could become.

That summer your mother came to see you.

I hoped for a chance to make things better, to lift my guilt. Instead, you hid me in the bedroom. I sat on the floor staring out the window, my jaw clenched, my fist tight, fingers digging into my palm.

When you returned, I let my rage engulf us both. I forgot to ask what it might cost you to be here. Drunk with entitlement, I screamed untruths about you, me, her. I expected you to yell back. Instead, you retaliated with silence. I filled in the gaps of what was left unsaid with the words I feared were lodged in your throat, and prayed for a future that would make the present a distant past.

It wasn't long before you and I came to inhabit different worlds, mine further and further away from reality, yours more and more grounded in it.

My love was self-serving because it wasn't a love of you or for you. I liked you in the now, so I could love who I thought you might one day be.

Between misunderstandings and miscommunications, you became someone I could hardly recognize. As the waves continued to crash on me, my emotions blurred, I pounded on my chest so I could feel something, anything for you and for me.

Sometimes when I'm half-awake my fingertips still look for the small of your back. In the darkness, I forget. I try to hold onto the possibilities I haven't yet let go. Then I realize I'm grabbing at emptiness.

Eyes opened, I retrace our steps, replay our arguments, relive the nights I've known you. An empty frame, mismatched socks, a lone pot lid. These are the vestiges of my life with you.

It took losing you to begin to see you.

From a distance I can see clearer than I was ever able to up close. I've learned you whisper what you want to scream. I've learned you take space to feel close. And for the first time in three years, I recognize who you are, who you hope to be.

So, I close my eyes and feel the wave recede.

Nicole Jess

Pedestal

AN EXCERPT

Broken sleep has marked my nights for some time. Tonight is no different. Half awake, my mind turns over things said and done. A blanket cocoons the lower half of my body, binding me to this merciless fate. The vertical blinds tap against the window, punctuating the night's gentle breeze. When the phone vibrates on the window ledge, I know it is you. Releasing the pillow from my clenched fist, I reach through the darkness. It's been six years since your name appeared on my phone, in my email, or anywhere else.

I hold my finger to the centre button and my heart freezes, both thrilled and terrified to read your words. You have responded to my call. I am not dead to you.

Hi Valery your message begins …

Three short paragraphs appear on the screen. The sharp scalpel of your trade is evident in words chosen so precisely.

I am married now.

This written confession traces the silhouette of my heart, causing it to collapse outward. I stare at the screen, reading the words again and again. How can this be? Why didn't you tell me sooner?

I imagine you telling me this news in person. I pretend we have just crossed paths, that we live in the same town, city, country. She is with you and we fumble with our words and you say, "Hi …" before adding, "This is my wife …" I pretend to be pleased and perhaps even shake her hand, excusing myself before the tears become evident.

I also imagine we have just crossed paths, that we live in the same town, city, country, and that you are alone. We fumble with our words and you say, "Hi ..." before awkwardly asking, "Do you want to walk down to the promenade?" Once there, you sit facing forward, gaze wide, your hazel eyes drinking in the horizon. Or if we choose to drive rather than walk, then we sit together in the car, perhaps with some music playing. For certain you hold my hand, because that is what you always did when we drove together. Keys in, music on, hand in hand. That's how we travelled. That's just how it was.

I want to be clear, as yesterday when you called I said I couldn't talk. It was not just that I couldn't speak in that moment.

They say absence makes the heart grow fonder, time and space having removed all aspects of doubt, disregard, and deception that lace a relationship. In our case your absence has taken with it the memories of your cruelness. Shrunken and shadowed in the mossy corners of my mind are the times you looked at me with contempt for wanting more of you. The times you paraded the notion of marrying a woman half your age, despite the mathematical fact that this other woman would be a child. How you called thirty-two "old" and white people bland. How you wondered aloud why you could pick on me seemingly without reason. These memories have all diminished in size, remembered only to shake the pedestal upon which I have eternally placed you.

In her book *The Year of Magical Thinking*, Joan Didion reflects on Delmore Schwartz, who once said, "Time is the school in which we learn." I wonder what I have learned in this time since we first met, since we last parted? If the details of the end had been more evident, would I have done anything differently? Would I have challenged you less, or could I have loved you more? Given who we were then, would either have been possible?

Your message itself is not a surprise, considering I called you earlier today. When you answered the phone your voice was dull and rusty, as though I had woken you. I had calculated that it was around 3:00 p.m. on Sunday afternoon in California, and I thought it might be a good time to reach you. But perhaps you had been on call the night before, or you were away on holidays somewhere in an opposing time zone? But this is not the point; your initial bluntness threw me off guard. My words gushed out while I desperately tried to sound positive and upbeat. "Hi, Sam. It's me, Valery." I feigned a smile, despite being alone, but was met with silence. I panicked and fumbled for my next words. " I wondered if you had a moment to talk?" Still trying to keep my tone casual and carefree, knowing I was far from either.

"I can't talk," you said flatly, followed by silence. Dead silence. I got the impression that someone was beside you, sleeping. Someone who should not hear another woman's voice down the line.

Quickly realizing that this whole idea was a crescendo of catastrophic collapse, I grappled for an exit. "Okay, no worries," I replied. "I hope you are well."

"You too," you said, your tone unchanged.

"Take care," I mustered. "Bye."

I hung up with the same unthinking speediness with which I had made the call. Time stood still, amplifying every minute detail of what had just taken place. There I was, phone in hand, the table, the lounge room, the day outside, and six years of not speaking to you capped by that call. A pitiful, inauthentic, unproductive call, laden with my inability to move on.

If things had been different, if we had never separated in the first place, we would be spending an afternoon in the hammock that we'd hung between the banisters in the courtyard under the bougainvillea. We would lie in the hammock, entwined and kissing, our skin warm and moist. Our eyes would grow wide and pour into each other in the way they do in the movies, the really beautiful French ones that show people deeply in love.

I always knew you could do whatever you wanted, your message continued.

Such films remind me of our trip to Hawaii. You met me at the airport with a lei of sweet, creamy white jasmine. Its fragrance and craft were exquisite, and you placed it around my neck before loading me into a shiny black limo. You held my hand in yours and looked out the window with a look of contentment. We spent our time on Maui in a small wooden house by the beach. It was raised on stilts, allowing the ocean breeze to reach its balcony, where we sat at the end of the day, smoking organic cigarettes and drinking Mexican beer.

During that vacation, we drove through rolling hills and stopped near a side road. You asked me to follow you to a gate that looked like something that belonged in *Anne of Green Gables*. I remember wondering if you were going to ask me to marry you then. You asked me to climb onto the fence because you wanted a photo of me there. I did, shining like a girl in love and about to be proposed to, but then we left. Perhaps you would ask later …

My wife and I have decided that we will not communicate with people from prior relationships.

You once told me you would never write of your love for me, because that would allow it to be proven. I found this odd, confusing, and hurtful. I didn't understand that it didn't need to be written, that it was already written in every action, every smile, and every shared sunset. In the way you held my hand, even while we slept.

I held so tightly to what you said you wouldn't do that I overlooked what you were doing. Like the time you took a fifteen-hour flight from Los Angeles to Sydney just to spend two days together. I missed the blatant messages because I was looking for you on the rooftops. I wanted to see you up there, singing our love story to the town that you had painted scarlet red. But in that desire, as I watched the rooftops for your silhouette, I missed your silent love song, a carefully orchestrated serenade directly from you to me. I missed it. I missed you. I miss you.

It brings a smile to my face to hear that you are thriving.

I push the window across its heavy runners, locking out the sound of the night, the gentle summer breeze, and the world. *If I can't have you, I will have nothing,* someone inside me whispers. I cover my face and weep.

When my breathing becomes slow, I am frozen as though mummified by the consequences of your message. I slump forward, saturated with mucus and hot tears.

I hope you understand and truly wish you all the best.

Sometimes I sat in the dark hallway of our house in Santa Monica, my back resting against the wall that was our bedroom. I was close enough to hear you sleeping, though you never made a sound. I have often mused at the profound silence you held in slumber. No bodily noises, moans, groans, or movement, seemingly absolute resolution of the occupancy of your body. Sometimes I watched you while you slept, unsure if you were still in there at all. I would cup my hand close to your lips to feel the evidence of life through your breath.

On those sleepless nights, I sat there thinking of you, just as I am sitting here on this night, thinking of you, the man I was going to marry.

Evie Gold

A Determining Train Ride

He had no reason to come to India with me.

I had mentioned a trip together briefly in a teasing manner one day. That was before we had ever held hands, before we had decided that "giving us a try" was a choice we both wanted.

We met on a university study-abroad program the night after orientation dinner. Our group was made up of twenty-two people thrown together in a hostel on the less-sexy side of Tel Aviv. One whole floor was dedicated to us for our living and learning needs. We all had different backgrounds, interests, and reasons for accepting the program, but there were a few things we had in common: a love of hummus, wanderlust, and a new country to call home for the next six months.

"I've never been so amused watching someone over dinner," he said, as we passed each other in the hall on the way to our rooms.

"What? What do you mean?" I was horrified to learn that someone had been watching me and I hadn't noticed, but I was a little flattered at the same time.

"Your facial expression—especially while Shana was chronologically walking the group through everyone that she had slept with—it was priceless."

I threw my head back in a laugh. "Shoot. I thought I was a lot better at keeping a straight face."

We naturally gravitated toward one another and began spending our time together. He'd recommend long walks and I'd suggest meals because the food in Tel Aviv was scrumptious.

The thing that I instantly knew about us was that we could make each other laugh, often so hard that people would stop to look at us on the street as I'd hunch over, my sides aching. Several hours together and my face would hurt; it's the best kind of pain there is.

Ezra grew up in an affluent suburb forty-five minutes outside of New York City. It was a quiet suburban life, with a father in banking and a mother who spent her time supporting the Jewish community. He always felt grounded and "ordinary." I'd share stories about changing schools yearly, my dad's different business ventures, and my mom's appetite for changing religions. He'd listen intently and comment, "If you don't write your memoir, I'll write it for you."

I wasn't blind to what was happening. I could tell by the lingering stares that we were slowly falling for one another. And so the dance began, with unfamiliar steps, subtle movements, closer, further, until our fingers intertwined on bus rides and we casually started planning for our future together.

"Good mornings, good sirs! Welcome to India!" a driver shouts in our direction as he grabs our bags and throws them into his rickshaw, an open basket attached to a golf-cart-like automobile with four wheels and a metal cage as the body. We position ourselves on the back bench as the driver sits down behind the wheel and turns to look at us, obviously waiting for instructions on where to go. I glance at Ezra, waiting for him to give our destination, but he doesn't say anything. He just looks at me with a blank expression.

"Lucky Hotel, please. It's on . . ." but before I can continue, the driver interrupts me.

"I know very well, ma'am. It is too much nice, ma'am, very good hotel," he says with a quick head bobble and puts the car into drive.

I sit back and try not to let the irritation seep into me, but it already has. Why can't Ezra give instructions? Why can't he take charge? I take a couple of breaths and steal a couple of glances in his direction, but he is absorbed with watching the streets pass us by.

I take a deep breath of air as we weave through the traffic and focus on all of the commotion that fills the streets. Cars zip in and out of lanes, traffic lights are disregarded, and a large succession of beeps and honks fills the streets with noise. At one point I realize I've been holding my breath, grasping the metal bar so tightly that my hand hurts when I let it go. Every new street reveals potential danger as we jam ourselves between donkeys, cows, motorcycles, tuk-tuks, cars, and humans.

When the car comes to a stop I am relieved that we aren't moving, until I realize that our driver is getting out and that we have arrived. In front of me is a tattered awning with the faded words Lucky Hotel barely visible behind the dirt that covers it. The carpet is disgusting, the air is thick and hangs as if there hasn't been a draft in years, and the paint on the walls has begun to chip so heavily I almost want to duck when I walk by certain parts of the ceiling.

There's an older man behind the front desk, sitting on a stool; his belly lies on the counter. He extinguishes his cigarette as we approach, and I watch the smoke depart from the ashtray. I want to pick it up and stub it out myself, but instead I force a smile. "Hi—we have a room reserved under the name Gold."

"Yes, yes, ma'am, the very best room for you, miss," he says and starts shuffling the paperwork in front of him, grabs the keys and makes his way from behind the counter. "I'll show you to the very best, ma'am."

I try to make eye contact with Ezra, but he's looking away. I wasn't expecting fancy for our budget, but I also wasn't willing to jump into the sack with bed bugs on my first night in India, so as we make our way up the stairs, I tug on Ezra's shirt and ask him if he thinks this is an okay place for us to stay.

"We're already here," he mouths to me as he shrugs his shoulders.

"Very nice room, miss. Here you have your bed. Here you have your light," the clerk says as he points to different things in the room that seem pretty obvious to me. "And here you have your shower." He gestures to a wall that protrudes into the room. I peek around and see a bucket with a shower hose on top of it. "Hot water is on at 9:00 a.m. to 11:00 a.m. in the morning. You fill up the bucket and you shower here."

"Oh … lovely …"

As he leaves the room, we are overcome by exhaustion after twenty-three hours of travel. I rinse my face with cold water from the bucket and cover my body with clothing even though it's humid and hot. I want as little skin touching the sheets as possible.

Bright-eyed and rested in the morning, we make our way to the buffet breakfast, consisting of several boxes of cereal, some containers of yogurt, and a brewed pot of coffee. Someone next to us is discussing Varanasi, the city of lights. They are elated with their experience, so I take it as a sign that we should go there for our first destination, and we make plans to leave later that day.

The trains in India don't stop at the stations; they roll through them. We are aware of this because every single person we encounter tells us this, including the very serious man who sold us our train ticket. "They will not stop. You will have to jump on," he says before handing over our stubs.

As our train makes its way into the station, I brace myself with a little squeeze of Ezra's hand. There's disorder and chaos as people everywhere hurl themselves off the train while the rest are trying to wrestle their way on. I see a small clearing in a car that is heading toward us.

"That one!" I point to a compartment three cars down and begin a fast-paced walk in the same direction as the train, but the train is going much faster than I anticipated and I have to pick up my pace to a light jog before I throw myself and land firmly on the moving metal. I frantically look around for Ezra, but he isn't in the same car with me. I stick my head out the door and see him still running alongside the train.

"I can't!" he screams in my direction as the train pulls faster and faster away from the station. I look in the direction that we are going. There isn't much platform left and any second now the train will leave the station. He will be left there and I will be stuck here inside without him. I grab at the closest men near me in the car.

"Please! Please, help me get my boyfriend up!" I plead. With an effortless movement, the two men grab Ezra by the arms and yank him up onto the train car. We both stand there panting, holding on to a pole and trying to catch our breath while the men snicker and laugh between themselves.

"I can't," I say quietly a couple of minutes later, finally breaking the silence between us.

"You can't what?"

"I can't ..."

"What?"

"I can't be with you ... I can't be the one in the relationship that jumps first ..."

Marian Dodds

The Man in the Cinnamon Suit

VIGNETTES FROM A MEMOIR ABOUT LIVING AND LEARNING IN ETHIOPIA

It's dawn in Addis Abeba when Demis secures our two giant boxes, marked *Marian* and *Shelagh*, to the roof of the non-governmental organization vehicle. We head northeast, coughing our way through acrid asphalt road construction, and finally ascend to clear air, fresh pavement, and a countryside teeming with people. Sheep, curly-horned cattle, and camels lurch unexpectedly from ditches, stopping traffic. Herders prod fully loaded donkeys toward the market.

We cut through a mountain tunnel Demis tells us was built seventy years ago by the Italian occupiers. The vehicle strains upward, from the steaming lowlands, hair-pinning to airplane height. Breathless from the altitude, I gulp the cooler mountain air. Rainy season just ended; it's lush and green. The sun glistens off leaves, terraced crops, people and oxen harvesting fields, golden stooks like top-knots. Circular compounds of thatched-roof huts sprout like shaggy-maned mushrooms. Double lorries overtake us on single-lane blind curves and I clench my butt at the near misses. Terror, exhilaration, and beauty. I'm fully alive!

Demis has driven many foreign volunteers to their placements. Is he calculating our odds of lasting? How stupid and predictable are our questions? How obvious are our fears and insecurities? I wonder how Shelagh and I will get on. It hadn't occurred to me that part of my cultural adaptation would be living with a foreigner from Nottingham.

Our final two hours are spent in twilight seeping into night while twisting up high mountains. Demis brakes hard to avoid an animal fleeting across the road. Shelagh gasps, "Oh my god did you see those glowing eyes?" Demis says, "Hyena."

Twelve hours after leaving Addis Abeba we shudder to a halt in front of our new home in a small town in Ethiopia's northeastern highlands. A loud ululation greets us. It's Alem, our landlady, wearing a gauzy white dress, the neckline and hem bordered with intricate weaving. Fresh green grass covers the floors of the four-room wattle-and-daub house. Alem takes her place on a low stool in the living room, welcoming us with a traditional Ethiopian coffee ceremony. The room is dim; only one bare bulb dangles from the ceiling. Clouds of frankincense and charcoal smoke spiral upward. Reaching for a wicker fan, she wafts aromas from roasting coffee toward us. I cup my hands, draw the smoke to my face, inhale, and murmur my appreciation. Next she pounds the beans into powder, spoons some into a graceful black clay pot, and fills it with water. When it begins to burble, she pours us tiny cups of *buna*, super saturated with sugar. Demis beams, spreads his arms, and says, "This is our culture."

The next morning the teachers college dean welcomes us with a coffee ceremony and tour. It's a befuddling ritual of greetings, different for male, female, individual, group, higher status, morning, afternoon, and evening. "Ato B will be in your class." The dean introduces me to the senior vice-dean, who is barricaded behind his desk, stacks of papers towering on every surface. I visualize the tornado swirl a breeze might make. Ato B reluctantly pushes himself upright, his dark suit jacket loose, bright white dress shirt bulging over an ample belly. Top heavy. He extends a cold hand, his big brown eyes narrow as he sizes me up.

"Ato B isn't happy about being forced to take my program," I tell Shelagh that night.

"Minalbat," she says. *Minalbat* is our favourite new word, generally translated as "maybe" or "possible", but depending on the context, it can also mean "possibly yes," "maybe yes," "maybe no," or "absolutely not a chance."

The following Saturday we're invited to a farewell celebration for colleagues who've been promoted. In the steamy night, high-decibel music backs traditional dancers pulsating on a giant screen. Squeezed around a tiny table, I watch the yellow and red labels with St. George and his dragon curl off our brown beer bottles in slow motion. When I return from the ritual hand washing (*lightly touch the sliver of blue soap, rub under cold water*), there is a round tray lined with flat injera bread covering our table. Waiters circulate with aluminum vats, plopping generous ladles of spicy sheep and onion tibbs over the traditional bread. We copy our hosts as we dig into the communal plate, tear off injera chunks to scoop up the chewy, tasty stew with our hands, and unceremoniously stuff our mouths. Am I really here, feeling so at home, so far from home? Suddenly I have a surreal sensation of flying out of my body, viewing myself far below with a bird's eye. I'm centuries back, enjoying a medieval feast. Then a sweaty insistent press of Ato B's thigh against mine returns me to earth. That night, I lie awake worrying. *What was that about? Am I misinterpreting something or is this just their culture?*

The men filter into class with a friendly ritual of hand shaking and greetings. Some now use the more intimate shoulder-bumping greeting that feels like acceptance. I ask them to translate my favourite Ethiopian proverb: When spiderwebs unite, they can tie up a lion. They're pleased when I say I've used it in workshops for years. Groups circle their chairs and begin to plan their active learning demonstrations. Our interior space may be dim and dusty, but the environment we've created buzzes with productive, positive energy.

Once they're immersed in their groups I glance out the window at the lush greens fields and mountains, glimpsing roaming animals and hearing the sounds of children playing. Contentment washes through me. Already, I love this group of instructors. Here we are, worlds apart yet connecting with a common sense of humour. I appreciate their culture of politeness, the kindness of their inquiries into how Shelagh and I are fitting in. We are all teachers; it's our common bond. Good teachers are willing to take risks, try out new learning, and reciprocate by teaching what they know. The one-to-one interviews I held this week have inspired me to seek out more resources. I've printed photos I took of paintings by an Ethio-American artist at the National Gallery in Addis for the art teacher to display. The geography teacher promised to loan me his master's thesis on the impact of peri-urban development on the town.

Suddenly Ato B appears and elbows his way into a group, ignoring me, offering no excuse for his lateness. Ten minutes before class is to end he jumps up, says, "I have an announcement," and proceeds to speak to the class in Amharic. The only English word I hear is *transformation*. When he's done, he dismisses my class. Ato B's group is voted winner of the group presentations at the next class. It kills me to give him the highlighter pen prize, but I'm committed to fairness. We all know he didn't do a thing. Yet they voted for him. Why?

"Two things seem clear to me" says Shelagh. "He expects special treatment because of his title, and the instructors are afraid of him."

"Well," I say, "he has the power to choose who can deliver and attend in-service workshops where they receive per diems to supplement their meagre salaries."

Ato B arrives the next week for a one-to-one make-up class. He preens like a peacock, wearing a cinnamon-brown suit so shiny it glints when the sun filters in. He nonchalantly flips through the blank pages of his workbook. I guess he expects me to dictate the answers to him.

"That's not how this works," I explain. "I will help, but I can't do the work for you.

"*Ishi*, I will try." He tips his head in a "yes boss" fashion.

After he leaves I tell Shelagh, "I'm so glad we share this classroom. I wouldn't want to be alone with him." We compare notes. As seasoned teachers, each of us has dealt with chauvinist colleagues and boys who expect to sail through on their charms.

Several months later, the supportive junior vice dean invites me to the workers' tearoom "to discuss." Once coffee is served, he leans in to shake my hand and says ominously, "You must be very careful." I open the small folded note he's placed in my palm. *There are people in your class who are his spies, reporting to him everything you say.* He pulls out his pen, writes *Biruk* on the note, and whispers, "He is the most dangerous." Then he plucks back the note, concealing it in his shirt pocket.

That afternoon I look around my class and the energy sucks out of me, like a reverse vacuum. I'm wondering, *Who are the moles?* When I chose the "spiderwebs unite" proverb, I only imagined weaving in my own small thread to advance quality education. I never expected to confront an angry lion.

Stewart Dickson

The Story That Never Ends

I heard somewhere that a story can only be told backwards. For the story to make sense there needs to be an end, a reason for the information and the narrative that is being spun. Please don't take this to mean reverse chronology, that you have to start with the end and tell the story from back to front. What I'm saying is, the story has to go somewhere—and mean something—for there to be a story. Even the simplest of stories, something that ends in a laugh, the punchline, the bit at the *end*, the *ending*, makes the story. The tale must have a tail, so to speak. This raises a question: Does every ending therefore have a meaning?

I think of the first time I saw a dead body so close I could touch it. I had seen death from afar or beamed to me through screens, but this was the first time it was right there, right where my fingertips ended. I was in Uganda, it was humid, and the windows in the lab I was working in were open to allow a soft breeze to pass through. The gauzy white curtains flowed in the current, swishing in and out of the barred windows. Suddenly, I heard shrieks and howls. They bubbled up as if they had come straight from the pebbled ground that surrounded the compound. There was nothing to announce their coming, only the sudden ululations. I had read this funny word before, *ululate*, but had never really known what it meant. Yet here I was, suddenly enveloped in a cacophony of shrieks and screams.

To ululate is to howl or wail as an expression of strong emotion, typically grief. I stepped out of my office. I asked a colleague, his nose in a file folder, "What're these sounds?"

He replied matter-of-factly, his thick African brogue rich and methodical like rolling syrup, "It is the women. They are grieving," briefly pointing in the direction of the greater hospital compound with a gesture of his head.

I went out to the compound and found a group of about six women on their knees or standing, gesticulating, howling, tearing at their clothes or hair, their hands scraping their faces; one was fanning another who was slumped in a seated position. They were spread out on the orange gravel that composed the driveway to the hospital. I remember stepping past them, leaving the sunlight that beat down on wailing women, and into the cool, shadowed hospital.

The hospital had two-toned walls and was filled with patients and their family members. There was no cafeteria, and the family members, not nurses, provided most of the caregiving. The ailments in this hospital were so different compared to the standard stitches, sniffles, and occasional broken bones found in any Canadian emergency ward I had been in. There were those rotting with leprosy; another was an undiagnosed epileptic, covered in burns after a seizure near a cooking fire with a vat of boiling vegetable oil. Many of the beds were filled with those devoured by HIV/AIDS. Today, though, the chaos was outside and the room itself was quiet.

As I stepped in I saw a man lying on a gurney with a white blanket pulled up to his shoulders. A doctor was there, writing on a notepad; he barely moved as I entered the room, stepped toward the body, and stood over the gurney. I looked down on a face, its eyes clenched shut. The man's face was frozen in a grimace, the brow furrowed and pursed, his jawline speckled with grey stubble, which stood out on his black skin. The doctor piped up, "Heart attack," and I nodded. Here was the end of this man's life and I, a pale-skinned stranger who had never met him before, stood peering over him as his loved ones sang their discordant song of mourning. Was it the end of his story? Was it the beginning of another? Was it the middle, or just a side note? Whose story must end for the rest to be told?

Some argue that a good story is like a ball of yarn: you can pull one part of a thread and find that it is connected to another, and the story will unfurl and reveal itself. A ball of yarn has a beginning and an end, though it can take time to find. With yarn, you can always exchange the end for the beginning, or back again.

As a laboratory administrator with an HIV/AIDS organization, one of my main jobs was to coordinate clinic days. Clinic days could be held out in remote communities with difficult-to-pronounce names, due to the Bantu proclivity to pronounce *c*'s and *k*'s as *ch*'s. Kigumba, Kiryandongo. Sometimes we held the clinics right in the compound we shared with the hospital. My main job was to organize people, which is a job I am uniquely qualified for. I've always felt compelled to join a queue, even if I'm not sure of its purpose. Sometimes, I have found myself waiting in a queue I didn't even have to be in, pulled in by the line's seemingly gravitational allure. This was not the case in Uganda.

The clinics were a swirl of humanity all vying for service, their fists clenched with documents that denoted the manner in which we would draw their blood. "First come, first served" was secondary to who could budge or push their way to the front as a tangled ball of faces and outstretched arms. I would arrive at these cement community health centres, find a table and chair, set up benches, pull out a ledger to record the tests and the results, and impose the law of the queue. I felt like an imperial administrator, swiftly meting out order in chaos.

The clinics tested those who were clients, those already confirmed as having HIV, to see if their condition had worsened. The clinic also tested for new clients by taking a drop of blood from one of them and applying it to a test strip. Depending on where we were and when we had been there last, we might test two hundred people and find that one-third would become our newly diagnosed clients.

Sometimes I would help perform the tests. I would take the index finger of the volunteer, swab it with alcohol, and drive a small metal prick into the fingertip, drawing a bulb of blood, which I would then apply to a test strip. I would apply a drop of solution to ensure the blood flowed along the strip and onto the magic lines that held fate. If the colour changed or a line appeared, depending on the test, the person was HIV positive. I dream of the fingertips. Sometimes the fingers are those of children, soft and supple, tiny between my rubberized thumb and forefinger, their faces buried into the breast of their nervous parents. Sometimes I would test farmers, their fingertips calloused and weathered, rebuffing the stab of the prick. They would wince as I tried again and again to draw blood, plunging the metal tip into their sandpaper skin. Often, I could only get a trickle from a finger; other times blood would jump out, speckling the table or my gloves. Sometimes there would be a young student, maybe sixteen, vibrant, full of life, and my heart would sink at the colour the test would turn. There were times when I could diagnose before I even drew blood. A frail baby, with discoloured hair like dried weeds and laboured breaths, or a middle-aged man, his clothes that once fit now draped over his body. He shuffles on a cane, smelling of urine and sweat, ravaged by the virus he was likely too scared to confirm, or confront, until now, far too late.

I recall lifting a woman, surprised at how light she was, another victim of HIV/AIDS. She was bone and sinew, and walking for her was agonizing. I carried her to the nurse's room to lay her in a bed; she was as light as a scarecrow stuffed with straw. She was like many others; their story had not ended but it might as well have. I heard somewhere that the story of our lives is suffering, the source of that suffering is our fear, and our most primal fear is death. In short, we suffer because we are always afraid of death. I think of these frail skeletons, all but dead, but still alive.

Viktor E. Frankl stated that it is the meaning of a person's life that fuels their survival in harsh conditions. Frankl survived a concentration camp and posited that those without meaning, without purpose for their suffering, were the ones who perished.

Here this story concludes, but it has no conclusion. There is no meaning, just words and experiences, and the meaning you choose to apply. Sometimes stories aren't like yarn but a bowl of spaghetti, full of starts and ends, some clipped and some long, all encased in a common bowl. I merely hope the bowl of spaghetti is good to eat for someone, or that a bite or two will satisfy someone else.

Sriram Iyer

The Busyness of Unemployment

USEFUL READING FOR THOSE AT PEACE

I am now convinced that Time is not merely an abstract concept but a living, breathing, scheming monster. I envisage a green octopod with large, red, oval eyes and a wide-toothed sadistic smile. In my vision, he holds the reins of a million horses, whip in hand, watching the havoc in our lives unfold.

This startling epiphany flashed across my mind's eye as I was huffing my way across Burrard Street Bridge on my bicycle. It took considerable effort to keep this image in focus as my toddler son, strapped behind me in his seat, insistently pawed at me to point out yet another yellow taxi.

We were going to be late for daycare, again.

I found myself wondering if I wasn't the victim of a wider conspiracy.

I had taken a long-awaited sabbatical from my busy job as a hospital doctor, ostensibly to slow down the pace of life and spend more time on other pursuits, discovering the artist in me, writing about it, and spending quality time with my son.

Three months later, these "other pursuits" felt hard done by, as I barely had time to breathe.

How could that happen?

I wasn't a slacker, at least I don't think I was. Well, this is my theory: When Time, capricious monster that he is, cracks the whip, the horses pull harder, and those unfortunate enough to be in the spotlight find themselves rushing.

And the evidence suggests the rest of the world is in cahoots with Him.

Take my case in point: my coffee queue is always the longest, my supermarket till the slowest, and even my omelette arrives late because—this is where things stop being funny—the chef ran out of eggs! I rush from pillar to post simply to live out the day.

This may well be reminiscent of a *Bruce Almighty* theme, but I assure you I'm not that important in this world. I'm just yet another naive puppet whose strings are being whimsically pulled.

"Honey, did you do the laundry?" is therefore countered sheepishly with "Sorry, ahem, I didn't find the time," much to the incredulity of my disbelieving wife, who works a seventy-hour week.

Under pressure now, I suggested, rather cleverly I thought, that Time was not interested in wrecking the lives of the working class, because how much can you flog the hamster already playing catch-up on the wheel?

I realized even as I said it that, without context, this isolated statement sounded like the ramblings of a madman.

My wife was kinder. "Are you doing drugs?" she demanded before storming off.

I went back to the drawing board (a.k.a. coffee shop) for further reflection and rumination. After several espressos, a wired-up version of me suggested I approach the problem as I would a research conundrum.

Problem: Why do I find myself running out of time despite being unemployed?

Approach: A head-to-head comparison of my previous and current avatars.

Note to self: Avoid scattered thoughts, odd personifications, or metaphorical visions—anything that suggests the beginnings of insanity.

It was quite simple once I bent my scientific mind to it.

I took an imaginary scenario, visiting a coffee shop, and played out how the two versions of me, busy professional and freewheeler, would approach the situation.

The professional rapidly orders a cappuccino whilst planning his ward round, lunchtime meeting, and afternoon clinic. In and out of the coffee shop in five minutes.

The freewheeler reviews caffeine options carefully before opting for the Tanzanian pour over. He is then curious about Tanzanian coffee and spends twenty minutes reading all about it on Wiki. He notices that employees from the bank next door frequent the café, spending an inordinate amount of time chatting about MLS and the Canucks. He gazes idly at the barista, who has dreadlocks, a nose ring, and a superstition about wiping the countertop in a zigzag pattern, like a final flourish on a work of art. It is fascinating to follow artists and their quirks. The coffee is delightfully pungent and citric with a hint of kiwi and blackberry. Actually, that would make an interesting wine. Merlot or Shiraz? Do vineyards in B.C. make fruity reds?

The whole experience takes a couple of hours, by which time I'm hungry and lunch beckons.

The results were the same no matter what the scenario, be it grocery shopping or doing laundry. Have you ever wondered why supermarket shelves are stacked in a certain way or how much research goes into visual merchandising? Or that nail polish remover can transfer ink stains from shirts to towels?

You see, Time was the driving force behind my working life—omnipresent, orchestrating every move and infiltrating every step. It ensured my work schedule had direction and focus.

So, when Time was removed as a key factor, I was effectively given a wide-angle lens with which to view the world. All my senses were peeled away and exposed; sounds, textures, colours, and ideas were all suddenly louder, brighter, and deeper. I realized I don't see and hear anymore—I observe and listen. Fascinating nuggets from strangers' lives enrich my day.

You could challenge my premise by questioning the purpose of carting around a lot of useless information. Well, I like the heaviness of knowledge; it lends balance and stability to my mindset, much like a mid-engine car.

The concept of Time becomes blurry as other aspects of life become sharper.

I'll stop my rambling; you get the general idea.

All I need to do now is box this concept up in clever, easy-to-read packaging for the missus and I can totally avoid doing the laundry!

It's time to hit the café again.

P.S. It is not my intention to be sexist by alluding to Time as a "he." He is a villain in my books, and my old-fashioned chivalry precludes me from incriminating the female sex. Plus, it's easier to blame my own kind.

Averill Groeneveld-Meijer

Circus

Family fracture and a transatlantic move turned my world upside down. A few years went by and I still hadn't quite found my feet. Ballet and music lessons didn't help, but when I was around twelve years old, I was sent to join Titia's Wednesday after-school art classes.

Titia was a painter, a dancer, and a trained potter. She lived by herself on the ground floor of a small house in The Hague. Her flat was divided between her private quarters, in the former living room, and the studio, in the old dining room, where she taught art classes to small groups of children.

At my first lesson Titia introduced me to the other children. Jan, a quiet boy around my age, and chatty Marieke, a year or two younger. Titia sliced up pound cake and poured mugs of tea for us, then placed Jan's finished oil painting of a train on an easel. She gazed fondly at short, round Jan, then turned our attention to his blending of cobalt and ultramarine in the sky and the sea and the delicate burnt-umber trestle bridge in between. She pointed out how the bright yellow train clanged in on rails from the left, drawn forward by the cadmium-yellow moon in the upper right-hand corner. Titia and Jan talked about his next project, and she promised Marieke a lesson on making saucers to fit the teacups she'd made on the pottery wheel.

After tea, Titia moved confidently around the cramped studio, showing me a cupboard full of oil paints, pallettes, brushes, charcoals, pastels, and sketch pads. Blank canvases and buckets of glazes were stacked behind the pottery wheel. A kiln in the corner vented through the outside wall into the backyard. She explained that students could work on anything they wanted, but she encouraged me to start with a still life in oils and set me up at an easel near the kiln. Diffuse northern light fell on the small canvas, as I clutched a pallette and brush and listened to her explanations about linseed oil, pigments, and blending, about starting with the background and letting it dry before moving on, and about turpentine and cleaning my own brushes.

For my first painting, I spent most of my time on the texture of a yellow stuccoed wall and swirling greens into a wild shag carpet. A week later I added a brown table, then a glass vase, and finally a bunch of red tulips.

I moved on to a portrait of my dog in the empty lot behind my house. First the sand, then titanium-white Tim, made fluffy with light strokes of grey. I added a stick for interest, but it looked like poop, so I yellow-ochered right over it.

Every week, Titia welcomed us with homemade pound cake and tea. We sat at a round table eating slice after slice of lemon or vanilla cake while she placed our work from the week before on easels for her students to admire and discuss.

One day, Titia wasn't there when I got to her house. Jan, Marieke, and I knocked on the studio door and puzzled over the clear tape stuck across the door and the woodwork, until Titia breezed in from outside. "Sorry I'm late. I was just buying cake." She carefully inspected the tape, peeled it back, fiddled with new padlocks, and led us into the studio. She apologized for the store-bought cake. "A problem with ingredients," she said. She boiled water for tea while we admired the shine on Marieke's newly fired cups and saucers.

Marieke was the youngest student, but she could kick the wheel up to speed and centre the clay all by herself. Week after week she turned out pieces for a tea set. When she took a break from the wheel to work on the spout for a teapot, I tried to make a bowl. Titia helped me select a lump of clay and work out the bubbles and grit. She helped me kick the wheel up to speed, then placed her hands over mine and told me to concentrate. The clay had to be in the exact centre of the wheel or it would fly away. She removed her hands, I concentrated, and the clay flew away.

She suggested I start with something flat instead and gave me a rolling pin and a new piece of clay. I rolled out a tile the size of a page, added snakes of clay, and drew in it with blunt tools. The following week I painted my tile with glaze, and a week later, Titia placed it on the table to be admired. The green on the grass was a bit thick, the clouds not quite white enough, but the sun was bright and yellow and round, and its beams slanted from the upper right-hand corner all the way down to the lower left.

As we settled into our tea and store-bought cake, Titia glanced nervously at the ceiling and whispered of trouble with the tenants upstairs. We couldn't quite hear her and she wouldn't speak up. "They're listening," she hissed, so we encouraged her to write it down. She wrote, "They are putting things in my food." She brought a package of ground beef from her fridge. We inspected its packaging and sniffed it. Titia seemed satisfied with our concern, and the lesson continued.

Jan began working on portraits, so Titia clipped an example of facial proportions to the corner of his easel. A wooden doll stood by, limbs ready to be bent into shape. Marieke went back to the wheel, throwing bowls and cutting hearts in their brims with a thin sharp blade. I took a huge canvas to my easel by the north-facing window.

I used charcoal to sketch a small circus ring in the centre of the canvas, rubbed it out with a dried-up bird wing, and drew a long arc across the diagonal. Impatient with the charcoal, I painted in the boarding around the partial ring and worked on the faces in the crowd. Young, old, some were funny looking, some wore hats. When I ran out of people ideas I painted the sand *piste* in a swirl of ochre and white. Titia moved the project along by pointing out that as the spectators rose up the stands, their faces would appear smaller, less distinct, and hidden in shadows. The painting was almost complete, except the spectators stared at an empty ring. The audience and I had to wait for the background to dry.

On my way home I thought about what I would paint as the central attraction. I walked along grey pavement and ran away with the circus, where I laughed with clowns and clumped down the sidewalk with elephants. I turned right at the canal and galloped alongside it in sequins on horseback, swinging a whip around my head like a lion tamer in a top hat. It didn't matter that the pottery wheel didn't work out or if the calligraphy pens spat ink all over the expensive linen paper. It didn't even matter that I couldn't draw very well. The next week I would paint something colourful, exciting, and alive.

A week later I sat at the table, ready to share my ideas for the circus ring, but Titia put one of her own works on the easel and with narrowed eyes asked us what we thought of it. We saw a dark abyss ringed with red flames on one side and pastel flowers on the other. A small armoured figure stood on a rose petal, holding a pike. Titia pointed at the abyss. "This is my womanhood," she hissed. "It is under attack, but I will defend it!" She spat at Jan, "You don't understand!" She pointed a paint-flecked finger at me. "But you, you understand." I understood enough to know it wasn't what we should be talking about, and I knew enough to deflect the topic. I hustled poor Jan off to his portraits and little Marieke to her wheel. I took my garish circus off to my spot by the window.

I painted an enormous teeter-totter in the centre of the ring, with a shadowy figure on the right, ready to jump from a great height onto the high side. On the low side of the teeter-totter I painted a woman in a shiny red leotard and a top hat. She had big pink thighs and skinny calves that disappeared into black high-heeled boots. I painted her in profile, thinking it would be easier, but her nose came out too big, her eye off-kilter. I smudged her face trying to fix it and had to wait a week for it to dry.

Impatient to complete my work, I rushed to Titia's the following Wednesday. I was uncomfortable to be alone with her and worked to keep the conversation neutral. Fortunately Marieke arrived later, full of innocent chatter. Jan never showed up. I fixed my acrobat's face. I painted her arms at the moment just before flight and touched up the background, adding balloons in the corners and brightening the tent's stripes. Titia didn't say much about this new work, but she promised to make chocolate cake to celebrate its completion. I signed my name in the lower right corner and left my painting to dry for the week.

On my walk home along the warm grey streets of The Hague, I bent my knees, straightened my back, and launched myself up, up, up, into the sky, arms swinging over my head for momentum, striving for each extra centimetre of loft.

When I arrived at the studio the following Wednesday, Titia wasn't there. No one was there. I rang the bell for the people upstairs, but no one answered. A woman came out of the house next door and told me Titia wasn't home, that she'd been in and out of institutions her whole life, and, "Sorry, no, this time she won't be back."

I never saw Titia, Jan, or Marieke again. I never saw my painting again except in my imagination, where a figure is launched into the air, somersaults above crowds, flies high in spite of her clunky black boots, and lands softly in a puff of yellow ochre dust.

Tamara Jong

The Will

My glider plane flew out our car window on the day of Grandfather's funeral. It was spring in South Bend, Indiana. Grandfather's service was held at River Park United Methodist Church, and he was laid to rest at Highland Cemetery. My family travelled twelve long hours by car from Quebec to pay respects. My sister Angie was six, I was four, and my little brother Tommy was two. This was our first introduction to Grandfather.

My grandfather Fee had died of a heart attack. He had been born in 1908 in a village near Canton, in China, and came to South Bend with my great-grandfather, a Taoist monk named Toon, around 1931. Grandfather owned a few Chinese restaurants with his brothers. He had a second wife, Mary, and two kids, Stephen and Debra. My father had two sisters, Alexa and Po. My father's birth mother had died of kidney failure when my father was ten. Grandfather married again that year. We had heard that my father was sent to Canada because the U.S. was in the middle of the Vietnam War. During this exchange my father had lost his birth and family names and so assumed the life of a dead man. We have borrowed his name like an overcoat; it is a name that is misspelled, mispronounced and leads to questions about my belonging.

When I was fourteen my relationship with my father changed after my parents divorced. My mother had been a Jehovah's Witness since I was two and this grounded me. My father disappeared, and I looked to God as his replacement. I hung onto childhood memories of me clutching my father's fingers when he'd take us to Chinatown to buy *Old Master Q* comic books. We'd eat crunchy Chinese noodles and pink, red, and white chips in waxy white bags as Tommy and I played in the back of our Buick behind the Chinese restaurant. Soon that was all I had, distant memories of someone who used to be my father.

My mother's sisters tell me that my parents were full of secrets. Ma is dead, so she cannot tell me the stories I am ready to hear. I don't know where my father lives, and communication with him is sparse. He is reluctant to offer any information. When we went to family weddings, we signed our name with one my father told us to write down. When I left my religion, I wondered who I was. I hoped that finding out more about my father and my kin would lead to answers. I wanted to honour my ancestors by acknowledging our family name. I am here because of them.

Grandfather made a will. We were told that my father and his sisters did not receive anything. My sister remembers seeing the will sitting on the fridge in our apartment. She had been searching for the candy my parents had hidden from us. When Grandfather died, they had been estranged. We heard my parents talk about this—something about my father having married my white mother or because my father's stepmother turned Grandfather against him. There were no family pictures, no letters. The will would hold the information that I was looking for, his name.

In researching Ancestry and Rootsweb, I was able to track down the probate number and get a copy of the will. When it arrived, my hands shook with anticipation. I flipped through the pages quickly and saw that Grandfather left his son nothing. Ecclesiastes 7:1 says that, "a name is better than good oil," and it was. *Ying* means "be full" and *nan* means "boy" or "man." My father is Ying-Nan.

There are holes and gaps in this narrative and relatives that are dead and cannot speak for themselves. They cannot confirm or deny what is true and what has been fabricated. My father's family is scattered, and time and language have separated us. These are the barriers in my story. A story that will continue after I am gone.

When I attempt to rewrite this story, I can't imagine Grandfather's face, what he sounded like or how life was for him as an immigrant, or if he was proud that he had made a good life for himself and his family in a new country. I do not know why my father no longer spoke to Grandfather. The only truth I know is that Grandfather loved my father enough to save him, and that is enough.

Nadia Ashley

"Say Goodbye to Daddy"

AN EXCERPT FROM A MEMOIR

One afternoon after school, I have to stay a very long time with my grandad and Aunty Kitty. They also live in Rothchild's Buildings, on the other side of the quadrangle.

The living room isn't meant for girls like me. The walls are bottle green. They look slimy like frog's skin, especially when the steam from the kitchen runs down them in squiggly lines. Grandad is sitting on one side of the scratched brown table, me on the other. Flakes of tobacco from his pipe are all over the place. I brush the bits off from my side onto the floor. *Aunty Kitty should use a tablecloth like Mummy. Then he'd have to be clean.*

The mantelpiece is bare except for the clock. *Five o'clock. Squeeze my eyes, wish till I shake, Mummy, hurry up. My feet can't reach the floor, this chair's too old it needs a nail, if I fidget it wobbles, Aunty Kitty's already told me off once.*

The smell of chicken soup sidles its way up to my nostrils and lands right in front of me in a china bowl. Yellow liquid with a shiny golden topping stares up at me. *Floating fat, that's what it is and it's not going anywhere.* Mum says that Aunty Kitty's too lazy to let the soup cool down and skim off the fat. *Fish fishing underneath with my spoon … catch a chunk of carrot with its head still on, stringy bits of chicken brown and smelly, like that cord she uses to tie up her old boxes she hides underneath her bed. Why doesn't she just get rid of those nasty dresses with buttons? They smell terrible when she pulls them out. It makes my skin crawl how she puts them up against me to see what I'd look like, all dressed up like a bloomin' Shirley Temple doll. What's this?*

Something mushy, an onion. She's supposed to take that out and only use it for the stock. I'm gonna be sick if I eat this muck.

"Aunty Kitty, I'm not feeling well. I can't eat. I feel sick."

Tick tock, tickity-tock says the clock. I concentrate on its numbers. Grandad's slurping up his greasy soup. She says in my ear, "Your mother will be here any minute. Be a good girl." The soup bowl is moved away from my placemat, only a little, just in case I might change my mind, I suppose. I take a peek at the side of her face. It's very wet and I just know a drop of her sweat is going to plonk right into my soup. *There it goes—caught in the nick of time.* A large, grimy handkerchief is waived in front of me, full of germs by the look of it, then goes into action as she mops up her face, shoving it back into her apron pocket. "My God, Willy, I'm *schvitzing*! You don't know how lucky you men are."

"So, go to the doctor and get it fixed, if it bothers you so much."

"I can't even get any decent shut-eye anymore."

"What are you complaining about? You can sleep all day if you want. And I'm out working my *tuchus* off. Listen, we'll swap places. You take the sweat shop, I'll stay at home. Then you'll get a taste of the real world."

The drab living room shudders into silence, broken only by the muffled sound of rubbish dropping down the chute.

Grandad looks at me with his watery blue eyes and jabbers, "What's up, Charley boy?" He sticks out his tongue, shows me his cavernous mouth with some half-chewed carrot still inside, and makes a kind of hissing sound. Then he flips his tongue behind his lower teeth and makes the whole row go up and down. He told me that the dentist ripped them all out when he was thirty, to save the trouble of toothache. At night he takes his teeth out and puts them in a special glass of cloudy water.

The door knocker bangs. *Two hard knocks—Mum's mad.* Aunty Kitty scoots to the front door, takes out her handkerchief and uses it like a flannel, into her ears, down her neck, even under her arms, then wipes her nose. "That's your mother. At last."

Mum's standing in the doorway. Her face is red and hot-looking. I run up to her, grab her hand, and pull. "Mum, where were you?"

She looks down at me and speaks with a cracked voice, as if she's been crying. "Now don't get all upset. Your father's home."

She pokes her head inside the living room, nods at Grandad, looks at Aunty Kitty, sighs, then gathers me up. I feel butterflies inside my belly but don't let her see my happiness.

"Wait up. Where's your manners? Have you said thank you to your grandad and Aunty Kitty for looking after you?"

"Yes, Mummy." I turn toward Grandad, blow him a kiss, and give him a wink.

We make the slow climb down the iron staircase, Mum holding onto the rail with one hand and clutching me with the other. Our footsteps make a clunky sound, but I'm not scared because Daddy's home. We make it down the six flights and out into the early night of the playground. There are three boys from my school, with mops of ginger hair and faces filled with freckles and dried snot, playing hopscotch near the big rubbish bins. "Ragamuffins" Mummy calls them. She holds my hand very tightly and steers me right away from them. "Don't stare and draw attention to yourself. They're nothing but trouble. Look at their trousers, hand-me-downs more like. All *yoks* from the same family—Irish. You're to stay away. It's those kinds of boys that have lice. And they jump from a dirty head to a clean one, and I've already had to delouse you twice this year. It's a big *mishegas*."

My tummy turns over and I pull her into our stairwell. *We've got to get to Daddy*. Up the first flight, then the second, with me in front holding onto the rail. By the middle of the third flight, we have to stop. A woman with a *tuchus* the size of an elephant is panting, then she sits down on one of the steps, her shopping baskets on either side. She's got a sour smell. Mum pulls me in very close to her body, whispers, "Hold your nose," then squeezes past her. "I would stop, Mrs. Pressman, but I left the chicken soup on a high simmer. I don't want to start a fire in the building. That's all we need."

As we move up the stairs, I turn to take a look at the old lady muttering to herself, "Worries go down better with soup than without."

When we reach our flat on the seventh floor, Mum tells me to stop in my tracks. She speaks very quietly, and her eyes glitter like black diamonds. "Your father's waiting in there. He's going to say goodbye. I don't want any fuss, do you understand? We're going to have a good life without him. A better life. So, don't you worry. Now go inside, and be a good girl."

Daddy's standing in the living room, looking very serious, wearing a dark overcoat and a brown trilby hat. I can hardly see his face, and something about him all covered up makes me stay in the doorway. A little push from Mum gets me closer to him. Looking down at me, he says, "Dinky, girl, it's time for me to go. Now listen, sometimes it just works out this way and mums and dads can't stay with each other. You're getting to be a big girl now and I want you to promise to look after Mummy. Do you pinky swear?"

I have to nod because that's what he wants me to do. He crouches down and I can see both of his eyes, watery like the oceans he travels over. He takes my hand and puts his little finger over my little finger.

Room spins, have to let go—of your finger, Daddy. Rest. Floor. Eyes closed. Dark spinning world. Cold, Daddy.

"Dinky, open your eyes. Drink a little warm water. Nothing to worry about. You're all wrapped up now in Grandpa's blanket with a hot water bottle on your tootsies. It's all over. Daddy's gone. It's just gonna get better from here on. You mark my words."

Maureen Duteau

Old Hands

The hands sit idly on the table. They are weathered, brown, and long-fingered. Old and worn out. Like the bark of an old-growth tree, they are creviced and bruised from battling storms. They are strong hands that have worked hard. They are gorgeous hands that tell the story of a life, the life of a man who has seen it all.

The hands pick up the deck of cards and cut the deck, deftly sliding the cards over each other—*sheh, sheh, sheh*. Tidy piles of cards stack up in front of each player—*shuk, shuk, shuk*. Shuffle, deal, drop. I'm mesmerized by these hands that I've seen a thousand times but never truly looked at, and I notice a small mark on the flesh between thumb and index finger.

"What is that tattoo on your right hand?"

"That's an anchor. I got that the time I joined the navy," says the owner of the hands.

"When did you join the navy? Didn't you run away?"

"I was sixteen and I wanted to make some money, so I hopped on a train for B.C. I lied about my age and got a job at a mill on Vancouver Island. I made good money back then—two bucks an hour. I sent half of it home to Ma. Eventually, someone started asking me questions about my age, so I skipped town early the next morning and joined the navy."

I scan my father's face. He grew up the oldest son of thirteen brothers and sisters from a French Canadian community in St. Paul, Alberta. Hopping on a train, working at a mill under false pretenses, and then joining the navy—this is all foreign to my own idea of childhood.

The hands shrug and select three cards.

"Where did you get your other tattoos?" I prod.

"This one is obvious," he replies, pointing to the word N-A-V-Y spelled across his knuckles, "and the one on my shoulder, that was a lady I knew before I met your mother."

This is a familiar line. "Who was Torchy, Dad?"

He smiles and looks at the faded tattoo that is as much a part of his fabric as the colour of his eyes. "She was a pretty lady that I used to know. Good ole Torchy. We had a lotta fun."

I imagine tawdry meetings with a curvy brunette in a cheap hotel room. I picture Jennifer Tilly from a mobster movie, all pouty sex. Suddenly, I don't want to pry anymore.

"Mom? You need to discard three cards to me." Mom is notorious for taking her time. It is especially hard now that she is losing her memory. My father's hands rest on the table confidently, resonating with strength. I want to learn more.

"Dad, didn't you take me hunting when I was little?"

"Yep. You were the best retriever a man could hope for. I would get home from work and you'd say, 'Daddy get your gun' and off we'd go. We mostly caught grouse and pheasant. You had a great eye. You could spot a bird a mile away."

"When did you start hunting?"

"There was always a gun around the house. But Dad wouldn't let us near one after Noel shot Jerry Murphy."

"What? Uncle Noel? What happened?"

"Well, we found a gun in the garbage. It didn't have any wood on it and it was stuffed with dirt. So, we used a coat hanger to clean it out and oiled it till it sparkled, but nobody thought it would ever work. Uncle Ray found some .22 shells and we tried to get it to work, but we eventually lost interest."

The hands rise to demonstrate the futility of the gun.

"When we came home later, Noel was playing with the gun. He was about eight at the time and we were twelve. He looked up and pointed it at Jerry and said, 'Bang, bang, you're dead.' And sure enough, he shot Jerry right in the stomach."

"You're kidding. What happened? Did he die?"

"Jerry was Irish, so he said, 'Call the priest—I lied in confession and I stole money.' Jerry's dad was an RCMP officer and he took him to the hospital and the bullet was lodged in his appendix, so they took them both out."

"Did he live?"

"Yep. And then his dad gave us a dog."

"Lorna, are you ready to play yet?"

The hands reach for a cup of tea. They are itching to play. For a while, the hands get what they want. They sort, select, and win. *Sitting ducks,* they smirk.

"Mom, you shouldn't play the queen of spades. You are going to win the trick."

"Maybe she's trying for a slam," I say. And the hands slyly put down the ace of spades, and win the trick. "Dad, have you ever been close to dying?"

The hands slowly rub together.

"A few times. I was a bit of a scrapper before I met your mother."

"That's right. They called you Black Bart, and you used to get into fights. You had a missing tooth in your wedding photo."

The hands close into a fist. They have a temper.

"I learned to fight from my dad. He said, 'Go in fast and get some licks in. If you're throwing a punch, hit him in the nose and draw blood.' It was all on account of a bully who used to beat me up until I finally got the courage to hit back. Tommy Berard. He picked on anyone he could and he was mean. Tommy was hung in Fort Saskatchewan for murder."

Mom pipes up, "Remember the time we met that beat-up man in the hospital with Michael? The man with the broken nose?"

The hands tense in rueful recollection.

"What happened?" I ask.

Dad reluctantly responds, "Well, we had to take Michael to the hospital when he was a baby and there was a guy in the waiting area in rough shape. He had a broken nose and was bleeding all over. When I asked him what happened, he said, 'You should know. You're the guy who did it to me.'"

"What? You beat him up? How could you not know?"

"I was working as a bartender in the evenings to make extra money. The night it happened, I was carrying a tray of drinks and this guy came at me with a knife. So I dumped my tray on him and started pounding him. I went ballistic. I was so mad that I just pummelled him and someone had to pull me off. Blood was splattered all over my shirt. After the shift, I was so tired that I forgot all about it."

"Oh my God, Dad. You were badass."

The hands nod in agreement. The fingers shuffle, *sheh, sheh, sheh*. "Lorna, you are passing to Maureen now. Pay attention."

"All right. Be patient. There's no rush."

But the hands aren't listening. They flush out the hearts. *Like taking candy from a baby*.

"Dad, how did you get that scar on your knuckle?"

The bear paws resting on the table suddenly pale. Two fingers reach over to rub the scar on the left hand, stretching over two knuckles in a neat white line. They remind the hands of the time they were of no use.

"That was from a canoeing accident. Back when I first started out as a surveyor in northern Ontario. You asked me if I had ever been close to dying."

The hands still in remembrance.

"In my early twenties, I was surveying for Ontario Hydro and living in the bush. It was spring and there was still snow on the ground. We made fifty-five bucks a week plus room and board surveying a contour for a dam in Thunder Bay. Harvey Lean was my partner and we travelled to and from work by canoe." The fingers rub the scar.

"Harvey sat in the bow so I could steer. One day we turned a corner and hit some rocks. Our canoe flipped over and Harvey hit his head. I got dumped too and the canoe landed on my knuckles, here, where the scar is. I scrambled to reach Harvey and I found him face down in the water with blood on his head. I dragged him to the shore but there was nothing I could do."

The hands tremble with nerves at the memory.

"I didn't know what to do but I didn't want to be alone, so I threw Harvey over my shoulder and took off to try to reach someone who could help. I must have covered ten kilometres with Harvey on my back until I got to the camp. The longest ten kilometres I've ever walked. Of course, there was nothing anyone could do. Harvey was gone."

The hands are motionless. The game is forgotten.

"Dad," I ask softly, "When did you meet Mom?"

The hands stir, then rub the ring. They love this story.

"I was twenty-seven when I met your mother. Ray Pledger and I worked on the *Stewart Cassiar* together. He said that he could find me a date—a great gal named Lorna McFadden—but he warned me not to get too serious with her."

"He warned me to stay away from Black Bart."

"He told her that I was bad news."

"But I liked him. He was dashing. I couldn't stay away." Mom's voice trills with the memory.

"If it weren't for your mother, these hands would have gotten up to no good."

I wonder about the kind of man that my father was. What would have happened if he hadn't settled down? I look at the photo of my dad in his navy uniform. He looks handsome and intelligent, and like a scoundrel.

The hands find hers and briefly touch her wedding ring. They close over her hands, dark skin against light. A laying on of hands. "Thank God I met your mother."

Georgia Swayze

Daddy Issues

AN EXCERPT FROM A MUCH LARGER PIECE THAT IS STILL IN THE WORKS

One of the only entertaining things to do when I visit my childhood home in Fort Langley (or Fart Langley, as I called it when I was a hilarious teenager) is to look through my old artwork, photo albums, and other items that my mother has kept from my youth. During one of these visits I came across something I had never noticed before, an aging navy-blue hard covered journal with a brown spine. I opened it up and quickly scanned a couple of pages. I was shocked. It appeared as though my mom had kept a journal about me when I was a kid, something I had no idea existed until now.

I turned to the first page.

March '93: As our cat Cosby is constantly knocking things over and in trouble, I can often be overheard muttering, "bloody cat." Of course you too, now refer to her as "Bloody Cat."

Next page.

February '94: Today you told me that you wanted to shave your legs, drive a car, and be a "cooker" like a mommy. You are three and a half.

Next.

Easter Sunday '94: Georgia, you refuse to acknowledge the Easter Bunny. You keep telling everyone that the Easter Duck came to your house! You seem to have come up with this one on your own.

Next.

Summer of '97: While I went to take surfing lessons in California, Grandma and Grandpa Craine came to look after you for a week. You had not seen your

Daddy for three years. He dropped them off outside our townhouse. You were looking out the window waiting for Grandma and Grandpa. I could tell by the look on your face that you had seen your daddy—hard to describe the look … Perhaps trepidatiously excited. You ran down the stairs and expected me to follow outside, and when I did not follow, you stopped as well. I explained that I did not want to see your daddy, but I encouraged you to go and see him, but you wouldn't. I told you that your grandma would go with you, but you still wouldn't go. I think you really wanted to. You were very quiet for a while. What a horrible, horrible thing for an angel like you to have to endure. I was so very sad for you.

Holy. Fucking. Shit.

What I'm about to tell you shouldn't be much of a surprise. I've got a shit-ton of daddy issues. Are you familiar with the term? If not, I'll supply you with this definition I gathered from the web:

> Daddy Issues
> [*dad*-ee ish-oos]
> *Daddy issues* is an informal phrase for the psychological challenges resulting from an absent or abnormal relationship with one's father, often manifesting in a distrust of, or sexual desire for, men who act as father figures.

I wouldn't say that this definition really encapsulates the entirety of my daddy issues—it merely scratches the surface—but yes, I can confirm for you that the cliché is true (for me at least). Little girls who grow up without fathers often become fucked-up adult women. I wish I could say otherwise. Do you think I enjoy being a living, breathing stereotype? I certainly do fucking not. I'd like to say that this is an essay debunking the "myth" surrounding daddy issues, but that would make me a lying sack of shit.

July 16, 1993: Today Cara's granny asked Georgia where her daddy was. Georgia told her that her daddy was "dead."

I was twenty-one when a friend and I went on a trip to Mexico. The general itinerary of the trip was drink, tan, and get slutty. I desired to be one of those feminists who sleeps with men purely for pleasure without it affecting her self-worth. Unbeknownst to me at the time, you probably shouldn't pursue this ultra sex-positive form of feminism if you have deep-seated attachment issues because your father abandoned you at a young age.

On the last night of our week-long trip, I slept with a local man who worked at the resort. Two days prior, my friend lost her virginity to a Dutch man we met at a nightclub whose name she couldn't remember.

The next morning as I boarded the plane home, instead of feeling like the empowered feminist she-hero I had expected to be, I felt worse than I had ever felt before. It was like there was a glaring pit at the bottom of my stomach, one that seemed to be growing bigger by the second. I couldn't quite pin the feeling. It wasn't shame. It wasn't a broken heart. I had only known this guy for seven measly days. We weren't in love. He had a garish cursive script tattoo that said "believe" scrawled across his chest and pierced nipples, for God's sake. Not to mention I barely knew him. But despite this, I had never felt so low, and this took the wind right out of me.

We found our seats and I was so thankful to be assigned next to the window. I leaned my head against the chilly glass as tears trickled down my face for the rest of the five-hour flight.

When I got home I was promptly overcome with anxiety and depression, all because I had some mediocre drunken sex with a semi-attractive Mexican dude. In the back of my mind I knew I was being an idiot, but there was nothing I could do to stop the constant wave of these thoughts.

Does he like me as much a like him? (No, of course not. You were just another notch on his proverbial belt, duh.) *When will I see him again?* (Never, because he lives in Mexico, you fucktard.) *God, I like him so much.* (But do you really? His English isn't that great and your Spanish is abysmal, so what connection could you guys really have?) Part of my naïve twenty-one-year-old self had managed to cook up some pathetic rom-com plot in my head. I so badly wanted to be his manic pixie dream girl. I so badly wanted to have a connection that transcended the barriers of language. I so badly wanted more. One taste of his affection was not enough.

Meanwhile, my friend (who, I should add, came from a stable two-parent household) remained unaffected by her tryst. Why couldn't I be like that? Why couldn't I be that badass feminist? Because I didn't have a daddy.

When I told my mother what was happening with me, she wasn't surprised. She had been waiting for this day.

"I always knew your relationship with your father would manifest itself somehow. And now here it is. I'm so sorry, baby girl."

August 25, 1993: Georgia's babysitter paged me at work to say that Steve had dropped off Geo's bike. When Geo saw him enter the co-op park she ran and hid behind the bushes and said, "No. Not going with Daddy." She would not talk to Steve or go up to him, nor say goodbye. Steve dropped off the bike and said, "Maybe she'll want to see me in a couple of years."

I'm embarrassed to admit it, but I repeated some form of that situation time and time again. I would meet an unavailable man, know him for a brief amount of time, and become inappropriately attached.

I guess it shouldn't have come as much of a surprise, because after all, daddy issues run in my family. Perhaps it's the reason my mother was expecting some sort of father-related fallout; she had first-hand experience.

My grandpa was in and out of my mother's life for as long as she could remember.

"How old were you when Grandpa moved out?"

"Oh sweetheart, he was never really there. It was always back and forth, back and forth."

Her father, much like mine, was an alcoholic. He met my granny when he was seven months sober and they married a few months later. Unfortunately, his sobriety didn't last.

For the most part, my granny was left to raise my mom and her two sisters alone.

I asked my mom what sort of daddy issues, if any, she had experienced.

"I never had anxiety problems when it came to dating. I just continually chose men who were inappropriate and unavailable. One of the things I did over and over again was choose alcoholics—not consciously, but I could pick an alcoholic out of the room."

Joseph Onodi

The Bicycle

AN EXCERPT FROM "INDIAN SUMMER"

Every kid remembers their first bike. In 1979 I was ten years old with no wheels, and I couldn't take another summer without a bike of my own. I said to Jacob, who needed a bike too, "I feel like a duck's dork running beside him." I pointed to the other member of our gang, Eric, who had a Moto-Cross. It looked like a dirt bike with big gnarly tires and grips that ran your hands raw. The village where I grew up had many families like mine, a single Native mother too poor to buy bicycles for her "Half-breed kids," as my mother often called us.

The three of us joked with Jacob's oldest brother, Charles, who said, "You think Marge Jumping-Mouse can afford thirteen bikes for her kids when she's in the bar with his mum?" His lips pointed in my direction. What could I say? It was the truth.

"Christ no!" Charles's eyes flashed, black saucers behind thick pop-bottle glasses. "They build what they can from the dump, and steal the rest from the white kids!" He pointed his lips at Eric, the only white kid in the room, who shifted his eyes and weight and looked for the closest exit to check on his bicycle.

To get to the dump we had three choices: hitchhike, pay Greyhound two-fifty a head, or hop the train. Hitching was too dangerous, and we had no money for the bus, so that left the train. In the South B.C. Peace Region, trains were long and slow, especially going through town. Most times it would almost come to a complete stop and there was always a flat deck or railcar empty enough for a kid. The trick was getting on and the hardest part was walking home; trains never seemed to come back.

That day it was easy pickings. The Alberta Wheat Pool express was right on time and we boarded without being seen by the caboose or engineer as it slowed around a bend and crossed Highway 2. It lumbered north along the highway, over the Dawson Creek trestle and past oceans of summer wheat and flickering yellow canola. The train turned west along Highway 49, The Old Spirit River Road as the locals called it. Soon the smell of rotten flesh caused my belly to reverse pumps. I covered my face with my shirt but it didn't help.

The train almost slowed to a halt as it approached the dump and I threw the tools off and quickly scrambled after them. Me 'n Jacob landed on the soft forgiving gravel that the CPR laid down after every spring freshet. Eric fell ass-over-tea-kettle in a dusty cloud of arms and legs, tumbling down a gravel embankment. I looked back at the mess and laughed. We shook our heads.

I said, "Good Grief! I bet you a buck he won't live till graduation?"

Jacob counted on his fingers and held up seven digits, "That's too long! Christ, Hunter, in seven years the commies could invade! No way! Besides, he's accident prone. It's just a matter of time!"

We laughed as Eric caught up. "What's so funny, guys?"

Jacob snorted, "You!"

Eric shrugged. "Aww, gimme a break. I'm left-handed, and I have asthma!"

We had to bush-whack a fair bit because the CN Rail wasn't like a taxi that dropped you at your front door. We navigated through chest-high wild grasses and gopher holes and hooked up with a gravel road that led to the dump. Jacob's brother said the scrap metal pile was where we'd find the bike parts.

We paused at the locked gate, signs everywhere warned: NO TRESPASSERS, but no one was around for miles and somewhere out there loomed an enormous pile of bike parts. Eric shimmied under the wire fence, followed by me and Jacob. Everything was there: washers, dryers, refrigerators, twisted and bent bits of this and that, some painted, some bare and rusting.

"We're almost there," I said.

"What the hell is that?" Jacob pointed to a heap of metal. We raced toward the glorious pile. Jacob and I heard Eric say, "Wait for me!" He caught up and took a deep breath using his inhaler. I figured the pile was taller than the three of us combined.

"Jesus Christ on a crutch," a breathless Eric puffed.

Jacob's eyes watered with joy. "It's so beautiful."

I discovered a nice CCM frame with a chopper look to it. Eric was a bull moose in full rut, he threw pieces every which way and piled them to one side along with the truest wheel sets. We used the tools we'd borrowed from Charles and soon had two rolling bikes assembled. Just in case, I tied two sets of wheels to Jacob's sissy bar and stuffed a few extra parts in the bag.

Eric asked Jacob, "Why a banana seat and sissy bar; you know what a sissy is right?"

Jacob answered, "The seat gives me room for the chicks, and the sissy bar'll stop 'em fallin' backwards when I wheelie through the intersection. Any more questions, professor?"

I wanted to be like Ghost Rider and pull evil souls to hell with my flaming Harley.

Jacob and I rolled our patchwork bikes to a gate, now mysteriously open. We heard the watchman's cigarette-burnt voice, "What in hell you kids doin' here?" He panted like a thirsty buffalo on a hot day, "You all know you can't be here. Can't you read the signs?"

Eric flashed his big, blue, heart-melting eyes and in the most Oliver Twist-like way said, "Please Sir, we were trying to find my stolen bike."

The watchman breathed cut-rate whiskey, "Was it new, son?"

Eric nodded yes and the watchman shook his head, "Better go to the cop shop, boys."

We took the back roads home, talking about our bikes and where we would go, and when we rolled into town we agreed to meet at Jacob's after dinner. I arrived to an empty house and all the makings for a ketchup and bannock sandwich. I filled the hole in my belly and enjoyed the rare peace and quiet.

Later, me and Eric met in the back alley behind Jacob's place, his Superman T-shirt stained with all the food groups. I knocked on the door and the smell of homemade pizza escaped. In the dimly lit basement, Charles instructed us on how to tune a bicycle. By 7:00 p.m., me and Jacob had bikes! Mine was a blue CCM frame with candy apple red forks, ape hanger handlebars, and an old leather single seat with two big springs for support. Jacob's was a green Raleigh with purple forks, half-length ape hangers, complete with a banana seat and sissy bar.

Eric laughed but Jacob's brother Charles said, "Hey, you know ugly wheels are better than no wheels. Right?"

Jacob said, "Now we won't be a couple of duck's dorks."

Charles said, "Nope, just a couple snot nose Indians on two shitty bikes. Now, piss off. I gotta get ready for a date."

We carried our bikes outside and rode until the sun went down. When Eric and Jacob had to go home, I rode late into the night and imagined better times.

Fiction

Lynn J. Salmon

Loss of the *Sea Dragon*

AN EXCERPT FROM CHAPTER ONE OF A NOVEL-IN-PROGRESS

Randolph Ross sat on an overturned bucket on the aft deck of his forty-two foot wooden fishing troller, *Sea Dragon*. He was untangling a knotted collection of colourful tin flashers from a pile of hooks and lines, jumbled together in a mass of mangled gear. It took a few minutes for his hands and fingers to warm up, the cold April air and his persistent arthritis escalated what should have been a simple task into a frustrating challenge.

While he weaved the flashers and hooks through the bundle of twisted nylon line, his shoulders relaxed and the pain in his hands eased. His mind idly processed a collage of memories from when he last fished for salmon in the frigid waters off British Columbia's northwest coast. Randolph hadn't fished commercially in over ten years but the passion he still had for the living it once provided remained as strong as ever. That, and his unabashed love for his cherished boat, *Sea Dragon*.

He missed fishing—it hadn't been his choice to quit, though selling the salmon license had paid off his mortgage. In the market today, that license would be worth double what he sold it for in the late nineties. But he couldn't manage fishing alone and his two grandsons—his crew—abandoned him for careers with the RCMP. His mind stopped short of intruding regrets sure to spoil this melancholy moment.

Water lapped against the side of the boat, an irregular lyrical sound punctuated by the occasional sharp cry of a strutting seagull demanding fish scraps despite none of the boats having any fish on their decks. The

Tyee Tie-up, where Randolph kept *Sea Dragon*, was a floating dock that extended four hundred feet from shore. It had seen heady days when Prince Rupert was known as the Halibut Capital of the World with three and sometimes four boats tied up outboard of each other—a far cry from the twenty or so boats that tied up in single-file these days.

Randolph's breath exploded in tiny puffs of vapour, the wheelhouse roof misted as the frost melted from it, and a low veil of fog skimmed the surface of the water. The sun, in cold mockery of its summer cousin, shone down without warmth.

An indistinct shadow crossed the deck.

"Randolph Ross?"

Randolph looked up from his task. The man who had called his name placed his boot on the gunwale of the boat as though he intended to come aboard. He was wearing a faux leather jacket, black polyester pants, and dazzling argyle socks showing blue and green at his exposed ankles. His face was vaguely familiar, but then, Randolph had lived in Prince Rupert for nearly eight decades. Everyone was vaguely familiar to him—and the more vague the better, he always thought.

"Who's asking?"

"Del. Del Hood."

"Now where do I know that name from?" Randolph scratched his chin absently.

Del hesitated, then spoke, "You maybe remember my dad. He said he used to hire your boat."

Randolph recognized the name now. "Your dad, sure. Del Hood *Senior*, the surveyor. I remember him." He looked with more interest now at the young man standing on the dock. "Does he want to hire the boat again? I'll just warn you up front, my rates have increased. Cost of fuel and all."

"No. He died two years ago."

Randolph felt mild irritation. "All right then, good to know." There seemed little point in continuing the conversation, so Randolph resumed his work on the tangled flashers.

"Look. I came down here because I was hoping to hire you. Hire the boat. Is that possible?"

Randolph put the gear down for a second time. "Charter work. Sure. But like I said, rates are higher now. Fuel costs more. Where do you want to go?"

"Taboo Island. Out by Green Island. Same place you took my dad."

A prickle of goose bumps flashed across Randolph's neck; he swatted at the sensation, ignoring the warning his brain was sending him. *Not again, Randolph. Some shady business going on.*

"Your dad never had a good thing to say about going there. What're you wanting with it now after all this time?"

Del leaned forward on his raised foot as if to share a secret, his weight pushing *Sea Dragon* away from the dock, her movement swift and unexpected. Del lost his balance, nearly pitching into the water as the space between the dock and the boat widened. He pulled his hands from his pockets, waving his arms to re-establish his footing, and grabbed for the rigging of the boat. Without being asked aboard, Del jumped onto the deck of *Sea Dragon*, the boat rocked slightly as he landed.

"Hey—" Randolph stood up to confront him.

"Geez that's dangerous!"

"Who asked you aboard?" Randolph kicked his bucket out of the way so he wouldn't stumble over it.

Del did not hear the question. Or he ignored it. "I own Taboo Island."

"It's a marine reserve. Nobody owns it."

"That's what everybody thinks. But I have the deed that proves it belonged to my dad. He bought it from the Crown, fair and square. He did all the environmental assessments and got all the proper approvals. It's all legal and all still valid."

"What're you talking about? Approvals for what?"

"For the fishing lodge he was going to build. Right on Oval Beach. The fishing lodge I now intend to build."

"Nobody is gonna let you build a lodge there. It's part of a marine reserve."

"It isn't. I told you that. It's only *surrounded* by a marine reserve."

"And that sounds like a practical fishing spot to you? Surrounded by fish you can't catch?" Randolph snorted at the idea. He'd had enough sparring with Del. He wanted him off his boat. "Never gonna happen. Never gonna get it approved."

Del wiped his hands down the front of his jacket, showing his anxiety. "Well, whether it goes ahead or not, it's still worth a couple hundred bucks for your time and the boat rental. You interested or not?"

Randolph considered the offer. "That's a couple hundred bucks *plus* fuel costs."

"Deal." Del glanced around at the other boats tied up nearby. "Yeah, so, I was sorta thinking this should just stay between us."

"You think anyone is gonna take your crazy idea seriously?"

"It's not crazy. The Ministry in charge said if I complete the last survey of the island—the archaeological component—then there's no reason to hold up the project. I'm so close!"

"That's usually when you get burned." Randolph hesitated; it was fuel money and a chance to run *Sea Dragon*. "But I'm not a man to stand in the way of progress."

"Great. I want to leave soon. I just have to get some—"

"I'll be here. I don't care about the rest of it. But I only take cash. Up front."

Del nodded, extending his hand to shake on it. He half-jumped, half-stumbled back onto the dock. A parading seagull squawked at him, hopping sideways as Del kicked at it, clearing his path to hasten down the tippy float toward shore.

Randolph watched him go.

"Who the hell was that?" A man appeared at the wheelhouse door of the fishing boat tied up across from *Sea Dragon*.

"Del Hood's kid."

The other man nodded. "Sorta resembles him, don't he?"

"Yup. Unfortunately."

Randolph sat back down on the overturned bucket, picking up the tangled gear. A charter to Taboo Island with Del Hood—was this a good idea? He shrugged off his doubts as his philosophy at age seventy-nine had become a simple one: Mind your own damn business.

Dayna Mahannah

This Girl Jane

I went to the beach with the woman who lives in my closet.

She's nothing like me. She has long, messy hair and faded eyes smudged with black. When she blinks, her eyelashes get caught in her eyebrows. I wish my eyelashes did that. Perky breasts poke through thin cotton—I know she won't be shy at the nude beach. I know I will.

I don't really want to go to the beach. I'd rather stay home and drink coffee until noon and spend seven hours allegedly working. I'll be anxious otherwise. It's hard to be in the moment when the moment is always somewhere else.

I'm in the kitchen of my one-bedroom apartment. It's my favourite room. In here, the philodendrons creep from clay pots on the deep windowsill, down the white walls, up the white walls, basking in the pools of butter-yellow sun melting through the window. A collection of old jars and ceramics filled with wild rice and spices line the blue-tiled counter. Little Morocco, I call it.

"What are you doing today?" Jane's voice flits through the morning quiet like a runaway reverie.

None of your damn business, I think. But I utter an "Mmm ..." and keep my back to her as I slice a banana into my oatmeal. Coffee sits in the press next to me. She doesn't hesitate to sidle up and help herself.

"Have some coffee."

"Thanks," she yawns, oblivious to my tone, passive-aggressive as it is. I wonder if it's because I use it so often? Maybe she thinks that's how I really sound.

"Come to the beach with me," she says.

"I have some work to do." I turn and shuffle over to the kitchen table.

"It's Tuesday. You don't work on Tuesdays." Sliding into the chair opposite me, Jane's foot finds rest next to one thigh; a knee rises up under her chin.

"Are you my secretary?" I retort.

"You haven't come with me to the beach once! I'm leaving on Saturday."

"What?"

"I'm leaving on Saturday," she repeats.

"I heard you."

"You said, 'What?'"

"I didn't know ... has it been a month already?" I say, thinking hard. Damn. Nearly four weeks passed and I barely noticed. "Like, *leaving* leaving?"

"Yeah."

"To where?"

"Seattle." Simple. Jarring.

"If you're leaving, then why didn't you tell me—"

"I just did," Jane says.

"—sooner?"

She looks into my eyes and I look into the depths of my nearly untouched oatmeal.

I knew that Jane wouldn't be staying long. I knew she was transient, a romantic vagrant. But it feels unexpected somehow, and as much as her presence is an annoying reminder of my own resolute sameness on a day-to-day basis, the thought of her absence makes panic climb up my throat. Is this fucking banana giving me heartburn?

I found Jane on craigslist, which I have an unhealthy habit of scrolling through when I'm bored. The Next 100 Postings are my own little guilty form of consumption, and the Next 100, and the Next ...

She was a quarter way down the first page:

$200 to live in your closet!

I clicked on it. Not because I was looking to fill closet space, but because I would never do that. Who was this person, and why did they want to live in a stranger's closet?

> *I'm Jane. I am coming to the city for a month & if you have an extra closet (creepy-crawly-free preferred), I'll pay ya $200 to sleep in it for a month. Couches are great but I like the floor and i like my own space. I'm quiet and I don't dream ;)*
> *(Creep-free preferred)*

I felt obligated the moment I read it. This girl Jane, whoever she was, had called me out specifically. *I* was free of creeps! This was craigslist—one thousand actual creeps would jump on this. A freewheeling girl in their closet? They'd offer her a couch, then their bed, then ...

I emailed her. She answered right away. The next week, I had a teeny tiny young woman taking up space in my hall closet, and she didn't even seem all that weird.

Jane looks more creature-like than human, sitting hunched at the oak table, my mug almost comically large in her curled hand. Everything about her accentuates her smallness, exists solely to contrast her fairy-like structure—her bushy brown hair with the thick fringe, the baggy jeans and shirt, the way the dark kohl around her huge eyes plays tricks on the rest of her face. It brings out the hollows beneath her cheekbones and the constellation of freckles that dust her nose like black stars in a negative sky. Even Jane's give-a-shit attitude bursts from her body like it was meant for someone else. She is magnetic. Sometimes I hate her for it. Sometimes I hate her because she is free. Today, it's both.

"What do you even have to do today?" Jane persists.

"A bunch of shit," I answer.

Jane rolls her eyes. *You look dead when you do that*, I think. *With all the whites showing*. Damn Jane. When she leaves, no one will be here looking at me expectantly to go play on the beach when I should, I should, I should be basking in the glow of my computer screen. Working. "Working." Working?

"Sasha, please come to the beach with me. It'll be good for you, I promise. Everyone should tan their nipples at least three times a year. I swear to god, if you haven't before, it can be quite humbling."

I bite my cheeks and furrow my brow at her. What the hell is she talking about?

"Oh, yeah," she continues, as if I'd responded aloud. "It doesn't work on the president because he uses a tanning bed. But I swear, Ra will do you well."

I can't help it. I laugh. "Ra?"

She nods, and with a flourish of her hand, gestures to the sun outside.

The beach is already crowded at noon, yet calm. The baked sand sears the soles of my feet and my face contorts to accommodate the pain. I move like a wounded gazelle past the free nipples and bare bums and floppy sun hats and curtains of chromatic beach blankets strung between spindly wooden poles. The wind rolls off the ocean and blows them into a billowed slant—a rainbow sailboat content to stay right where it is.

We find a vacant spot against a giant knot of driftwood. Jane spreads out an old bed sheet and the corners flip up against the wind. Fluidly, like she's made of liquid, Jane unbuttons her denim shorts and they fall and she lifts the thin cotton shirt over her unruly head of hair and spills her body onto the sheet, leaning back onto her elbows, tilting her face, her breasts, her nipples, toward the sun. Tan-line free.

I glance around, but nobody is looking. They are talking quietly amongst themselves, or sleeping, or reading. Some are wading into the cool water that, from here, sparkles like a sea of crystals. I sit next to Jane on the old bed sheet, removing my clothes from a position barely above sea level.

"Take off your bra," Jane says.

"I am," I retort. I do. No one looks over as my bra hits the sand, or as my translucent breasts squint into the sun. When I close my eyes, the only one watching me is Ra.

Jane leaves on Saturday. The skin around my nipples is still peeling on Sunday, and on Monday, too. On Tuesday, there's still too much coffee in the press—I can't finish it all by myself. My shirt rubs against the burn on my breasts. I take it off and, as I sip my coffee, alone at the table, half-naked, I can't help it—I laugh.

Gillian Tregidgo

Seagull

I felt safe when we moved into our new condo. I loved to look out the tall windows at those leafy green trees. There was a swimming pool in an area shared with the apartment next door, and on waking, I could hear the sound of children's laughter as they splashed in the shallow pools. It grounded me, helping me drift back to a time of innocence, playing in the orchards in the Okanagan with my kid sister, Sam.

The swimming pool was on the south side of our building, so I placed my desk to have it in view. I would get up in the early morning and head to the pool. I loved the stimulating feel of the water, clinging like warm mercury to my limbs. Once I had completed my lengths, refreshed, I would head home.

On one of those idyllic days, while I was completing my fourth length, I noticed a large seagull soaring above me. It was breathtaking to watch its body arc over the pool, its underbelly and wings tinged azure by the water's reflection, and eventually tip to skim the glistening surface below. Mesmerized by its shape, I cupped my hands over my eyes to follow its flightpath. It flew upward and then appeared to float in front of the neighbouring building, casting a dark shadow across the window—an eerie Hitchcock image. The sun had momentarily gone behind a cloud, and I shivered. As I watched, I noticed two figures moving in the apartment, behind the bird's shadow. The sun, once more partially blocking my view, created shapes, blanked out by the low morning light. I returned to my lengths, a fluttering feeling in my belly tugging at my senses.

As the summer cooled, I woke one morning, my husband Josh's body crooked into mine. So as not to wake him, I slowly moved to the edge of the bed. A slight chill in the air made my teeth chatter together, and I reached for something warmer to cover my shoulders before I got up and tiptoed to the kitchen for my first coffee of the day.

I saw movement in the window of the apartment opposite. It was two young women. Were these the two figures I had seen when the seagull had flown in front of the window the other day? Their blinds were open, and they were semi-clad—and very loving to one another. I tried not to look but was mesmerized by their open show of affection. It stirred something in me that hadn't been stirred for a long time. I could not look away.

As the light was now kinder to my eyes, I saw the women clearly. One, tall and slim. Long red hair and pale features. *A Klimt girl*, I thought. The dark-haired woman was shorter, but also slim and lithe. I tried not to stare as they embraced and kissed. Eventually, I got up and closed the blinds.

After the first week, I told Josh about it. We were having our Friday evening meal, a lovely end-of-the-week ritual. We would order in food, drink wine together, and catch up.

"What do you mean, you couldn't look away?" he said when I told him what I'd seen. "Why don't you just move your desk?"

I was lost as to how to respond. I dropped the subject. But as the weeks brought the full onset of autumn, I still hadn't moved my desk. When I talked to Josh about it a second time, he grew less amused. He seemed preoccupied with his ever-increasing workload, working in a technology department at a nearby hospital. What had once been both a vocation and a passion was starting to stress him out, due to the long hours and fewer technicians to assist him.

When we spoke of it again, he told me I should simply pull our blinds down, stop looking. I tried. It worked for a while, but the compulsion was just too strong. After a couple of months, I opened the blinds again.

The apartment now appeared empty. The furniture was still there, but the young couple were not. My heart sank. Watching their lovemaking had fueled something inside me, and I felt a pang of loss and sadness at their apparent absence. I sank down onto my chair, acknowledging that I had no right to feel this way, sharing in these intimate moments uninvited.

January drew in with its icy early morning chills. I lifted the blinds one day and exclaimed. There was someone there. At first, I thought it was someone new. She looked like the shorter dark-haired woman, but her shape had completely changed. Fully clothed and many pounds heavier, she sat on a chair by the window. She seemed to be alone. I watched her on and off for several hours. From time to time she got up and came back with a cup in her hand and a tin of cookies, and appeared to eat the whole thing.

This went on for several weeks. She ate a lot. I told Josh about it over breakfast one morning. "I think maybe the Klimt girl has left the other girl. Comfort eating, you know?"

Josh shook his head, stirring his coffee aggressively, an action I had grown to hate. "I thought you were done with all this." He got up and left the table. He would not hear more on the subject. However, I had grown attached to these girls. I wanted to know what had happened.

In early March, another woman appeared. No longer the Klimt girl, I thought. Whereas I had witnessed the change in shape of the dark-haired girl, the Klimt girl had visibly shrunk and was bald. As I watched over the next few days, it was apparent they had not fallen out. They were always fully clothed now, and still very affectionate to one another, but there was no more sex. I felt preoccupied with their story. What was going on? How would I ever know?

That Friday night Josh came home and did not perform his usual evening ritual of a quick peck on the cheek followed by a question about dinner plans. Instead, he walked into the living room, his face slightly ashen, and sat down in a chair.

I went quickly to his side. "What is it? What's wrong?"

He looked up at me. "You're never going to believe what happened to me today."

"Go on."

"I was called to look at a computer we had loaned out that crashed. Part of an assistive device for people who can't speak. It's usually lent out to patients with neurological disorders, ALS and the like. I started to work on it, checked the usual IPO settings, but then … Well, I saw … There was a file. A 'living will.' I don't know what prompted me to open it, but … It said …"

Josh fumbled in his jacket and pulled out a wrinkled piece of paper. He had obviously printed it out, and he passed it to me with trembling hands. I read the words, stark on the white paper.

"In the event of my succumbing to any kind of illness or disease that stops me being able to make my own decisions, or be able to verbalize them, I request that the person who I designate will help me take my own life, by whatever means is possible to him or her."

I looked up and our eyes met.

"At first I felt this was very personal. None of my business," he said. "I'm the only person who's looked at this device. Apart from that 'significant other.'

"I was asked to return the device. Normally one of our techs would do it, but we're so understaffed, and the address is in our neighborhood.

"The address … It's the apartment across the street."

We both stood up and walked to the window. The blinds were now partially drawn. We could see one of the women, half sitting and half lying on the bed. She was looking at her partner with deep love in her eyes, her face paler than ever. Blue veins protruded across the top of her head. It was dusk, the magic hour, and a lovely magenta glow suffused their bodies and cast an ethereal haze on their faces.

As we looked out the window, a seagull flew over the pool between our buildings. Its wings were tinged by the azure of the pool. I followed its trajectory across the front of their window, watching as it dipped its wings to skim the cool water below.

Debbie Bateman

Your Body Was Made for This

AN EXCERPT

1

Brianne joins the outside world puffy-eyed, with a furrowed brow and a flattened nose. Her crinkly mouth yowls and her blueish fingers clutch the air like claws. Bowed legs dangle from her distended torso. Her oversized head sinks into rounded shoulders. She is neckless.

And everything is out of proportion, not the least of which her potential. She contains two million eggs, her lifetime quota—or so the world believes at the time. Later, the notion that females can't generate new eggs proves false, but by then the damage has been done. Brianne and other girls like her have learned their most essential purpose is to guard an ever-dwindling stash and hope one day a smooth, pure egg hatches into a new neckless creature yowling at the open air.

"It's a girl," says the doctor.

Sloppy with anaesthetic, Brianne's mother smiles. The faint red stain on her baby girl's cheek will soon disappear. Most babies need to be tugged into the world, as her mom well knows. She's delivered twice before.

2

Brianne has baby dolls with luscious cheeks. She tucks them under a blanket in a miniature carriage and feeds them with a milk bottle that magically drains without ever losing a drop. She's practising for later, getting ready to be a grown-up mom. The dolls wear pink bonnets with elastic chinstraps and white leather shoes that fit over their stiff plastic feet. Watch out for those feet. They're likely to get punched in, twisted, or cracked should the doll grow too adventurous for her own good.

From the minute she's able to keep herself upright, Brianne never stops twirling and skipping and hiding from adults. Her braids are forever coming undone, and the pink barrettes meant to hold them in place are always getting lost under the pine needles below the row of trees in her backyard. She climbs whatever tree she chooses faster than her mother cares to notice. Where the branches have been trimmed, she knee-pinches her way up the trunk. Then she comes to rest under the cover of sticky boughs with needles that poke her if she's not careful.

"Brianne, you crazy girl. Where are you now?" Her mother's hands are on her hips, elbows pointed outwards sharp as arrows. Above the cat-eye glasses that twinkle in the open sun, her mother's penciled-in eyebrows pinch.

If only she'd think to glance upward, she'd catch Brianne. Instead, she walks away and Brianne grows bored of hiding. It isn't any fun without somebody looking for you. She slides down, creeps through the back door and tiptoes up the steps from the landing, but she doesn't make it past the kitchen. Her mother snatches her by the ear with long red fingernails and drags her to the bathroom where she scrapes off the pinesap with a nail brush. Brianne loses skin in the process.

Afterwards, her mother fixes the braids, changes the dress, and returns Brianne to the bedroom where the dolls in the baby carriage have been waiting.

"Here," her mother says, handing Brianne the dripless bottle. "Your girls look hungry."

3

By the time she starts school, Brianne has plenty of spine for the white cotton turtleneck she wears under an orange jumper with fat buttons down the front. A matching orange band holds back the shiny black hair her mother gives one hundred brushstrokes to every night.

In those days, public schools have "standards" and girls aren't allowed to wear pants. Every morning, Brianne pulls on her cotton panties and tugs up the leotards she's forced to wear, winter or summer. There are two colours to choose from: black and white. Not that it matters. Whichever pair she's wearing, the crotch is forever sagging. The egg-white folds of firm skin where her legs meet do nothing but sweat, stick, and rash. She's constantly scolded by teachers for squirming in class and she can never say why.

A week into Grade 1, Brianne already knows life is unfair. She's tried on her brother's pants.

4

In Grade 5, all the girls are herded into the school gym for a top-secret assembly. With the knees of their skinny leotard legs pressed together, they sit on fold-out metal chairs arranged in a tight semicircle. The lights go off and a young woman fills the projector screen with a face pure as milk and auburn hair flowing over a peach sweater that shows the curves of her breasts. Her image grows smaller and moves to the side. Text flows onto the screen: "Congratulations, you're becoming a woman."

Each girl receives a brochure and a maxipad in a pretty plastic wrapper of white lace over powder blue. The brochure features the same beautiful girl they saw in the film, sitting pensively in her bedroom one minute, cycling through a city park the next. "Having your period should no longer be thought of as a curse." That's what the brochure says.

For months after the assembly, all the girls whisper, "Do you have your period yet?" Brianne is the first, not that she tells anyone. The place where her legs meet does more than rash now. She's not allowed to call it blood and it feels like diarrhea.

Now she's reached puberty, Brianne has half a million eggs. All the others—one-and-a-half million bubbles of infinite potential—gone without her even noticing.

Jonathan M. Bessette

Freud to Frisco

FLASH FICTION

Wind blew warm against the shaking eon of Western Civilization, like a car rickety on the road.

I had planned the trip with some long-time friends. It was my first travelling experience outside of family vacations. The Ford Aries was several years old. The licence plate was stained with rust, its grey metallic body glimmered under the muggy July sun. Its windows were spotted with little brownish, granular specks: splashed dirt from coastal meandering. These bodies we called our own were bound to the movement of that vehicle. We pretended there was a destiny for us as young adults trying to overpower the history of our *tabula rasa*, searching for something like the '60s to imprint with more gravity.

We had decided to drive down through Washington and Oregon, navigating the scenic routes along the coast. Our arrival in San Fran would be heaped with beautiful images: the Golden Gate Bridge, Alcatraz, the windswept beaches, the charming trolleys, Pride week, fog rolling in and coating the cityscape like a magic trick. Our neuroses told us that we could borrow from the stories of old and merge them into the way we experienced our constructed reality.

There were three of us: Ryan, Alexander, and me. We were all familiar with the American West Coast, since we grew up right above it, teetering at the 49th parallel. This wasn't supposed to be a contrived journey, rather a minor experiment in ourselves searching for a past we were still too ignorant to know didn't exist anymore.

Frisco was that city where the beatniks had published a new wave of American language experiments; jazz had been played everywhere, coaxing the city into hepcat coolness; hippies had coalesced at the frontier of psychedelia where Joan Didion's slouching had occurred; the vibrant wave of LGBTQ+ had culminated into Pink Fridays, pride parades, and Burning Man. We wouldn't realize until after our arrival that this past spirit of the city had crashed against the erection of the tech industry, like what Hunter S. Thompson wrote about the transformative power of the middle '60s. How, "less than five years later, you [could] go up on a steep hill in Las Vegas and look West, and with the right kind of eyes you [could] almost see the high water mark—that place where the wave finally broke, and rolled back."

"Comfortable?" Ryan mocked.

"Never," I joked.

The interior of the vehicle was packed too thickly. There were our backpacks, sleeping bags, camping gear, a tent, tarp, cutlery, a Coleman stove, a cooler packed with wine, cheese, bread, kosher hot dogs, apples, Dijon mustard, ketchup, mayonnaise, lettuce, cucumber, pepper, salt and pepper ... We had also packed bongos, a box of CDs, an acoustic guitar, harmonicas, some blow-up sleeping mats, extra shoes, hats, blankets, a small 3-channel recorder ... and a kitchen sink.

I read the poetry of e.e. cummings for a while, then we each stared out our windows, seeing how the light bent through the refraction, listening to the spaces between poems. Something about the words distributed on the page, the dirt on the window, and the sense of excitement that we were out there on the road—on our own—made me sad. My brain wanted to organize the brittle symbols and pull them together. Words were one thing, but the dots of mud—could I really convince myself that I knew what those meant?

"This coast is so beautifully prehistoric," I sighed.

"We drove down here when I was a child, my family and me," Alexander said.

"I can't wait to see Frisco sparkling on the horizon as we drive in through the sunset," Ryan exclaimed.

"How do you know we're going to drive in during sunset?" I asked.

"Oh, trust me," he assured.

The clutter of stuff shivered as we ebbed and flowed down the asphalt highway; I often had to lean my weight onto it in order to keep it from slipping down all over me. I read *A General Introduction to Psychoanalysis,* looking back and forth between the glass of the window and the scenery behind it. The Mamas & the Papas twanged from the stereo and the molecules of motion and sound coalesced along the whirlpool of my eardrums. The paperback I held in my hands had a broken spine, torn corners, and smelled of mildew. My eyes blurred over while I tried to focus on the writing, explanations of the ego, id, and superego. Sometimes I saw myself as a bystander to my own bodily processes.

I sat with my outstretched arm through the gap in the window, hot breaths and cool drafts mixed around my face. A tranquilizing sensation convinced me to lean on the door frame, using my pillow for support. Other cars flitted by in blinks, each a little microcosm of the world. I considered the depth of Freud. Though I disagreed with his overall analysis of humanity, there was a fascination with his empirical explanations: his delineation of the mind and the bestial parts of self; the most natural and sexual.

In the motion of my reading, moving, thinking, seeing, being, an epiphany occurred as we drove beneath the canopies of coastal pines. At some angles, when the car swayed around corners, the sunlight patterned through the glass and the trees looked momentarily like dancers of the mazurka. Black gradations of shadows intermixed with bright shades of amorphous shapes and saturated the inside and outside of the vehicle, causing a tremble in my vision. I felt a tinge in the back of my brain.

We had brought drugs with us, and I knew we hadn't taken any yet, but the varying slats of stroboscopic flickers transported me as if I had been sitting before a Gysin/Burroughs Dreamachine. Hallucinations overlapped reality. The black blotches of words on the page swirled up off the white and consumed me in images ... or were they symbols: lambs, doors, hands, pens, crosses, clouds, clocks, lips, cars, knives, hills, trees, houses, eyes, hats ...

Was I really in a car with two other people? Were they merely projections of my own internal psychology? Language began to disintegrate, I reached out and touched what I thought was the seat in front of me where Ryan sat, driving. A recent memory of reading Descartes's idea of the brain in the jar overtook me—the totally illusory external world, the parts of my grey matter being stimulated by electrodes. Shivers bent me toward the window as I hoped for the light to remove my anxiety-ridden vision from darkness.

Were we only pretending to search for something real in the graveyard of Frisco? We were still young enough to be idealistic about freedom and the way we could strive in existential states through drugs or drinking to find some new world. But maybe we would just end up like Kerouac, going crazy in Big Sur and later dying from cirrhosis of the liver. Faded hallucinations returned as I started to yawn, blink, and snuggle into the surrounding wasteland of possessions.

Then I became an indigo elephant and forest fires blazed high up into the sky, where a mandala of overlapping circles and squares emerged. My trunk whipped through the air trying to breathe above the smoke. I groped at myself, feeling my flesh dissolve into a void balanced on the edge of nowhere. I spoke, unsure if anyone heard me, "I haven't forgotten about you, yet ..."

I woke up. We were parked in a gas station. Ryan filled the tank with gasoline. Alexander paced and smoked on a nearby curb. I yawned and started to explain the dream I had been having to Ryan, surmising how confused, vulnerable, and isolated I felt in life. He smiled and agreed with me that he was equally unsure of who he was or what he was going to become. The pump clicked. We got back in. We continued to drive toward that place we thought could make something certain for us.

Felix Wong

Chinese Funerals Are Weird

I showed up to the funeral hall in a cheap tie and a dress shirt I couldn't iron because I didn't own an iron. According to my aunt, I had overdressed. She was in a T-shirt. That was the first time we spoke in two years.

To be fair, I should've known better than to move in with my aunt in the first place. When I landed in Hong Kong in 2014, I had told her I was there job-hunting. But in reality, I was *kind of* "soul-searching." She was ecstatic to have me back until she realized, after years spent overseas, I had grown into someone she couldn't relate to and therefore didn't approve of. Everything I said and did only triggered her disappointment, and it probably didn't help that I had developed a taste for cigarettes, booze, and pizza. In my aunt's eyes, I had become a *gwailo*—a white devil. She kicked me out within the month, and we were practically estranged after that.

Then my grandpa died.

I had never been to a Chinese funeral, so I expected one of those fancy ceremonies you'd see in triad movies, with the incense, paper money, dancing priests, and funny hats. But my grandpa had apparently converted to Christianity some time before his death, which put the funeral in this weird limbo of having both Western and traditional Chinese elements.

You'd expect my aunt to apologize and attempt to reconcile, but she didn't. Instead, she stuffed a red envelope in my hand. It couldn't have been a bribe, because inside was only a one-dollar coin, a White Rabbit candy, and a tissue—the hell was I supposed to do with that?

My aunt ordered me to bow three times to this big photo of Grandpa, then sat me down in the first seat of the front row, closest to Grandpa's body, which was kept in a back room. Her implication was that, as the sole grandson, the figurative torch was in my hands now, along with the fate of our entire lineage.

"Stay here," my aunt said. "Bow to each guest as they come in. And keep away from walls and dark places. There are—" she dropped to a whisper "—evil spirits."

The crazy kook was serious.

"So how old was he?" I asked.

My aunt thought for a moment, then turned to ask my grandma, who was further down the row and looked a lot angrier than usual.

"Who knows!" I heard my grandma yell.

I found out later that all Grandpa left behind was about a dozen rolls of toilet paper, stolen over the years from his senior's home. I guess I'd be pissed too.

I was mostly nonchalant about the whole ordeal. I'm no psychopath, but I never got to know my grandpa. It wasn't that I didn't see him often—in fact, I visited regularly—it's just that for most of my lucid years, Grandpa had been unlucid. Though at one point, he was lucid enough to move himself into a senior's home, mostly just to get away from my aunt and my grandma. Whenever I visited him there, he'd identify me as my father, and I'd nod and sneak him a Filet O' Fish, then we'd sit in silence. So really, sitting there at his funeral wasn't so different from our usual interactions.

The first guest was an elderly woman who claimed to be my childhood so-and-so, though I could swear we had never met.

With a hand on my shoulder, she said in Cantonese, "Came back just for the funeral? You're such a good boy!"

"Oh, no. I've actually been in Hong Kong for the past two years."

"Ah! You work here!"

"No, not really. Odd jobs here and there."

"You're going to school here then?"

"No. University's not really for me, you know?"

She didn't know.

"Then what *are* you doing?" The woman pursed her lips.

My aunt immediately pulled me aside and gave me a fucking lecture. Said I can't say that shit. "Live your Western lifestyle all you want, but don't advertise it!"

For the rest of the night, when someone asked if I flew in specifically for the funeral, I'd say, *I just landed, still jet-lagged*. When they asked what school I was attending, I'd say, *University of British Columbia, for business*. When they asked about my career aspirations, I'd say, *I want to be a freakin'* CEO.

As more people arrived, I saw that I did indeed overdress. Only one person there wore a dress shirt: me. Everyone else was in casuals, looking like they were only stopping by on the way to dinner.

To make matters worse, I had a sneaking suspicion no one actually knew my grandpa. Instead of sharing their memories of him, each stranger talked about their memories of *me*. They were all—allegedly—major formative influences on my youth. For fuck's sake, one dude said he used to be my dentist. The funeral, weirdly enough, began to feel more and more about me.

A Christian priest conducted the ceremony. Halfway through, a choir came to sing a few hymns. They tried to get us to sing along, but as far as I could tell, no one in the audience knew the lyrics.

I didn't mind the religious thing, but I could tell my aunt hated it. My family didn't believe in that sort of stuff, and I wasn't sure if Grandpa did either. I had never seen him pray or go near a bible. Unless there was a church hidden inside his usual dim sum restaurant, he certainly didn't attend service on Sunday either. My aunt would later mumble and groan about how someone approached my grandpa at the senior's home about converting and he just went along with it, not fully aware of what he was doing.

I didn't hear him at first, but the priest asked me to address the crowd. Not my aunt, not my grandma—just me.

All eyes turned in my direction.

I didn't know I had to prepare a speech. My mind was blank. After thinking for a second, I stood up and just said, "Thanks for coming," and sat back down.

The room went silent. I thought I heard my aunt sigh. I don't know why, but I sort of expected a round of applause.

Grandpa's casket was rolled out for us to say our goodbyes. Some cried, or at least pretended to. My aunt simply power-walked a lap around the body without looking at it, presumably out of fear of "evil spirits."

When it came to my turn, I thought I'd feel something—anything—but I didn't. It was rather anti-climatic. As bad as this sounds, I thought that with all the makeup, grandpa looked more alive then than he ever had alive. I was actually a bit envious of him. Shit, at least he no longer had to deal with my aunt.

I knew my aunt would take the funeral as an opportunity to talk me into leaving Hong Kong and finishing my schooling. Once the ceremony ended, I slipped away as fast as I could. But she caught me and dragged me into an alley.

My aunt asked if I had any tissues.

I remembered there was one in the red envelope from earlier, so I gave her the whole thing.

My aunt freaked the fuck out.

"Oh my God! You're not supposed to keep this! You'll bring the spirits with you!" she shouted, shoving the candy into my mouth. She made me promise to spend the dollar before I got home.

As for the tissue, she crumpled it up, lit it on fire, and set it down on the concrete. A tiny bonfire in this dark alleyway, struggling to stay ablaze.

"Hop over," she demanded. "Quick! Before it goes out!"

It was another paranoia-fueled, crazy moment of hers, which was one too many for me in one day.

I stood my ground. "No," I said.

So she pushed me over the fire.

Shane Leydon

Three Flags

Right on the crest of my shoulder, just before it meets the collarbone, is the spot that's keeping me awake out here—the one spot the sleeping bag won't cover. It lets the frosty temperature of the middle of the night creep its way across my back and down the left side of my ribcage.

It's more than that, sure. JT should be home soon. I miss him, even if he's still a little shit at thirty. I've been sleeping in a tent on our property. By choice. My father's been warning me about coyotes on the property since I was in Sparks, but a sighting of one is rare, in my opinion.

They're definitely around, though. Most nights out in the tent, their shrill yelping can keep me awake until dawn. Or, believe it or not, it can be quite soothing, depending on what kind of mood I'm in. See, I'm the oldest of seven. The only girl. I'm used to high-pitched howling and growling at all hours of the night.

Kyle, DJ (Donald Joseph), JT (Justin Thomas), Chris, Tyler, Josh, and Cody, youngest to oldest. Kyle's named after our father and I share a name with my mom, Julia.

We've had this property on Zero Ave for twenty-eight years, since I was four. Kyle Sr. ran the long-haul trucking outfit he "built with his own two hands" years ago, and Julia's had a hair salon off the garage for as long as I can remember.

They started a clandestine romance, Julia not wanting anyone to think of her as a "cradle robber." She made him swear on his grandmother's grave not to tell, and he did so. Not much can be kept secret in high school, though, and so of course all of the hockey team knew. Not until JT, their fourth kid, did Kyle Sr. let Julia in on his little secret: that he'd shared their secret with his pals. They argued about it in front of us. I can't believe she let him off the hook, even all those years later. He's always being let off the hook, it seems.

My dad is proud of his American roots. Too proud, if you ask me. Outside our house are three flags: one Canadian, one American, and one Confederate. I'm positive that if he'd had it his way, Kyle Sr. would've shipped us all back to the interior of Washington State, but at the rate my mother was giving birth up here, it made no sense to go south. Health care is just too good and too cheap.

His work kept him from being drunk 24-7. He worked hard, I'll give him that. He'd be gone for weeks at a time, hauling freight all over the continent. He'd send the odd postcard. I still have one he sent from New Orleans, a place that, by the pictures, still seems foreign to this landmass we're on. I'd like to go someday. The note he wrote on the back has faded since, but it was only a few words. Just saying hello. As my brothers got older, he'd take one of them along on rides with him. They all look up to him. Still. He never took me. "The highway wasn't meant for a lady," he'd say to me. He thought this was a compliment.

He's retired now, and has since passed the business down to DJ and JT. His only friends are Fox News anchors, who he watches on a loop. If he had any sense left in him, he'd focus his energy on making it easier on my mom since her MS diagnosis, but that's too far out of his comfort zone. God forbid he learn how to adapt to a change in his life. Right, I should've mentioned the MS sooner. Julia needs my help, but I can't live within those walls.

"Go put a jersey on, you little shit," I recall him yelling once to Chris upstairs in the kitchen, while I watched *Buffy the Vampire Slayer* in the basement. Chris couldn't have been older than thirteen. Kyle Sr. wanted to teach him a lesson in the only way he knew how: a hockey fight.

"What are you waiting for? Christmas?" he yelled, gaining on poky Chris as he headed for refuge downstairs with me. Kyle Sr. didn't like to treat his sons like that in front of me, and I could never figure out why that was. I suppose he thought he had a touch of class. He wound up and drove his bare foot into Chris's backside, kicking it as one might kick a football for a field goal.

Chris went down the whole flight of stairs airborne, crashing back-first into the retaining wall in the basement. I remember the look on his face, lips opening and closing like a fish out of water, gasping urgently to bring air into his lungs, his body writhing on the ground, pelvis slamming from left to right. After he caught his wind, he let out a coyote howl.

I let Chris snuggle up with a blanket beside me that night. We pulled the hide-a-bed out and had a "sleepover." We watched the episode where Buffy's mom dies. We both cried, and Chris fell asleep shortly after.

"It's been bad like this all day," Julia said as I looked at the harvest moon outside her bay window.

"Well, let me take you to the hospital if it's the same tomorrow. Or worse. You gotta keep me in the loop here, Mom!"

"No, not that. Him!" Her eyes looked down the hall into the blue of the living room.

"Oh, Mother. You gotta know by now just to tune him out. Have you tried listening to music on those headphones I bought you? They're the top of the line!"

"He sounds like a crazy person. He sounds like he's scared." She seemed legitimately worried, a notable change from her usual laissez-faire approach to his cantankerousness. "Will you speak to him? Those idiots on TV, I'm telling you, they're no good."

"I'll ask him to kibosh the right-wing propaganda for a night, let you have your rest," I said as I touched her forehead.

She sighed in relief, her energy for the day on its last legs. She had always been able to sleep through anything. "How's Raj?" she said through a smile as she closed her eyes.

I stopped breathing, took my hand from my mother's head and placed it over my neck, feeling it get hot instantly.

"I'm not stupid, love," she said, still smiling. "Thanks for your help."

As Julia drifted off and I dimmed her lights, I heard the front door close.

The howling was noticeably loud tonight. We live right close to Campbell Valley Park, where there are plenty of wild animals to see. Plenty of rabbits, raccoons, and other small furry things for coyotes in the neighbourhood to stalk and dine on. It was the loudest it'd been since I'd been coming back here. It felt like I was surrounded by a fleet of fire trucks, all sounding off in an emergency. I considered taking the high-end headphones from inside, but I saw Kyle Sr. out along the edge of the property, pacing back and forth. He was armed with one of his rifles.

"Dad! Get back in the house!" I yelled. My attempt to discipline this domesticated beast got lost in the mayhem of screeching from the wild dogs.

I trotted toward him, the wetness from the grass leaking into my shoes. When I was within ten feet, I said, "Dad! If it was a mountain lion, the coyotes would be quiet! It's time for bed!"

He rang out a shot from the rifle. The coyotes stopped howling. "I know you're in there! You think you can just come and go as you please? We got rules here on this side of the world!" he blurted, louder and deeper with each word.

I barrelled into him, knocking him to the moist ground. He stank. His body smelled as putrid as his breath. I couldn't remember the last time I'd touched him.

"I'll kill 'em all! Enough is enough!" he shouted proudly, smiling into the moonlight above me as I pinned his broken-down shoulders to the ground.

He jerked himself loose and gathered his rifle. Then he looked right through me and headed back to the house for another drink.

Kate Flannery

The Rat

AN EXCERPT FROM "BECOMING OF AGE," A NOVEL

All that was left of the rat was its hindquarters. Tail, legs—stiff and bent, seemingly ready to spring somewhere—and the lower half of the torso. Mary Flanders had found it earlier that morning, when she was out in the garden working to clear away the debris in the back flowerbeds. She supposed it was a rat, but it could have been a young possum. Or something else. Maybe just something caught by her cat who liked to stay outside at night—finding his nocturnal self—and then leaving a treat for her to find in the morning.

But this half-rat had been casually left behind, discarded by whatever predator had torn or chewed it in two. It was no token, no gift, no treat. It was just left behind after the predator had had its fill of kill. Mary wondered whether the death had been quick or slow, merciful or played out. She knew cats liked to play with their prey. Was this a kind of honing of the cat's skills to keep it at the ready? Or was it just to tire out the target, leaving it exhausted and less ready to fight back and injure the cat?

Mary had been in the garden for most of the morning, doing what she could to get back on her feet again following a feeling of sickness that had hit her during the past week. Her husband, Bill, was gone from the house, up the coast somewhere. She had forgotten to ask where and he had not given her any details. But, prompted by a growing contrariness, she had confronted him as he was loading up his classic Goldwing motorcycle two days before. As Chair of the Board of Trustees of Mansfield College, he always took more than enough clothes with him when he traveled, fund-raising for the college, making a professional impression. But he packed light when he was riding.

"Bill. I know where you're going."

"What?" He had looked down and paused. "I don't know what you mean." He had the decency to colour as he said the words.

"Bill. I know about Rachel," Mary had continued calmly.

"What? What are you talking about? Rachel Epstein? What makes you bring her up?"

Mary had just stared at him until the silence prodded him to say more. An old lawyer's trick she used to use in court when she was still practicing. The need to fill in the gap of silence was irresistible and had prompted Bill to keep talking.

"Look. Obviously we need to talk. When I get back, we'll sit down and talk about all this, but I have to go now," he floundered.

"Of course you do." Mary had heard rather than felt the steadiness in her voice.

And with that she had let him go.

With Bill gone, she was left alone with the aches that accompanied the sickness she had felt when he rode off. And so, this Thursday morning she decided to go into the back of the garden and start clearing out the debris—debris she had happily neglected in the last several weeks. Some of it was from the pine needles that had fallen in the recent Santa Ana winds—the so-called "devil winds"—that roared in from the East. But mostly it was the now-dead leaves leftover from the bulbs that always bloomed in Southern California long before spring; she knew she should let those spent leaves turn yellow, then creamy white. The leaves would die their slow, natural death as the nourishment sank back into the bulbs.

She was working in the cutting garden. The more visible part of the garden, where guests were entertained, was always kept in good order. In fine fettle. Ready to be on display at any moment. But this other part of the garden was where Mary always felt much more at home. It was the place where the bulbs grew in season, where the flowers bloomed in planned disarray, where weeds came in and went out, and where things were nourished with compost to make them grow lush and strong.

She had been on her way to the trash bins beyond the cutting garden, to dump the garden debris, when she had seen the stark fragment of rat that had been left behind. It got her thinking. It was the kind of thinking that used to frustrate Bill during their lunch and dinner conversations. Mary's mind would fly across her mental landscape and perch on whatever point caught her attention. Bill would look at her quizzically after she had made one of these mind-leaps and say, "I don't follow."

Mary wondered how long he hadn't been following, and why she hadn't noticed it before.

Bill had no patience with her "odd" turns of mind, as he called them. Her mind-flights, careening off into unexpected places. He liked things simple and straightforward. He would make a pronouncement. And that was the end of it. But Mary enjoyed the journeys her mind embarked on when she let it run free. However, with Bill's disapproval heavy in their home, she tried to keep her fanciful musings in check. Except at parties, where everyone agreed she was a lively and charming addition.

After her dinner party two weekends before, Mary knew what she was facing. She had seen the quiet, knowing looks between her husband and Rachel Epstein, and after seeing the letter from Rachel on his desk, Mary knew what those looks meant. She also knew that Bill's riding up the coast probably had something to do with Rachel. Rachel had a small rented house in Santa Barbara where she worked as an adjunct professor. It was a good hide-away.

After her realization about Rachel, Mary's first thought—oddly—was not anger at her husband, at the thought of his betrayal. Her first reaction was an icy freeze in the pit of her stomach. A kind of growing weight that left little room for food. She didn't know precisely what was happening or why it was happening, but her first reaction was not to strike out in anger. It was to grow quiet and still and move very little.

Perhaps that is what had happened to the rat. Perhaps that is why he had been caught by whatever had killed him. He hadn't moved quickly enough. And if he had fought back at all, he had clearly lost.

She left the rat remains where they were on the path to the trash bins, and turned back to the house. Without Bill, it was more than empty. After all the years of worry, the ache in Mary's heart was now finally real. She felt the surprise of betrayal—which in itself surprised her: how could she feel surprised *now*, when she had spent years wondering if Bill was susceptible to the attractive secretaries at his law office? Weren't there any fat or unattractive secretaries in Los Angeles? Apparently not in the legal field.

After her morning's work in the garden, Mary began to feel a little stronger. She went upstairs to clean up and get on with the rest of the day. She took off her clothes and got into the shower where she stood with the hot, almost scalding, water stinging her skin. The pain felt right, almost as if she deserved it. Stripped down, the feeling of aloneness hit her as if someone had thrown it at her. Hard. It was as if she was looking into a void, an absence that took away everything and left nothing behind. She had felt lonely before, but this wasn't the same. This was different. It was as if there was no landscape around her, no ground beneath her, no color, no sound, no smell. As if all her senses had been nullified and neutered. *It must be like this when you die,* she thought. *And there is no bright light waiting ahead.*

On top of it all, she wondered if she had been hoodwinked. Lulled into believing things were fine. Her life was good. She had all the trappings to prove it—the large house, the successful husband and her social position—and the ground was firm and steady beneath her feet. Then, all of a sudden, it wasn't. Should she just let things take their own course, staying still and quiet? Or should she stand her ground and fight?

Mary Flanders considered the rat.

Matt Brandenburg

Bone Chandelier

AN EXCERPT FROM A SHORT STORY

Mabel's only explanation as to why she stole the Bible-shaped container from a group of drug-dealing cult members was because it seemed like a good idea at the time. The Apocita Doom howled and screamed behind her as she sank deeper into the woods. They promised her the rumours were true, her skin would become a part of their spellbooks, her soul ground up into the drugs they sold. She batted away the threats like the mosquitos that buzzed by her head. She focused on the house by the beach, the freedom that was so close. Once she lost the men in the woods and unloaded the drugs, she'd finally be free from the heroin and the words, "unfit mother," that plagued her every step.

Fog enveloped her, erasing the world. Mabel followed the trail, not trusting herself to find a way through the trees. The backpack with the container bounced on her shoulders. All around her, insects chirped and mammals barked. Under her skin, she felt the steel wool itch of addiction, something she hadn't felt for weeks. Old scars on her hand throbbed from when she had put her fist through a window because her dealer had cheated her. *Just focus on what you are doing now, you don't need it anymore.* As she pushed forward, slick tree trunks slipped in and out of view.

A stray branch cut her cheek, another grabbed her bag. Mabel's heart froze and she balled up her fists ready to fight. She'd rather die than go back to that place filled with flayed bodies and pathetic cries surrounding the man in the bull mask as he melted down souls into black tar. She thought she smelled their lust for her soul behind her, imagined their heavy hands gripping her shoulders. She pulled with every ounce of strength, the snap of twigs sounded like bone as she ripped her bag away. A bird cried out. Frantic energy propelled her deeper into the nightmare-like forest.

The path wound through the trees, rising and falling. She imagined stumbling into a hole hidden underneath some brush. The Apocita cult watching as she squirmed on razor wire and sharpened sticks. Would they kill her over one tin of drugs? Or were they mad because she duped them into believing she wanted to be a dealer? When she had visited the cult, she had no plans to steal the drugs. But when they left her alone it had come to her. If she didn't have to be under their control, she'd be free to start fresh somewhere far away from the memories of her stolen child.

A branch slapped Mabel's cheek, bringing her back to the present. Her heart wheezed and sputtered like an old station wagon. If not for the grunts and yells bounding amongst the trees, she knew she'd collapse on the forest floor. But the horrible noises reminded her of the chants that haunted the cult's headquarters. As she struggled to push her body, Kim's voice came to her, "Honey, if you want cash, get to those lanky robe-wearing sons of bitches. It flows down that dead-end like nobody's business."

The path took a sharp turn to the right and then ended at a gloomy clearing. Her body sagged and felt as empty as the promises the boys gave her on prom night. Next to the path stood a large bush with spindly branches and ragged leaves. Mabel squeezed her way in, doing her best to ignore the sting of thorns. The smell of urine mixed with rotten berries filled the tiny space as Mabel studied the fog and listened for hooded men.

The longer she stared into the mist the more she could make out the dark silhouette of a house. Within the expanse of the clearing it brooded, like a deserted dollhouse forgotten by its owner. Catching her breath she studied it, the black windows reminding her of the eyes of a junky.

A howl broke the silence. She edged deeper into the bush, curling into herself with the backpack next to her chest like she used to do with her baby.

An icy finger traced a skeletal path down her spine and she shuddered. Her hand instinctively reached for her neck, swatting at a drip of water. She listened for the cult, trying to determine how far away they were and if she could double back without them knowing.

Mabel tried to concentrate on forming a plan, yet the clearing tempted her. She couldn't help but think of the unknown possibilities hidden within. It felt like her future, a space where anything could be, she just needed to forget the past and take the leap. Mabel craved the fresh air, the freedom from the confining woods, the chance to explore the house. She struggled to her knees, shaking water from the bush. The dripping matched the sound of rain in the Apocita's headquarters. She inched out of the bush and crept into the open.

Would the house be filled with the same horrors? Could there be a chance it was worse than what chased her? The pros and cons weighed on her as much as her bag full of drugs. She danced back and forth on her feet until the house seemed like an obvious place to hide. She decided she'd do better going back into the woods hoping the men would assume she had headed into the clearing.

As Mabel turned from the magnetism of the house a strange sensation came over her, like she was missing something. Her heart pounded in her ears, breath steamed past her face. Then it hit her, the forest was silent. No birds or bugs or animals scurried about. She froze on the edge of the wood, feeling dread like a deer before a hunter.

The inhuman growl that exploded from the path shattered the peace.

Mabel made a break for the house. Her veins and fingers vibrated with anticipation like the second time she had picked up a syringe and tied off her arm. The clearing welcomed her to its domain.

Avalon Bourne

The Other Woman

The theatre is full of people awaiting the next film screening at the festival, but Dominic's attention is captured by the girl walking down the aisle to the stage. He watches her, rumpled skirt and thick, sleeveless sweater already sticking to her in the heat. She is lugging several large blank canvases and an overstuffed messenger bag with a bottle of wine poking out of it. He sees the obstacle before she does—an unruly cable freed from the thick electrician's tape attempting to hold it in place. But he waits, leaning against the stage, eyeing her approach to their inevitable meeting. He watches as her foot catches the cable and—quick as a flash—he's at her side, steadying her burden and preventing her fall.

"Careful," he says. "The cables are loose."

He is already justifying this decision, excusing himself from the consequences of her gratitude. There wasn't room for him to turn back after her grateful thank-you drink that turned into *drinks*. Not when he kissed her and she tasted of salt. Not in the cab with her pressed against him, nor in her studio with him pressed against her. Not after, as he drifted off in unfamiliar sheets in a stranger's bed, silently congratulating himself for telling his wife that he'd stay in the city during the festival.

Consciousness comes to him slowly, rousing him from deep, comforting darkness. He is cold and bewildered as his memory fills in his immediate surroundings. He glances around and sees the source of the coldness—an open window. A ghostly figure sits on the ledge. He watches her, falling back to sleep.

June feels his eyes sliding over her, though she doesn't turn from the window. She knows that married men are not for the faint of heart, but she has never liked to deny herself what she wants. She waits until he falls back asleep before turning from the window. The lights from the street dance across the canvases in her loft, rendering them unfamiliar.

She moves silently from the window, an apparition amongst her painted figures. Her pieces are her version of tapestries, immense continuous scenes of storytelling keeping the shadows at bay. Her latest is unfinished. She glances toward the sleeping figure in the bed, wondering what role he could play in its completion.

Dominic is dreaming. It is the kind of dream where he can tell he's asleep. The girl is in it—no longer a girl but a cross between a fish and a bird. He is trying to determine where she belongs, but every time he releases her into the sea she tries to fly. It is a frustrating dream with a deep current of desperation threatening to grab hold of him. Fear rises through him like steam, forcing him awake.

The early morning sun floats through the window, caressing the girl wrapped around him. In the light, she looks faint and spectral. Dominic plots his escape. He's not sure he can extract himself without waking her. He glances around the loft, noticing the canvases for the first time.

There are four of them arranged against the walls and another perched on an easel in the centre of the room. At first, he thinks there is a layer of gauze covering the canvas, but on closer examination realizes it's part of the painting, a thin layer of brushwork creating the illusion of looking through water. There is a figure shimmering in shades of green and blue. The early morning sunlight shines through the window to dance with the brush strokes, and the shimmering intensifies. Dominic blinks, sure the sun is tricking his eyes.

The painting is moving, the dancing sunlight mirrored by the shimmying figure within. Dominic wonders if he's still dreaming as the aquamarine form pulls itself from the canvas and steps amidst the dust motes on the floor of the studio. He stares transfixed at the figure, the girl in his arms forgotten. The scene before him is not quite three dimensional. There is a hint of fullness as the figure sways back and forth, almost easing into completeness, but falling back into colours and shapes. The figure turns suddenly, fading away into light and dust, and Dominic yearns to follow.

June stirs. The night floods back into her, and she pauses when she realizes the coldness of the arms around her. The chill of the embrace fully jostles June into the world of the living. She pulls herself away, turning to examine him. His lips are blue. She stares at him, knowing what is in front of her and realizing what comes next.

June grasps her phone, the room whirling around her, light shattering against every shiny surface. She has never called 911—this thought bubbles up in her head. By the time the paramedics crash through her door, June is as icy as the man in her bed. There is constant motion, orders she obeys without conscious thought.

"How long has he been like this?" "What were you doing leading up to this?" "What is his name?"

Time passes or doesn't at all. June feels herself a stranger surrounded by the familiar artifacts of her life, looking at herself through a funhouse mirror, a jarring and unnerving reflection staring back at her.

She is surrounded by faces, the only familiar ones staring at her from her canvases. She wonders if she should call Dominic's wife. She wonders if this is something she should have asked sooner, if the absence of her asking has marked her somehow, made her suspect. She supposes it won't make a difference either way.

June notices one of her canvases is askew and fights the urge to fix it. She is self-conscious, aware of every gesture and movement.

The paramedics continue their work in feverish constancy, a clinical choreography of imperfect motion. June silently surveys.

Dominic is deep under water in the dark, save for a flickering circle of aquamarine light far overhead. It doesn't interest him. He's chasing the painted nymph deep into the cold blue of the water. He almost has her—his hand around her ankle—when the same action is mimicked on his own. He kicks it off, intent on his prize, but the tugging is persistent. He glances back, only for a moment, but it's enough to break his concentration. The figure vanishes into the endless water and Dominic panics. He glances toward the light, focused on a new quarry, and starts to kick.

In a flurry of green and blue light, Dominic kicks back to the surface, sputtering for breath. He is face-to-face with a stranger.

"Can you hear me? Do you know who you are? Do you know where you are?"

The light is harsh, the air dusty and bitter in his lungs. He has no idea where he is. He glances around frantically, gulping in burning air. A familiar girl in a green silk robe stands above him.

The paramedic is arranging for his transfer to the hospital and his wife is meeting him there. She has been told little. "A close call," is repeated often. Dominic wonders how much breathing space a near-death experience will grant him. He wonders if it's enough for forgiveness. The girl won't look at him, her eyes pulled to any face but his, her expression unreadable save for a hint of disappointment. He reaches out to her, demanding her attention.

Exhausted, June meets his eyes. "It might have been better for both of us if you had let me trip."

June has always thought love affairs should end with drowning. It seems a fitting way to extinguish the passion of what preceded. But how to determine who should take the plunge? She wonders again why she allowed this to happen, when the sequence of events had been so clear in her mind. She knew what would happen from the moment the cables came loose—and yet, she did not turn away, she did not refuse his offer. She looks at the not-quite-finished canvas and sees his face in every corner.

Isabel Spiegel

Refuge

AN EXCERPT

Aunt Marianne picks me up at the Gare d'Avignon, where I descend the steps of the train, clutching my cardboard suitcase, coughing from the black cloud of coal dust. She reminds me of a rhino, with her large shoulders and muscular calves bulging over red boots, as she lurches through the crowd and drags me behind her. We exit out of the station to cerulean sky and spindle trees, the clamour of passengers a thunder in the distance. Marianne glances over at me, my eyes watering from wind and dust, and mistakes them for tears. "You'll be safe here, *ma fille, ne t'inquiètes pas*," she says. Don't worry.

I stand still, relishing the heat of the sun through my favourite blue cardigan. I inhale the scent of the south, thick with rosemary and sage. A lizard darts over a rock near my feet, swiveling its yellow eyes in my direction, and I hold its gaze until Aunt Marianne realizes she's left me behind and leads me briskly toward the rusty automobile parked outside.

During the ride home, the car jumps with every rock in the road, and Marianne never takes her foot off the gas pedal. She squishes an old straw hat on my head, remarking, "You're so pale! You'll burn quicker than a crème brulée!"

I see fields and trees go by in little squares of bright light through the weave of the hat, and clutch my one-way ticket in my hand as if I can use it to get back to Paris, back to my parents.

The house looks out toward fields of lavender, stretched like fuzzy purple caterpillars basking in the sun. The salon is filled with the sweet smell of hay, so different than the damp apartment I had shared with my parents. While I unpack, I hear Aunt Marianne sing "Sur le Pont d'Avignon," plucking her mandolin strings with the same fingers that will circle the chicken's neck, gut and prepare the limp white body for dinner.

Days later, with her glasses perched on her nose, her hair piled on her head like one of those old-fashioned matrons, she tells me my parents died because they knew too much. I remember the story of the Parisian boy who blew up Librairie Rive Gauche with a book. How, crawling under my parent's bed to play hide and seek, I saw papers and pamphlets tucked under the mattress, and the way my father came home after his job at the newspaper, completely spent, dragging his satchel as if it was made of stone. I remember telling my father about the camels in Morocco who wear little red hats, and he said it was the men, not the camels, but I was determined to be right. "Let's go there," I pleaded, like I was begging for sweets.

He laughed and said, "You're just like your mother. We're not going anywhere. France is our home."

At night I shiver in bed as I stare at the shut door. Shadows move with open arms to pull me into their mouths. I wander downstairs to press my ear against the salon door and listen to the hushed conversations with guests from the city. Their accents are smooth, unlike the twang of my aunt who adds a *g* to the end of *bien* so it sounds like a guitar losing its string.

DeeDee LeGrand-Hart

White Lion

AN EXCERPT

Seven hours of nothing but flat. Our train rattles and wails and rolls into Nevada before nightfall can throw a curtain over what it should hide. Windsor. It's a good name for a cocker spaniel but this place is a hairless chihuahua with sunburn wrung out from the heat. But by morning, our big top will turn this Dog Town into Glam City.

Even in dumps without Wi-Fi, I've seen museums of farm tractors, gummy bears, and funeral hearses. My squad, the trapeze twins and I, have the night to find a pulse in Windsor. It takes ten minutes. This is it: a mall, a Dairy Queen, and a liquor store that sells pork rinds, fishing bait, and camouflage baby bibs. We intel the mall. Meaning, we steal. Watermelon lip-gloss and toe rings from Claire's. We swap circus tickets for Cinnabons. Walking home, we laugh like horses whinnying, and our high heels clop like hooves. I go, "Check out the ball caps in the windows! Redneck townies are rubbernecking to see what they can't see." They're the kind who want to catch every act in a three-ring circus.

Opening day, our free sideshow is crawling with beer brand T-shirts. Crowds flock to our Animal World—tigers, bears, and monkeys in a train of red and yellow cages like giant boxes of Barnum's Animal Crackers. Chocolate-smeared kids shove their way to see the main attraction: Wild Bill, World's Only Ghost Lion. To me, he's a toothless old man. To them, he's supernatural. They form a line to take selfies with him. I'm like, "Can't you read? The sign says, 'No Pictures!' It's a scientific fact—flash hurts a white lion's sensitive eyes. It turns him into a demon." Brats try to pet him, so I give Billy's tail a yank. His jaws rip open and belt out a haul-ass thunder. Kids run, except for this ratty-haired runt who says, "He's not a ghost! What's so scary?" I go, "You'll find out. He eats fast, so the first half-hour will hurt the most." I flick my cigarette and smudge it with my heel. He scrams. Wild Bill yawns and sinks into a sprawled-out sleep.

It's after six, almost show time, and the desert's cooking us to a hundred degrees. The crowd trampling dead grass sounds like a knife scraping burnt toast. Our tent is steaming with the smells of popcorn, draft beer, cotton candy, hair spray, perfume, deodorant (or the lack thereof), and something I can't see but it's heavy like a rainstorm's coming. The musty tent smell will outlast cigarette smoke in cheap hotel wallpaper.

Backstage, the fam argues, as usual. Tightrope swears a talent scout from a competing troupe is in the stands. "They pay better," he says. Ringworm flips him the bird and peeks into the tent, "I'd pay more if it weren't for all those empty rows." Unicycle goes, "Everybody's at a tent revival getting baptized. It's hot as Hades, the dunk tank's heaven." Ringworm says, "Our clown's dunk tank gets a good laugh." My dad, the World's Greatest Fire Eater, goes, "But it doesn't sell tickets." Ringworm shoots a look at me. "What don't sell tickets is that damn ghost cat! I got a bid on him for ten grand! Would've got more if a disease didn't make him blond and blind. An exotic pet collector wanted him. For his kid, remember?" He knows I do, that's why he's reminding me.

Billy was a cub still missing his mama when they first tried to sell him. Our lion tamers couldn't train him for the ring because they had to stop whipping him. It put red scars on his white skin, and animal rights protesters crowded outside our tents. Our trainers tried to starve him and lure him with food, they even pulled some teeth to make him less dangerous. Billy didn't have to listen to them because I fed him. I trained him to let my dolls ride piggyback. Easy squeezy. I still don't know why Billy didn't sell. Rumor was the collector's kid freaked out, thinking the growl was a ghost.

My take? Ringworm got greedy. He got wind trophy hunters would pay fifty GS for him, but held out too long. No one will pay a cent for the old boy now.

Suddenly, I'm glad to hear our cranky organ. It sends Ringworm to the stage. He drones on for an embarrassing kind of forever while the audience plays with hand-held circuses, a.k.a. smartphones. Our sound system buzzes electrocution-style, moms shush their kids, and the crowd wiggles to a stop. Ringworm looks all serious. "Ladies and Gentlemen!" voice quivering like an opera singer or a mad preacher. "You are about to witness death-defying acts never seen on stage. For the safety of our performers, please turn off your cell phones." When the lights go out, little screens blink on and off like fireflies in the dark.

Dad and I are up after the arthritic contortionists. Dad doesn't flinch, the World's Greatest Fire Eater never will. While the drum rolls, I light torches. Dad juggles two, four, six, eight. He catches a torch in his teeth and swallows it. If he breathes, he burns. He pulls the flaming torch from his mouth. Applause! Then he tosses spinning torches to me. We play catch without even blinking. But tonight, I lose my groove when I hear a roar I know better than my ringtone. Billy's in danger. Whoosh! A flame swipes my arm, the crowd gasps. I feel a sizzle, no burn. Dad's eyes lock, which make mine steady. He nods an okay, and I'm totally back in.

Next, for our new bubble stunt, the drunk clowns on tricycles buy me two minutes to shimmy out of my leotard and hop into a white bodysuit covered with plastic bubbles. I come out juggling water and shampoo bottles, and pour suds on my hair. When I tug a string on my jumpsuit, millions of bubbles make me invisible. I soak my long hair in a bucket and toss it back like in those TV ads. Dad gets soaked. He mimes pissed-off, shaking his fists. I mime clueless, shrugging my shoulders. Then he breathes fire into a huge fan, faking a turbo blow dryer. Instead of smoke, millions of bubbles fly out into the crowd. While they're going nuts catching them, voila, my hair is dry! Dad hates this act because people laugh. He hates it more when they don't.

Eight years ago, I started doing Mom's job when she ran off. I was six, no one expected me to be any good, just cute. One night, a torch melted the fringe off my costume. The crowd goes, "Aw!" like I was a puppy. I curtseyed like it was no big deal, which it wasn't. We got a standing ovation! Dad hated adding that burning fringe to my act. Earth to Dad. Crowds get bored way faster now. Squad manual says, "Fire it up or go down in flames."

After my bows, my trapeze buds are up. The crowd sees pink ballerinas who could fall to their deaths any second. Ha! The air under a trapeze artist doesn't let them fall, and they're the only ones who know it. I usually watch, but tonight I slip backstage to see what's itching Billy.

I hate being right about something being wrong, but sure enough, someone's nosing around. I light a torch. A bald head shines out of a costume rack. Too old to be a cruelty protester. A thief! I charge at him with flames blazing and back him against Wild Bill's cage. Billy's growling like mad. The man's bawling like crazy. Saying his little girl's a huge circus fan. Saying she couldn't see the show—she's dying in the hospital. Saying she has a brain tumor. Saying he'll bring the circus to her. Saying she wants autographs from performers. He hands me a program, "Would you p-p-please sign?" Then he bends over so I can use his back for a table and a box of SweetTarts falls out of a shirt pocket, then a glow-stick, then a ticket stub, then a sticker book. He's not lying about the girl.

I write, "To a brave kid." I wonder to myself if she'd prefer the fire eating or the bubbles act. People want her to be strong, so she'd say the fire act. Deep down, she'd totally prefer the bubbles. By this time, Billy's looking cuddly, like he wants a teething ring more than flesh. I'm like, "People get fined for taking photos of this lion. But I'll do it this once for your daughter, got it?" He nodded. I snap a picture with his phone. It bothered Billy, but I think that dying girl is the only thing this man's got in the world. And lame as he was for sneaking backstage, he might be all she has, too.

The man hurries off, then Dad walks up, "Who were you were talking to?" I don't lie unless it's for someone's good. Squad Manual, page seven: "A white lie's okay if parts of it are true." I go, "This man comes by saying the white lion spirit can heal his kid with brain cancer. I get a photo with him and Billy in case her believing it can make it true. He could've seen a tent revival healer, but he came for Billy! Ringworm will see Billy's a healer, earning his keep outside the ring. He'll fix Billy's teeth and feed him steak!" Dad sighs real deep and says he believes Billy's special—he'll keep a closer eye on him from now on. He takes my hand and we return to the ring for our last bows. Our old organ plays an awful hymn.

Windsor's behind us. The next town has a Museum of Alien Remains! Like the Squad Manual says, "The next gig must be better."

The windy plains are waving goodbye, our train whirrs past power lines, road signs, and cuts across grasslands like a river running home. I fall asleep brushing Wild Bill's mane, his deep purr rocks my head back and forth with the train's music: the strumming of railroad ties, spaced evenly, steady on the tracks.

Dianne Carruthers

Schadenfreude

John invited me to lunch. I was five minutes late. When I arrived, there was a white envelope on the table with my name on it.

He was the picture of health and impeccably dressed, wearing his signature million-dollar shoes.

"What's that?" I asked, reaching over and picking up the corner of the crisp, white rectangle. It was made of beautiful paper with an impressive heft.

"We'll get to that," he said. "Order first."

John and I were childhood friends. It didn't matter how much time went by, it was easy to pick up where we left off. John was godfather to my kids. He sent them letters and made an effort to make them feel special. He was the kind of friend that never failed to send a card, bring nice wine, and ask after your mother. He chose his friends carefully and I was honoured to be one. In truth, I probably didn't deserve him.

Unfortunately, John wasn't under the lucky star of relationships that I was. I had a good friend in him. I had married a woman I loved, while he had a heart-wrenching break up with Jim, his partner of nine years. Neither did he have much of a connection with his family. They were cool and distant because of his "lifestyle" choice. His sister, despite his efforts, positively glowed with *schadenfreude* when she moved into first position in the family.

I was glad to see John. We had had a falling out a few years earlier when I double-booked—and cancelled—a ski trip he had carefully planned. John is detail-oriented and I am not.

"You buying?" I asked.

"You cheap screw," John said, affectionately. "Yes. Be reasonable. No lobster."

John seemed anxious, so I took my time perusing the menu to prolong his discomfort and guess at what he wanted. This was, by far, the most formal outing we'd ever had. He wasn't going to spring news of a divorce or a pregnancy on me and he looked great which made me wonder if he was considering changing his name. He had often talked about disliking his last name, Waskowitz, mostly because he was tired of spelling it.

As soon as I ordered, he relaxed, but I was surprised at what he had to say. He exhaled. "I want to talk to you about my last wishes," he said.

"Oh God, John, are you dying?" I was alarmed at my insensitivity. Why hadn't I called him more often or gone golfing, even once? He had stopped asking me. I was not as good a friend as I imagined.

Although he'd ordered an expensive wine, I resolved to buy lunch.

"No!" he said. "It's nothing like that."

I changed my mind. I didn't have to buy lunch. He'd invited me after all. "So what's this about then?"

"It's about how I would like things done *if* I pass away." He was watching me like a hawk. "It was awful going to Charlie's funeral last year, wasn't it?"

He was right. A chum from school had passed away and his sparsely attended service in a dusty funeral home with soggy sandwiches had been depressing. There was no evidence of the life Charlie had led or the fact he was the undefeated beer pong champion from university.

"Am I the executor of your will?" I asked.

"No! I would never ask you to do that. That's a job for an enemy. I made my sister executor. You're the party planner."

"For your funeral? Do we really need to talk about this?"

"We do. I can't trust that any one will take care of these things properly. What if there were devilled eggs and a cash bar? I would die ..." He laughed at his joke but he wasn't joking.

"Yes! Of course I would," I promised—with the best of intentions.

We finished lunch. John paid the bill and, as we got up to leave, he handed me the envelope on the table with an earnest look. Holding me affectionately by the shoulders, he said, "You're the only person I trust with this."

When I got home and opened the envelope I realized I had agreed to a contract before reading it. The directions were elaborate and painstakingly detailed.

In the event of his death, there would be money provided for me to spread his ashes in three places. It seemed like a good movie plot. One of the locations was St. Andrew's golf course in Scotland. He would finally get me on the green.

The second place made me nostalgic. It was the river near his parent's place where we used to while away our days when we were boys. I remembered us standing knee-deep in freezing water, fishing for hours, never realizing our chances of catching anything were close to nil. We had tried to build a weir, dig a hole to China and, once, we accidentally set a grass fire.

The third place, the instructions went on to explain, would be revealed to me in the will. That was very John—in control even from the grave.

He had the menu set and the "guest list" was alphabetized with full and secondary contact information for anyone with an asterix beside their name. I figured this demarcation either meant most important or most transient.

He had included my ex-girlfriend, which seemed like another excellent plot line. My wife and I had recently separated.

The instructions that surprised me the most in their detail were for his wardrobe. He wanted to be buried in his Savile Row navy suit, a white shirt (the kind he always wore) with small monogrammed initials on the cuffs, and a silk tie my wife had given him. He had included his brown alligator loafers from Harry's Shoes, South Audley Street in London.

They were beautiful shoes and I, not without shame, had always coveted them with the green envy of a high school girl. It felt a waste for them to be in the ground, but these were his wishes.

To my surprise, only thirteen months later, I received word John had died. His sister filled me in on the details. Apparently, John was struck by lightning in a hot-air balloon in Anatolia. I was deeply saddened but knew John would have approved of this dramatic exit from the earth. She asked me about the details for the funeral. That's when I remembered—the envelope!

I commenced a mad search for the document John had entrusted to me. I located it under a pile of paper in my den with a curling sticky note that said, "File!" I cringed. John would have hated that it was not in a safety deposit box or at my lawyer's office for safekeeping.

I phoned the golf club, and it turned out they were already apprised. I then forwarded his self-penned, beautifully written obituary to the newspapers on his list. The service had been set and John, being a good Catholic, had arranged for an open casket at St. Mary's Cathedral. The music had been chosen and the bar bill at the golf club had been prepaid. The only thing left to do was take his beautiful clothes, as instructed, to the funeral home where his body was being prepared and would later be cremated.

I had yet to find out where the third ash drop was to take place. I hoped it was Switzerland for some reason, and immediately gave myself a good self-flagellation. Vietnam would be cool too.

On the day of the funeral I arrived early at the church. I couldn't look at the body. I didn't want to remember John lying in a coffin. I wanted to remember him alive and as my dashing best friend.

The church started to fill up. His mother, usually stern and well-heeled, looked a disheveled mess. His sister's face was set with her mean jaw and his father looked defeated.

My ex-girlfriend waved at me from across the aisle. She was glowing. I patted the seat beside me. She looked surprised. That was when I saw her burgeoning belly and a guy, at least five times more handsome than me, take his place beside her.

Some of John's friends had sent their condolences but were not there. The service was short and perfunctory. When it was over I stayed in my pew, wondering if I believed in God and what I was going to do now: divorced and without John.

As I considered this, I noticed a slight movement from the coffin. A deep pit of fearful disbelief knotted my gut. John rose up and turned to look at me. He was angry. We locked eyes. I felt sweat under my armpits. A look of disgust crossed his face. My mind was racing. I would never find out the third location for the ashes.

Then John spoke the last words he ever said to me.

"Give. Me. Back. My goddamned shoes."

Griffin Tedeschini

Sticktown

AN EXCERPT

Lee stands on the corner, watching people stream by as they head toward the warehouse. Sweat trickles down between her shoulder blades. It's still warm out, but really it's nerves that are heating her up.

She can hear the music, pulsing from the space, a methodic *phwump phwump phwump* that feels like it's pounding her in the middle of her chest. Flashes of light escape from the top windows, the lower ones blacked out. Abandoned warehouse-turned-nightclub, even if just for tonight.

Lee was surprised the day before when Gabriel invited her to the party, right there in the middle of the cafeteria. She's started going there more often, foregoing the expensive coffee stuff down the street. Truth be told, the cafeteria coffee is cheaper, but it's terrible. But Lee isn't going there for the coffee. Gabriel's smile, and those sparkling eyes, more than make up for the bitter black brew disguised as coffee.

As Gabriel set Lee's Americano down on the table, she asked, "Hey, my friend is DJ'ing a gig tomorrow night, you interested?"

Lee sat there for a moment, stunned. She looked around, wondering if Gabriel was really talking to her. She'd imagined that maybe—somehow, someday—they'd go on a date. Maybe something more than a coffee conversation in the cafeteria would be possible.

"Yes, I mean you," Gabriel said, shaking her head, laughing. "You do dance, don't you?"

"Uh, ya … yes, I do … I mean dance … uh," Lee finally stammered out, her mouth dry, her face warm. "Yes, yes I'd like that."

And now here she is, standing on the dimly lit street, watching people stream by, in pairs and groups, laughing, talking loudly, glow sticks hung on belt loops, joints passed between hands, the occasional clink of a beer tin tossed into the garbage before their bodies jostle into line.

She scans left, right, left, right. Checks her phone, no new message, just Gabriel's *on my way* text from half an hour ago. She knows Gabriel is coming, but part of her feels maybe she changed her mind. Maybe she's not really interested. Maybe she's just messing with me.

Lee hates moments like this, waiting for people. It reminds her of when her father forgot to pick her up after practice—or from school, or left her waiting at the train station after coming back from a visit with Nonna. It leaves an empty feeling inside of her. Like she's been forgotten. Abandoned.

Stop it, she tells herself. She looks back down at her phone, rereads the message, *on my way*. Lee takes a deep breath and goes back to scanning the street.

She sees Gabriel striding down the street toward her, hair down, clad in a tank top and cut-off denim shorts and the black boots Lee's only ever seen her wear. She looks like a cat—no, a lion—all golden and lithe and slinky with energy under her skin that Lee can feel from across the street. She's talking with a guy who must be the DJ, headphones slung around his neck, bulging messenger bag bouncing against his hip.

Lee takes a step forward, wonders if she should say something, hesitates, and then Gabriel sees her.

"Lee!" Gabriel bounds over, face lit up, all smile and teeth, her hair shining golden under the streetlight. Lee feels something looping in her stomach, feels herself smiling back, just as wide, as open. There's a moment, a pause, and all Lee wants to do is step forward, grab Gabriel's hand, pull her close to her ... and then it passes, just as Gabriel grabs the stranger and pulls him toward them.

"Lee, this is Dominic. Dominic, Lee."

Lee smiles, pushes her hand out toward Dominic, who takes it in a firm grip.

"Nice to meet you, finally," he says, smiling.

Gabriel gives him a look, grabs his messenger bag and pushes him into motion. "Come on, someone has a show to do."

She looks over at Lee as they head toward the growing lineup outside the warehouse doors. Lee thinks that even with the dim light shining down from the street lamps, she can make out a pink flush on Gabriel's cheeks. She smiles, then looks down at her feet. Maybe she's not the only nervous one after all?

It pays to know the DJ. Lee follows Gabriel, following Dominic, as he makes his way through the crowd, right to the front. He takes the door person's hand, the two give each other a shoulder bump, and then waves the three of them inside, much to the dismay of the growing crowd.

"Line cutter!" someone calls out just as they're about to step through open doors.

"He's the DJ, we're his groupies!" Gabriel calls out, pausing to blow a kiss to the disgruntled crowd as she pulls Lee into the pulsating space.

Inside the warehouse the air is thick with smells—sweat and weed and beer all mixed together, kept aloft by the warm fog from the smoke machines on either side of the DJ booth. Even with the overhead doors pulled up and open on either side of the space, Lee feels heat coiling around her.

"Want a drink?" Gabriel says into her ear, close enough Lee can smell the fresh laundry scent of her tank top, a hint of soap underneath. All she wants to do is get Gabriel on the dance floor, pull her body close against hers, feel all of her skin and curves beneath her fingertips.

"Lee," Gabriel says, snapping her fingers in front of Lee's face. "You take something tonight or what?"

Lee laughs, shakes her head. "No, I don't do drugs. Just a bit overwhelmed by all the music and lights I guess." Which is a lie. Overwhelmed by Gabriel, but she isn't about to give that away. Not just yet.

"Stay here, I'll get us some beer," she says, and then Lee watches her disappear into a moving mass of bodies. She looks around, orients herself in the space so as not to move, not lose Gabriel when she comes back.

As she's scanning, Lee sees someone across the room, lit up momentarily by one of the strobe lights slicing through the darkness. She keeps her eyes fixed on the spot, even when the space goes black, squinting, focusing. The lights flash once, twice, then for a few moments the space is lit up in a clear, bright opening.

It's the man from that night, with the white hair. The one who had watched her from under the streetlight. Even from across the room, with the space full of people, he's watching her watch him.

She looks away for a moment, and just as she looks back the space goes dark again. A shiver travels through her body. Involuntary, primal. She shrugs, tries to push the sensation out of her body and back into the writhing space.

What the fuck? It's a coincidence, just a coincidence.

Sweat trickles down her neck, to her back. She reaches up, wipes it away from her neck, grabs the elastic she always has around her wrist and puts her hair up into a ponytail. She hoped she could wear it down tonight, to show Gabriel her curls, but the heat's too much. Or maybe it's nerves.

Or fear.

She watches the space across the room, waiting for the light to open it up. When it does, there's no sign of him. He's gone.

Lee jumps as she feels something cold pressing against the back of her neck.

"Whoa!" Gabriel says, jumping back as Lee whips around. "Sorry, didn't mean to scare you, here's your beer."

"It's okay, I thought you were ..." she starts to say, then smiles, shakes her head and takes the beer from Gabriel. "Cheers." She holds the can out.

"Cheers," Gabriel says, clinking tin against tin, tilts her head back and takes a long drink. Lee lets out her breath and does the same, all the while her eyes scan the space on the other side of the room.

Ann Svendsen

The Man Who Came Through the Window

The three ladies charge down our long driveway. Adele Pershinsky leads the way with her trademark curlers under a garish red-and-yellow scarf, Sophie Seymour follows in her flowered cotton dress and dark purple sun hat, and Freida Blackmoor brings up the rear in her usual drab green skirt and droopy sweater.

I'm standing over the heat register beside the kitchen window, glad to be home from school on a Monday when it's my mother's turn to host the coffee party. I hope she'll let me stay with the ladies—because of what happened last night.

"Hi everyone, come on in!" Mom says as the four women fit themselves into the narrow space on either side of our aluminum-edged table in a flurry of jostling and chair scraping.

"How are you, Adele?" she asks, not waiting for a reply. Adele often hogs the conversation complaining about Pete, her miserable Polish husband who lost his arm in an accident at the shipyard. He has a hook for a hand and a pot belly from all the beer. My mother puts up with Adele because she's a spy. Everyone is afraid of her. She's no one's true friend.

"Love your hat, Sophie!" Mom chirps. Mrs. Seymour is my favorite. She's quiet and shy, like me. When I clam up she doesn't prod or push, she just carries on like nothing's wrong.

"How are your sick boys, Freida?" Mrs. Blackmoor's face is a dark thunder cloud. If the ladies were in the army, she'd be the Sergeant Major.

"I noticed your lights were on at midnight last night, Sylvie. Did Robert get home early? He's usually not home till Wednesday, right?" Mrs. Pershinsky sees everything. My dad sells office supplies. Every week he leaves Sunday morning and comes home Wednesday night after dinner.

"I was going to tell you what happened," Mom whispers. "But, before I do—Jayne, please take a square and some milk to your room." I shrug my shoulders as if I don't care. By the time I'm on my bedroom floor with my ear against the heat register, she has launched into her story.

"Last night we had an intruder, a peeping Tom. I was just going off to sleep. My bedroom window was open to let in the air. It was unusually hot and muggy." She is just warming up—Mom is a great storyteller.

"Then I saw the curtains move. I saw a leg and a foot come under the curtains and step onto our dresser."

"Oh my God," says Mrs. Seymour. "You must have been terrified."

"I didn't have time to be scared. I just jumped out of bed and pushed him out of the window. Unfortunately, he only had a few feet to fall. I ran down the hall and locked the front door as he ran along the front of the house and catapulted over the fence."

"Who was he, Sylvie? You must have some idea? If you don't, I certainly do ..." Mrs. Pershinsky again. "It's probably Mr. Hussein who moved into the old Hardy place. He's weird and his wife is, too. They're from Egypt and they smoke marijuana in a hookie pipe. God knows what else they get up to. I also heard that his wife has gone back to her country. When the wife is away ... Well, you know what happens." Mrs. Pershinsky snickers in her cutting way, but I know she's just mean and a big fat liar.

I babysit for Mr. Hussein and he's a nice man—not like Mr. Pershinksy, who tried to stick his tongue down my throat at the neighborhood Christmas party last year. If I suspected anyone, it would be Pete.

"Now, Adele, let's not jump to conclusions," says Mom.

"The important thing is that you aren't hurt. How is Jayne?" asks Mrs. Seymour.

My mother says sharply, "I'm fine and Jayne is her usual stoic self."

I feel the heat rising from my toes, up through my stomach and chest to my face and cheeks. I am not stoic—if my mother only knew. My father should be here. Why is he always leaving us to fend for ourselves? I feel hot tears roll down my cheeks.

Mom calls me as she opens the front door and leads the policeman into our living room. I sit beside her on the sofa. The officer sits in my father's chair beside the fireplace.

"I'm Constable Millar and you are Mrs. Clarke, I presume? Who is the lovely little lady?"

"This is my daughter, Jayne. She was also home last night when the intruder intruded . . ." She giggles nervously. "My husband wasn't home. He's a salesman and is away until Wednesday."

"Jayne, where were you when all this was happening?"

I wipe my sweaty palms on my dress and sit up straight. My stomach is in knots and my voice is lost somewhere. I clear my throat. The officer leans toward me and holds his pen just above his notebook.

"I was sleeping in my room. Then I heard a noise and my mother shouting. I ran to her bedroom and saw her push someone out the window."

"Did you recognize this person?" he asks.

"No, I don't know who it could have been. I don't know why he would be trying to get into my parents' bedroom."

"Do you usually leave your bedroom curtains and window open, Mrs. Clarke?"

"Yes, I do. To get the air on hot nights."

"I suggest you leave your curtains closed and your windows locked in the future. A peeping Tom—if that's what he was—is more likely to come around when a woman is beautiful and alone." He offers us a varnished smile, his perfect teeth glisten in the morning light. "But I could come by this evening to make sure you're safe, especially if your husband isn't home." Mom doesn't see a weasel, just a policeman doing his job.

This is too much. I choke and cough, words catch in my throat, and my knees shake, but I won't be quiet. I jump up and shout, "My father will be home tonight. I'll find him and tell him he's been gone too long."

My mother stands up and puts her arm around my shoulders. "Jayne, your father won't be back for two days. You know that."

Pulling away, I say clearly, "I know where he is, Mom."

She gasps. Her eyes open wide and her tiny mouth clamps shut in a thin straight line.

"He lives with that lady—Stella—the one who paints pictures ... and his other daughter. He goes there from Sunday until Wednesday and he lives with us the other days."

She collapses on the sofa like a puppet whose strings are being cut one at a time. Then she doubles over, covering her face with her hands and moans, "Oh, God," in a long, sorrowful cry.

"I've known since Grade 3—Debbie Pershinsky told me." Her chin drops to her chest and she whimpers.

Mom shows the officer out. She wraps her arms around me, pulls me close and whispers, "Jayne, I'm so very sorry." I stand absolutely still in her arms, feeling warm and happy for the first time in ages.

"I've been meaning for us to visit your grandmother Marie in Montreal," she says. "Now seems like the perfect time."

Later, when the taxi arrives, Mrs. Pershinsky watches from her kitchen window. Mom stands for a moment on the front porch, locks the door and turns, ignoring Mrs. Pershinsky's wave. We get into the taxi and are finally on our way.

Karla Kosowan

The Lady in the Cake

A MOTHER AND DAUGHTER PRACTICE SAYING GOODBYE

Even though the kitchen is at the back of the house, warm sugary air wafts out the front, making Nora thirsty and tense. She knows her dress is too tight. Middle-age is creeping up on her, making the fat cling to her back and sides, where curves should be.

Sucking her stomach in, her shoulders raised higher than they need to be, she rings the doorbell. Helen, as if waiting only for Nora to make the first move, jerks the door open.

"Late," Helen says. Yes, she is late.

"What do you call this?" Helen continues, pulling on the strap of Nora's dress, letting it go with a snap. Helen is wearing a wispy, mauve dress that reaches mid-calf and has her good diamonds on.

"How are you, Mom?" Nora says.

"I'm almost done."

They walk down the hallway, their heels banging on the hardwood. There is no music playing, no other guests making noise so the footsteps are a singular assault to Nora's ears.

"Just in general?" Nora jokes.

"Don't be ridiculous," Helen says, shrugging Nora off. They enter the kitchen. Helen picks up a spatula and continues icing the cake, her hand zig-zagging, making little divots all around. Beside the cake is a plate of vegetables.

Nora points at it, surprised. "We're having salad?" There is a sliver of excitement in her tone. A refresh. A change in the routine.

"You'll see." Helen smiles and puts her reading glasses on. "Go get the champagne."

The cake is for her brother Tom, to mark his going away to college in California twenty years ago. Every year it's the same, Helen wants to celebrate this milestone with Nora.

"I don't think I'll drink this time." Nora picks up an empty shopping bag, shaking out bits of onion skin into the sink.

"You're going to make me drink by myself?"

"When I get drunk, I make terrible decisions." Nora smiles, but it's not a lie.

"Do you remember what kind he wanted? A Kahlua cake."

Tom and his friends, Luke and Nick, were inseparable. They had even become nearly identical over the last year of high-school: tall, slim, and blonde-haired, dressed almost year-round in surf shorts and baseball hats, listening to ska punk, skateboards always under their arms or feet. California was the promised land to them so when Tom landed a spot at the University of California in San Diego it was like he'd won the lottery. It was bolder, cooler, and better than anything Vancouver had to offer with its grey skies and outdoors; nothing famous or hip, just the CBC.

A trip was planned. The three of them would drive the Pacific Coast Highway in Tom's ancient VW van. They would stop and camp at a beach in Oregon for a few days before making their way down.

They had the going away party in the backyard. Tom and Nora stood together, watching Helen entertain a group of Tom's friends, gesturing like a marching soldier. She squatted and popped up quickly, a look of fake surprise on her face. There was a pause, then a chorus of polite laughter, like from a TV audience.

"Maybe we're adopted," I said.

"I'll miss you, nerd girl," Tom replied.

They died that night. On the I-5 in Washington state. The trucker—Mom had insisted on talking to him—said their car came at him, "Straight as an arrow." He told her he'd never forget how unavoidable it had seemed. The police figured Tom must've fallen asleep at the wheel.

"Well?" Helen asks.

It is in decorating the top of the cake that Helen has given 110 percent. No, "God bless, Tom" or "We miss you, Bub," or even a simple presentation of the year of his birth and death like she did last year. Rather, Helen has used a collection of vegetables to create the shape of a sexy woman's face. Two thin gashes from the curve of a green pepper for eyebrows, a wedge of a cherry tomato cleaned of its mushiness for her nose in profile, black olive crescents for half-opened eyes, and the lumpy bottom of a red pepper sliced in half for a full mouth. For hair, she has used something long, thin, and brown. Nora can't even guess what the substance is. She appears to be singing, or swooning. On closer inspection, Nora knows if this lady were real, they wouldn't be friends. Her face, one eyebrow permanently raised, her sultry lips parted just slightly, the way her mouth curves down. It looks to Nora a hell of a lot like she is judging. Like, if there were more space, a wagging index finger wouldn't go amiss.

"She's meant to be Latina, like they have in California," Helen explains. Her eyebrows cave in, two deep wrinkles like gashes, permanent records of previous thoughts. But then, for a moment, her mother's eyes are as blank as a four-year-old's. "Or, Nora, even a woman who is happy at the beach."

Tom was dating Pam back then. She had long blonde hair, permed to lifelessness, such was the style. Nora called her "Monster Head" or "MH" for short. MH had kept in touch for a long time afterwards, taking a protective role, asking her brother, Raymond, to take Nora to the prom since she was notorious for being Tom's sister, but not pretty or with any particular skill that would get her a boyfriend. She really didn't want to go, but felt that saying no would be rude—as if she was saying it to Pam and Tom—and so she went.

Raymond tried to neck with her at the after party. They were all smoking hash and drunk on coolers so she didn't take offense or pride in that. She just pushed him off and called him an asshole, and he called her a cunt, which made her cry when she thought of it as she walked home by herself in her bare feet, her high-heels stuffed and poking out of her purse.

"Why don't you wear makeup?" Helen asks, nudging herself in behind the loveseat to turn on the AC. "If I were you, I would. Make the most of your face."

"What's wrong with my face?" Nora says.

"Nothing." Helen's own face is pale and lined. Her grey hair is disheveled, as if she'd rubbed it while climbing around the furniture.

The last time her mom ran the AC was a year ago; it was no wonder the stiff smell of dust filled the room, making Nora's eyes sting.

"Today is a special day—" Helen says, but interrupts herself. "—how sad is it, Nora, that we'll never see him again?"

Nora continues the dialogue, which she has come to memorize, where he mother left off. "Today is a special day. We had the AC on. You told him everyone in California has AC."

"ACDC, he said." Helen cuts the cake, the Latina's face still in rapture.

Spencer Lucas Oakes

Team Building

AN EXCERPT

"Swing, batter, swing!"

Sometime before now, maybe a week, maybe a month before, a woman from the executive team with wire-frame glasses and a blue suit had walked over to my cubicle. I couldn't tell you the day of the week. Workday memories melt together. It's hard to separate any one from any other.

"Excellent work!" she had said to me, smiling, arms crossed in a non-confrontational way. "I've been hearing great things about the work you're doing."

I readjusted in my chair, not knowing if I should stand up when an executive enters. I almost saluted, but refrained and took a sip of my coffee instead.

"This merger is going so well and it's people like you—taking the lead without being told—who are making it a success." Her smile didn't disappear while she spoke. "I'll see you at the softball game, I hope you're on my team."

"Swing, batter, swing!" A woman from the office yells it again into the afternoon breeze between mouthfuls of sunflower seeds and swallows of warm beer. Not a soul at home plate. She looks like the executive that invited me here. She looks different, too.

Off to the side, behind the home plate and a high, metal fence, a few rough boys are sitting. They're from a world far different from the office. They talk about their bets and their scores and Oklahoma and Pittsburgh and a two-six of Grand Marnier someone's boss had given them.

"He's soft!" says one of the rough boys with red cheeks and years of wrinkles aged by the sun.

"I know, I know," says his friend, "but he's a good guy. Gave me that two-six, didn't he?"

The first rough boy, the roughest of them all, extends his closed hand out to the knowledgeable one and encourages him to fist bump, which he does. Then he extends the same offering to the third rough boy in a gentle way, the way a child would treat the family dog. These rough boys, for all their years and wrinkles and stubbly faces, are just boys in a park enjoying the company. A world separate from mine, a better world, maybe.

More talk of winning bets and being buzzed and old ladies along with fist bumps so tender and sweet I forget about team building and the office and whatever world I live or don't live in and I get swept up in their daze and feel drunk with them. They elbow each other in the ribs, play-fight and lean into each other's shoulders while sitting on the bleachers and opening cans and letting their heads fall, in time with the sun, back into the slow afternoon.

The first rough boy crushes a can—*bang*—beneath his boot against the metal bleacher. His friends watch and plead with him not to litter but he does anyway and he tosses the can up to himself and pretends to knock it out of the park. The can bounces under their seats into the weeds and uneven pavement.

I stand off to the side while a game of softball is played. The park is close to the water and in the distance oil tankers and freighters sit in the blue, puffing black into the air. They've been there so long they appear to be natural. I recognize few faces from the office, but everyone thinks I'm Steve or that I've replaced him. Softball was something he did. The sun would liquefy this whole place if it could but it can't. The sun is weak sometimes.

"Good to see you again," says the auditor, Maggie.

"I'm not much of a ball player, not really sure why I'm here," I say.

The game itself is happening without anyone paying attention to it. Seventh inning. Many of them are sitting on the ground now. The same man has been batting, swinging violently, since it started and the pitcher is actually a pitching machine. It's constantly ejecting softballs toward the home plate. Most of the balls land in the red dirt and roll into the fence and there are fifty balls and counting piled up. The machine is toying with the drunk man. Music plays through a speaker, along with advertisements, and sometimes the music is the advertisement.

"Everyone's drunk." I almost don't recognize Maggie outside the office. We're all different in the natural light. People are sitting on benches and bases and on the grass getting drunk from bottles and cans and cups.

She shakes my hand and we are two people shaking hands under a hot sun near a baseball diamond while brain power dissolves all around us.

"Are you auditing athletic ability, too?" The handshake ends. Two hands lose touch.

I look around and no one comes off as athletic. People look the part but the drunken malaise has descended into something uglier than a game. Flames are having a fit on a grill and people are chewing meat and spitting seeds and drinking beer and spilling everything all over each other in their revelry and a wind runs over the field, briefly cooling the world.

"Athletic ability, sure, that's all part of it, right?"

"Part of—"

"Oh, looks like I'm up to bat!" She disappears into the madness and the sun settles into another twilight.

"Pop fly," someone shouts and I see Maggie is up to bat. I look up to catch the ball in my glove and when I look back at the plate she is gone. Someone else begins to shriek for the ball to be thrown home. I didn't see anyone running the bases.

Three coworkers are rolling in the dirt and grass fighting over a ball beside the pile of a hundred balls and one woman is passed out on third base while crows nervously hop around her and the music is getting louder and one man is vomiting in the dugout and there are cans and empty cups and foil wrappers and sludge and napkins littered everywhere on the green grass and red dirt and the white lines on the field have been trampled away and two people are carnally tangled in the outfield and the advertisements get louder and I can see one of the men in the tussle is now bleeding all over and when the fight stops another man throws up on himself.

The rough boys, in their gentle way, are watching the horrific scene, their heads hanging lower and lower, eyes fading from the beer or the sadness or a combination of the two. They are the only ones who look like they belong here. This party of aliens has landed and taken over their time, their world.

The scoreboard towering over the field buzzes bright over the field's slow darkness and informs all that one side has points and the other side has none and that we're well into the final inning. I guess this is team building, becoming effective, and finding common ground. The deconstruction of restrictive company lines. Giant white lights on tall poles slam with power as each one turns on, humming like generators, circling the group as we all soften into a newer form. The neon-red numbers on the clock flash down to zeros and continue to count down to nothing over and over going faster and faster.

"Team building!" is yelled from the crowd. "Reinvent yourself, eye your objectives, focus on fun!"

The sun nearly gone, I wonder how long this can last. A long time, I imagine. I try to focus on fun. With no horn signalling the end of the competition, I think we'll be here forever. I don't feel reinvented and my eyes are tired. No end in sight.

The executives start beating their fists down on one of the folding tables on the sidelines, while the presidents and vice presidents drink as much as they can between breaths and the chief officers are shouting out orders, indecipherable to all yet important to them—because what would they be without orders—drink spilling down their faces and chests, turning the red dirt to mud under their feet. The workers are hyperventilating and hitting the ground hard and getting back up and sprinting at other workers and those having sex start to slap and scratch and the vomiting occurs almost simultaneously with the drinking and the yelling and a pack of dogs enters the field, heads low, scanning for scraps of anything.

Naked bodies climb the metal fence, bottles crashing below and bouts of dust surround the field. They turn the bats toward each other while laughing and singing a fight song and some maniac has found a mic attached to the speakers and starts shouting about profit and growth, saying:

"Is everybody having a good time?"

"Is everybody having a good time?"

"Is everybody having a good time?"

Walking away from the field and bleachers, arms around each other, the rough boys cuss and share their feelings of disgust, really listening to one another.

"Fugazi," the first rough boy says to his friends. "Fugazi."

Three more fist bumps and they escape into the night.

Kathleen Kerwin

San Domenico

Tristan stood on shaky legs at the edge of the piazza. They trembled from the bus ride he'd just experienced, not jet lag. Tristan silently thanked San Domenico for delivering them safely.

He'd deeply regretted sitting in the first-row window seat of the bus. To his left, unimpeded views of oncoming traffic, passing so closely he'd expected to hear metal scraping on metal. To his right, a sheer drop down to a deep gorge.

Next to him, Tony had seemed unfazed. Right hand playing with the gold crucifix he always wore. Eyes closed, ear-buds in. Leaking Metallica's "Master!" into Tristan's air space. The apocalyptic music had been perfect.

Tristan listened to brakes exhaling, low and long, after the arduous mountain journey. He exhaled, too.

Tony's earbuds and iPhone were already in his back pocket and his shades were on. He gripped his friend's shoulders with both hands and shook him.

"Welcome to the real Italy, *paesano*!"

Tristan and Tony had been planning this trip to Tony's familial hometown since the summer before high school. Tony promised that the festival of Villalago's patron saint would blow Tristan's mind. Sombre religious processions followed by all-night dance parties. Lazy, four-hour *al fresco* meals after mass. Maybe a summer *romanza*.

Tristan didn't care if reality matched the hype. He just wanted to live for a while in a place where people had lived for centuries.

On the plane, Tony had briefed Tristan on San Domenico and his four miracles. One puzzled him. About a thousand years ago, Dom got so pissed off with a guy who wouldn't share his lunch that he'd turned the food into a snake. That didn't seem very saintly to Tristan. He wondered if it had been a mistake to thank a vengeful saint for safe delivery.

At their first meal, Nonno Alfredo nicknamed Tristan "Mercurio." He thought this *soprannome* was obvious because Tristan's blonde hair, golden tan, and long muscles made him look like a god of eternal youth. Tony's eyes almost rolled out of their sockets.

Nonno Fredo ignored Tony's reaction. Fredo recounted how Mercurio was assigned to guide Larunda, the water nymph, to the underworld. She'd been banished for having an affair with some god, whose goddess wife wasn't amused. On the way to hell, Mercurio made love to Larunda. Nonno Fredo couldn't remember what happened next. He carried on by teasing his grandson about his *soprannome*, "*il buffone.*" The comedian. The teasing made Tristan uneasy.

Tony didn't comment on Tristan's nickname. He sat in uncharacteristic silence until Nonno finished. Then he thanked his nonna for dinner and told Tristan they were going out.

Once free from the villa, Tony introduced Tristan to the locals. In those first days, Tony offered occasional morsels of information about Tristan. Like how skilled Tristan was at soccer, provoking a pick-up game, from which Tristan emerged bruised and aching. Tony implied that his friend had great success with the ladies, triggering raucous encouragement for Tristan to pick up a local girl at the pizza parlour. All in a confusing dialect that was not in any learn-to-speak-Italian audio book.

After these incidents, Tony started giving Tristan advice about how to behave with the guys, muttered in *sotto voce* English. Tristan guessed

Tony was worried about losing face. That was rich. At home, Tristan worried about what Tony might do or say next.

It was early evening. Tristan leaned against sun-warmed stone, listening to Tony as a procession passed by. Every year, pilgrims walked from Fornelli to Villalago in honour of San Domenico. They would billet overnight, then join the townspeople the next day for the final procession to the saint's ancient grotto.

"Look at these Fornellese. They don't smile, they don't wave—they don't even look happy to get that crazy-heavy cross over the finish line. I mean, I know San Domenico is religious, but Christ! You don't have to look like your mother just died every minute!"

Tristan's eye was drawn to a girl who looked to be about their age. She wore a simple sack dress and Adidas sneakers. She looked straight ahead, small smile turning up the corners of a generous mouth. Forehead smooth like an alabaster bust of a Roman noblewoman. Bare arms glowing in the pre-dusk light. This must be what pure looks like, Tristan thought.

The girl looked directly at Tristan as she passed. Her expression didn't change in response to Tristan's frankly admiring look. She gave him a single nod. Tony turned, disbelief on his face.

"Hey! Mercurio! Snap out of it." Fingers snapped in front of Tristan's nose.

He ignored Tony, eyes following the girl as she moved towards the central piazza.

"Don't be an idiot, Tristan. Fornelli girls don't mix with Villalago boys."

Tristan hadn't expected to see her tonight. Tony said the pilgrims didn't dance. They'd appear in the morning, pious and hangover-free, to join the procession to the grotto.

But there she was. Sitting at the end of a broad stone step, in a coat that looked like bubble-wrap. Adidas-clad feet demurely crossed at the ankles. Tony was engrossed in conversation. Tristan decided Tony wouldn't miss him.

"Ciao." Tristan sat down next to her. "Do you speak English?"

She shook her head. Didn't look at him.

"*Mi non parlo Italiano.*" Tristan had no idea if this made sense.

She kept her eyes on the piazza, where a live band was hamming it up with Justin Bieber's version of "Despacito." Screeching toddlers, solo teens, and middle-aged lovers with pot bellies danced enthusiastically.

Tristan stood, gesturing for her to follow him up the steps, deeper into town. He was headed for the church with San Domenico's statue. To Tristan's surprise and relief, she followed.

"*Mi chiamo* Tristan," he said at the church's entrance.

The girl looked at him directly, green eyes steady. "*Mi chiamo* Lara."

Tristan walked through the open church door, with Lara one step behind. They moved through thick silence and breathed the memory of burnt incense. Votive candles threw other-worldly light onto San Domenico's sorrowful face. Tristan thought the saint must be contrite about his bad behaviour, but then wondered if he disapproved of Tristan's hidden desire.

Tristan felt Lara's arms encircle his waist from behind, embracing him. Before he could comprehend this, she put a small hand into his, led him to a dark wooden confessional, and pushed him in. She pressed his back against the wall and her body against his. Tristan's confusion roared through his ears. He froze when she stepped back out, quickly shutting and bolting the door.

"Lara?"

Soft footsteps ran away. Tristan's hands passed over the wooden door, searching for a way to release the bolt, finding a sharp sliver instead. He closed his eyes and imagined he saw a serpent slither away.

Soon, well before Tristan could collect himself, he heard boots striking the stone floor and loud male voices obliterating the silence. The bolt slid back, the door opened, and Tony stood before him, eyes cold and mouth set. The guys surged past Tony, pulling Tristan out of the confessional. He was pushed along the centre of the boisterous swarm all the way to the piazza, where the band was now playing slow music. Lara was in the arms of some stick of a guy with a bad haircut. Someone shoved Tristan in Lara's direction.

The guys, who'd mocked Tristan the entire way back, watched closely. Tony watched closest. When Lara saw Tristan, he saluted her and bent deeply at the waist in a courtly bow. She turned her head away. The guys broke into spontaneous applause.

Later, on the walk home, Tony turned to Tristan and said, "Damn, you got her good. Your legend might live as long as Mercurio's."

Tristan silently thanked San Domenico for delivering them safely.

Erica Hiroko

there was nothing festive about The Fair at the PNE in 1942

FOR MY BAACHAN AND OTHER JAPANESE CANADIAN WOMEN AND CHILDREN DETAINED AT THE LIVESTOCK BARNS

march 24, 1942
hastings park, arrival

it's so cold here. drafty. even with the blanket pulled tight.

how can this straw mattress be lumpier than the porridge at breakfast? felt hopeless to wash up tonight. dust and stench still cling to every surface of my skin, bit of clothing, strand of hair. constant smell of animal feces and cut hay. so foul.

a far-off cry pierced the air last night. baby woke up, wailing into darkness. *hurry!* okaasan cued me, rattling the steel bed frame. down the bunk bed. under the bed sheet curtain. took a deep breath. counted to five. walking, walking, running. heart and feet beat in sync.

turned corner—bright light—frozen in place. moonlight cut through the barn window to bare concrete.

illuminating nothing, everything.

july 9, 1942
hastings park

summer here is dull and hot. embarrassingly clammy. sweat glands triggered by blistering heat and adolescent hormones, or so i am told. apparently i am supposed to be aware of that sort of thing now.

they set up a "school" for us in the arena. fifty of us teenagers thinking the exact same thing: *back home we wouldn't be sitting in class in this heat, let alone jammed into rafters pretending this was an education or anything else normal.*

what's the point? what else is there to do? the future drips with unanswered questions.

no more peeing in a trough anymore. at least. baby sister cries less at night now. same with oka-san. more accustomed to hunger, cold porridge, otousan's absence. less fear lies in darkness when it's the only thing constant.

september 6, 1942
departure, eastbound

packed. we sit shoulder to shoulder. knees and elbows squished tight against body. suitcases bounce with every bump in the road.

fidgeting young ones. *mama, where are we going this time?*

veils of mist shroud grey skies and forested valleys. speeding along winding mountain roads. bypassing a whole other world. no more stable. what is home anymore?

a sixteen-by-twenty-four-foot shack for eight of us. just imagine! unfamiliar voices dream out loud.

maybe i will cook again for us, for your otousan, okaasan whispers to me, wistfully. she clutches baby tight. the bus slows, signaling our arrival.

here we are folks, just past Hope.

journal/journey. Digital composite by Erica Hiroko.
Photos used with permission from Kayla Isomura.

Author's note: Of the 22,000 Japanese Canadians who were uprooted from their homes in 1942, it's estimated that around 8,000 people, including babies, children, and the ill, were detained at Hastings Park, or what is commonly known as the PNE Fairgrounds in East Vancouver. From here, individuals and families were moved onto remote internment camps in interior B.C., labour camps and sugar beet farms in Alberta and Manitoba, and prisoner-of-war camps in Ontario.

The Livestock building, Garden Auditorium, Rollerland, and the Forum still stand at Hastings Park today.

subject line: babymaking

AN EXCERPT FROM "AFTER THE U-HAUL"

Kiyo and Jes are a queer couple who want to start a family and raise a kid together. The only problem is they don't have a road map for how to become moms and have struggled with the adoption process so far.

Even with most of the lights off, the room was bright enough for Kiyo to notice the bed had been made up with extra pillows. A faint earthy scent wafted through the air. Her nose perked up. *Incense.* A single candle burned atop the dresser. Its flickering light revealed a portable speaker in the shadows, the source of a smooth R&B croon. She smiled to herself. *This was so sweet. Jes was really putting in effort to make her feel comfortable and set the mood.*

"Babe, do you have everything ready?" Jes interrupted Kiyo's thoughts. The clock flashed 5:05 p.m.—they didn't have much time.

"Right here," Kiyo gestured to the night stand where a zipped bag sat nestled between her phone, a folded towel, and a bottle of lube.

"How are you feeling?" Jes reached for Kiyo's hand, gently stroking the soft skin between her thumb and pointer finger.

"Nervous ... excited ...?" A grin shyly spread across Kiyo's face. She unzipped the bag on the table and carefully pulled out a syringe and a narrow plastic container. "I hope this works."

"C'mere." Jes placed her hand on Kiyo's waist and gently pushed her back against the headboard. She leaned her face into Kiyo's. As their lips touched, Kiyo felt the world around her start to tremble—or was it just her?

Jes noticed her quiver and pulled back. "I love you. No matter what. You know that, right?" She dropped her voice, "if this doesn't feel okay, you can tell me. We can stop anytime."

Kiyo nodded, taking a deep breath. "I know. I trust you." She nuzzled her face into Jes's shoulder and closed her eyes, expelling a warm breath of air on her partner's neck.

Jes held her tight. "Are you ready?"

"Yes." Kiyo looked Jes straight in the eye and gave her hand a quick squeeze before crossing her arms to strip off her cotton T-shirt. She pulled it over her head in one swoop to reveal a lacy bralette underneath.

Jes beamed at the sight. "Ooh, must be a special occasion." She teasingly fingered the strap along Kiyo's shoulder before steering her lips toward Kiyo's bare skin.

"Mmm," Kiyo moaned softly, "yes, more of that."

Bzzzz! Kiyo's phone vibrated atop the dresser—an incoming message.

"Ignore it, babe." Jes pulled Kiyo closer.

They were interrupted again only a few moments later. *Bzzz! Bzzzz! Bzzz!* The phone buzzed incessantly, almost knocking the plastic syringe off the table.

"Augh."

"Here, just turn it off."

Jes reached across Kiyo to silence the device, its bright screen demanding attention, like a small child. As her finger hovered over the glowing surface, she paused. "Omigod." Jes sat up straight and looked at Kiyo. "Did you tell your ex we were trying to conceive tonight?!"

Jes dropped the phone between them on the bed.

Poetry

Tamar Rubin

Tablet Fragments

א Moses discovers adultery, breaks dishes.

Shame is a ragged edge
that grips. Something with traction,
loved,   hated.   That left
a hot and sticky mess, cooled: tarnished, sacred,
and you're not sure which,
in what measure.

Shame is the remnant of anger. *It sticks,*
by the broken ends of the tablets shattered,
still pointed, dangerous
as a knife in butter. *Shame is fatter*

than the hammer that bludgeoned the golden calf,
smashed stone into fragments you could scatter,
and now lingers,

terrifying in your hands.

ב After Sinai.

You promised yourself
you'd never skip away   a   perfect   stone.

But then you found one, had to
test its will to dance
                                         above   water.

The arguments weighed on you.
If you didn't drop something,
you thought you might
drown.

You threw the tablets in,
a reckless fling that missed
the real thrust: you weren't
                                                 stone
                                                 would   never   be
                                                 water.

ג The pieces are a reminder.

You couldn't leave commandments where you broke them.

You packed your suitcase full of bygone
dust, wandered through the parchment desert,

as a fraction. You moved each lifeless fragment,
out of honour for the body, or to bury

the bones of evidence, later.

ד Rabbi Yehoshua Ben Levi instructs us to take the broken with us.

You gathered up the sacred stones,
the tiny mass of every atom
adding up, but never reproducing

whole. You kept the parts
even though they had no function
for anyone, anymore

ח

ה

ט י

ו

ז

Except for you so you could hold them.

Sareh Donaher

Beginning

The air crisp
          arid

clean   marmalade light
                                        slowly fills the slate street buildings

a city stirring from slumber,
in quiet prayer upon
                    rectangle
                    silk
                    carpets

paisley pinks and blues, sit softly, beneath clean morning
feet

before the trucks

under midnight amethyst skies, spotted with stars
    my maternal grandmother
climbed the rooftop of her parents' one-storey house,
    awaiting the euphony
of businessmen coming home on
camelback trade-expeditions.

her father and uncles rode gentle golden beasts
to foreign lands and back again,
    before King Reza Shah Pahlavi decreed mandatory
motorization.

    a musical procession she could hear from afar
breaking silence   growing louder
families crowding quietly on rooftop verandas   hearing

camels adorned with wares from the marketplace
around their necks and bodies
clink clank, clink clank in tempo to
their tough tired hoofs as percussion to
whistling from fathers
poetry recited by uncles
sing-song echoes from sons

returning home.

Revolution

It's in this chaos I grow

slowly lifting the sides of the ancient rug

my family bestowed upon me

,

God's Country

Dawn broke the desert sky—
we crossed the border into new territory

in my ribcage,   all night
                    I was holding,   the dreaded anticipation of the
          border-guard exchange with my parents— everyone could
          feel it   in their lungs   on their chest
          its tight grip on the flow of oxygen in the clenched
          corners of the Volkswagen bus.
          a vise.

we crossed   into safety   breathing.

holding pearl-white earrings in pistachio shells,
you turned to me
          pretending you were not crying

your grief now had room in my ribcage.   I held it
          with you   from you   for you
          give me all of it, if only my two-year-old body was not so
small.

          looking for answers: the peach-skin sun spoke to me
softly: *will we ever be back home?*

          Dad's laughter rolled with his tears
let's pretend this is not the end.

Diaphanous

lightly stitched, we are

with heavy hands,   thick knuckles,   thin skin.

lightly stitched

between one another,   we tenderize   small wounds

callus the walls   of our heart chambers.

Deborah Harford

She Sings to Me

What is left of that comfortable
tuck in time
where my mother lived
now she has become one
with sky, crows,
small blue flowers on the rosemary.

The air floats still,
unthrummed by her kind tones
sweet greeting,
warm as her hand in mine

and yet
the low note of her love
murmurs in my veins,
her kindness sparkles
in sunlight pathways on the sea.

She sings to me in the blue mist of morning,
in the thousand-winged thrum of starlings
as they throw their net of life across the sky.

Merry Go Round

… a crow in the tallest tree
in the copse outside the French doors
beyond the curve of the white jug
shaped like a fish
tail curled back up to its head for a handle
on the broad wood expanse of the kitchen table
where I sit surrounded by
plastic and chrome, glass, wood, fabric, china,
the odd bit of silver and gold
the spoils of war, heaped up
with all the world's creatures in rout,
fleeing or dead
but at least there's …

Hump

we have made honey and macaroons
and filled the kitchen sink with washing up
and planted plums and churned cream
and entwined the spruce boughs of our arms and legs
and become joined through skin
that tastes of campfire smoke
and eaten cake and made pickles and
it's only Wednesday

Turnstile

I have come to a stop.
Far behind me the screeching
days of the city,
hot sweat of dance floors,
bad choices, bleary mornings.

Gone now the endless walks
of the toddler times,
brave bend and strong set
of mother shoulders.
Gone too the black eye
and punched stomach.

Love held us up,
strong as a vine
grapes in sweet bunches
hung through the framework
of days   as you grew.
Till you grew.

Now fall has turned towards winter,
the chatter and laughter
have faded to silence.

I sit on the turnstile,
searching the clouds
for meadowlarks.

DEBORAH HARFORD

A Bright Spark

Stephen Hawking said
the universe will dissipate into blackness and cold
the golden globes fizzle out
the miraculous skeins of matter
unravel and drift as their glowing coals
wink out, cease in pure solitude

like the cold of my mother's skin
after, in the closed peace of ending
hands folded, the gold on her fingers
the last warmth left to her body

the universe will go where she has gone
beyond my sight

shot from her body, I, round rose of babe flesh
warm twinkle of fingers, the shine of new eyes
my son from mine, then, spiral ladders entwined
double helix of happiness twirling through blackness
towards light

should not the dying body of the universe
at some stage
produce a bright spark that will wing its way
in a new direction

outgrow the failed body of its parent, carry on
as I have, as he will

Rowan EB

Ancestral Kites (Dozing Lover)

The quiet is dialled low in the pauses between
snores of a gentle lover sprawled in sleep. She might be
dreaming.
In her dreams, she might be running or she might be writing. In my dreams, she is a summer kite made of used
notebook paper and cotton thread
made swiftly by dark grandfather fingers,
thick-skinned numb but still nimble. She is the gentle furrow of my grandfather's brow as he folded paper, smoked
a cigarette, pinched the rim of a ceramic coffee cup
between two fingertips.

Domesticated ironworkers welded two girls who walked
in a halo-swarm of masculinity
like queen bees escorted away from the hive.
In the pit of a flower they met while drinking
alone. An obscure nectar tasteless to others,
shimmering-savoury to them. She is a bee who rubbed legs
with me in the privacy of gathered flower petals
and the friction caused the sound that echoed
across the expanse of a flower-face open to the sky.
The sky: sometimes blue sometimes black,
like the veins under my eyes that carry
blood heavy with the sight of her, down through

limbs capable only of one skill: to dance
to the brown proximity of a dozing lover
too unfolded to fit neatly down only one
side of the margin.

She is the homeland neither of us has ever had. In her teasing,
she questions with the intonation of a would-be accent. She
speaks with lips as soft as Nile-fed soil and in them there is
blood held back by pressure and silk.
Cotton pulls moisture from my hair but it
sits dry and hungry in safety around my neck.

In my dreams, I spin the coarse quiet of rattling sleep-breath into thread for a kite. Paper folded from old notebooks of poems trail neatly between my fingers. I will wrap string around my finger again only if my lover is a kite.

Mother, I

Mother, I shake my head with you
at the tongues whipping girls,
who lick unfurled phalluses.
Those tongues click in disapproval as
you shake my head, while
tender tongues give head
to the whipping boys of patriarchy.

Father is a sky dripping in electric ecstasy,
drops strike the pearl-hard calluses on your skin,
and you are stretched/hammered/bent tin.
A metal roof on my stick shack of
daughterhood.

Mother, I press my cheek to you
as my tongue tip traces cracks in dirt.
Thirsting earth is me under you.
I am dry as I watch saliva released
from the purveyors of masculine deities
like divine precipitation.

Wetness is dispatched
onto dirt punctured by sticks.
I am a shack
top-rimmed with thin chiselled tin
of you. Mother, I
raise my head with you.

ROWAN EB

Safety

sitting in a coffee shop, you wonder: if you talked to the other patrons,
would they sound
like the people leaving comments on online news articles about refugees
and pipelines? would they
have an opinion at all? the voices that shout are
whipping arms, and your head is a pinball banging
back and forth between them.
between rage and resignation,
hope and fervour. back and forth,
up and down, diagonally and in all other directions:
your mind is a dry wad of rubber slamming
endlessly against the inside of your head.

how can safety be tallied? is it by the number of people
who are not beaten to death or
unjustly held captive
each day? or by the number of moments
where a person does not fear for their life,
counted for each person?
is safety a perception or a count?
qualitative or quantitative?

one formula for safety = (# (of?)moments of not thinking about death or attack in one day experienced by one person) / (# (?) moments of feeling fear, insecurity, hunger, worry, sleeplessness, helplessness, powerlessness, sorrow, the acid-burn of injustice, torture, anguish, suffering) *100 [calculated for each person on earth within a single day and added up]

[divided by the number of people on earth]

safety is a construct. danger is real.
danger is a construct. safety is real.

safety might be in the moments of half wakefulness
when the recollection of the self is not
complete, and awareness is only of light, firmness
or softness of where you sleep, and of how alone you
feel in that moment. It is unfiltered,
the ego not yet roused. Your head not swirling with declarations of who
you are or of time.

April Lewis

Knotting Memory

AN EXCERPT

Like reels playing at the same time, I can't be sure of our sequence and our end.

In the city, our music was thrumming cars and barking dogs

and the beer was always plentiful in Ireland

we were drowning in accents

sexy, but I felt homesick

we went to class in towering stone buildings

that felt like Camelot

and yet

I felt so alone, like I was making friends with ghosts

I wanted to escape, sink into my room, disappear.

And did you know how much I treasured our friendship?

Smile so wide at seeing you, hoping you didn't think I liked you like that just missing a friend

What is the point of carrying another's number but

never having the courage to call?

Now I cling to those memories of you and I, because you made the hard times bittersweet.

The music beating in my ears no longer matters

or catty, arrogant girls

We thought Ireland would be a land full of enchantment but we were sick with the cold and tired of drinking.

And still, my friend,

I want you to know that you have not been forgotten

those moments loop in a perpetual Knot.

Alex Duncan

A Relationship in Three Parts

A CLUSTER OF POEMS

I: A Light in the Attic
a poem inspired by a conversation about Shel Silverstein

There's a light in the attic
it's flickering there
A place that has long been kept dark
A place crowded with boxes
that hold heavy past
it's felt dusty and cluttered, yet stark

So the door it got locked
and the key it got thrown
to the furthest far edge of the woods
As I dusted my hands
and I nodded my head
thinking, that place is closed up for good.

But then you came along
like a spark in the night
my heart a drain you might unclog
And I felt like a ship
after too long at sea
when a lighthouse appears through the fog

You're quite unexpected,
entirely sweet
after silence a siren's alarm
and it's strange 'cause it's new
and yet somehow familiar
to fall asleep wrapped in your arms.

So I want you to know
that I think you're a light
I've felt it from the very start
And this dark, dusty attic
a mere metaphor
for my tentative, curious heart.

II: Delicate
a poem written in aisle 28

I walk into Canadian Tire wearing a baseball hat ironically.

Do I look like I belong here, amongst the tires and things?
I wonder.
Do I look like a woman who can fix the chip in her own windshield?
I hope so.

I cruise the aisles, casually.
I peruse the Permatex selections, confidently.

I have no idea what I want.
I'm sure it shows.

Can those who pass me feel the rapid frequency of my heart as I frantically question what to do—

with this cracked windshield
and unsure heart
and possible career
and tentative rash

You say: I better fix it now before the crack grows and spreads—
I'll need a new windshield then.

I think: Is there a product to fix myself with similar ease and convenience—a permanent glue to repair my weathered heart: easy-to-use, no mixing or special tools required.

I want to buy a whole case of that.

I use the self check out and feel tempted by the selection of house plants,

they always look so healthy in the store.

As I leave, Taylor Swift sings:

it's delicate.

III: Sirens
a break up poem

on the way to your house,
I thought I heard the sound of sirens
emergency vehicles racing through my cluttered mind
I checked my rearview (sweet bitter past)
blind spot (unseen obstacles)
all around (you)
yet the stinging sound of sirens droned on
alerting me
that the heart can break
even if it isn't whole
I searched for red flashing lights
evidence of accident
but none were there.

on the way to your house,
I cast down every past and future memory
—each distant hope and wonder
like a child plucking petals from a daisy
he loves me
he loves me not.

my heartbeat is visible through my worn white shirt.

Brad Akeroyd

Just Give Up

Admit it.
You started with good intentions about injustices that needed to be addressed
about people whose stories
the historians seemed to have missed.
You intended to write about complex issues
but you just ended up
writing about yourself.
How sad.

It's not that you aren't a worthy subject
it's just that you intended
to do so much more.
In the end it was your stories
that needed to be told.
Now you've decided what it is you want to do
give it your full attention, give it your all.
Don't scrimp, don't save, don't obscure
any part of it.
Once you start, you will never stop.

The Enigma

As a child running in the woods climbing trees
splashing in the creeks
filled me with joy.

Those solitary pursuits
calmed my mind
made me content.

Activity helped me deal
with the stress of being
treated differently.

My persona developed
a protective layer a crust
that shielded me.

But that crust turned into a wall
made it difficult to communicate
to understand others.

As a youth I only felt comfortable
with those I perceived to be
different too.

I gained the confidence formed relationships
made good friends at work at school
with minority misfit kids like me.

I felt loved respected connected
but a part of me was withheld
unknown even from myself.

As a young man I recall late one night
I stood in front of the bathroom mirror
puzzled.

I didn't recognize the person looking back
"Who is that man," I pondered,
"Is that really me?"

I wanted to look like a regular Canadian
for too often was treated like an alien
carried that feeling like a cross.

I would search for an identity
in people places pursuits
join a group for awhile.

I would be comfortable until something
disrupted that sense of belonging
I would flee not knowing why.

Many a friend did I leave confused
by my sudden departure
often without a word.

The confounding behaviour
reflected my belief I did not
fit in did not belong.
When I was a member of a community

I became the mediator the glue
the one who organized activities.

I tried to ameliorate conflicts
maintain the group harmony
I was a participant a leader.

I valued cohesion collegiality
but my personal sense of insecurity
was never far from the surface.

When it was time for me to leave
or the community met its natural demise
I would be left depressed wistful.

I would spend an inordinate amount of time
genuflecting on lost relationships
which made it difficult to move on.

I regretted my lack of confidence
recognized work needed to be done
to overcome my fears of connection.

My central focus became understanding
addressing my childhood experiences
began to look at why I disengaged.

I looked through the losses that I imagined
had happened and went on long journeys
searching for a cure.

I started   to unravel   the tight spool
of confused   contradictory   emotions
I vowed   to stay focused   on the present.

In my   late 40s   I gained   new perspectives
about my pain   a wisdom   by reflecting on
my fragility.

I still   struggled   to maintain   my sense
of self   made   a conscious effort   not to
fall prey   to worry   doubt   fear.

Slowly   gradually   improving   until
I came   to see   the problem   involved
my   self perception.

I am fortunate   to have   a loving   understanding
caring   partner   and   good friends   family
supportive   writing group.

With   exercise   daily writing   a vitamin regime
I am   succeeding   managing   better
than I have   for years.

I am   on the path   to healing   myself
One day   I will be   an enigma
no more.

Sabyasachi Nag

How to Raise Them in Moss Park

You are with a counsellor sipping Chardonnay.
Soon the cup is empty and her cardinal-red lip stain
On the glass rim stands out, each line distinct like a flute
Feeding a choked estuary—you suppose
Because she hasn't spoken a word since you ranted
About raising kids, here in Moss Park.

Meanwhile addicts twitching in withdrawal
Take turns to hand out on sale—a bag
Of summer gowns, pop tags intact.
A girl in a shapeless blouse is slouched
By a homeless sign stood up against
An orange witch hat.

Way before they can stand up straight, she says
Drowning out the cars and construction drill
Before they walk past the sorority years in cheerleaders' uniform, licking
the afternoon glacé. Before they bear
the cross of your meaning—
Before they become the reason; the whole idea;
The song in its entirety—that's when they are perfect.

You shake your head in disbelief.
How could your blood become the bitch?
Go away. Get the fuck out.
That's all you hear. That's all they want.
And reduced, redacted you sway out
Or drop down on your knees begging for a piece
Of the dirt to squeeze up close and dream
From the same dark space, as you once did.
What a scandal!
You say that without pausing to breathe.

Everyone's entitled to their one private Hiroshima
She says. *Yet, when the jury is off radar,*
And truth takes off in a thick mushroom taxi—
It's Okay to stay back in town
With the pumice stone of your own failed history—
Like the lip stain on the rim of a wine-washed glass—
You have no use for guilt, blame, denial, regret.

In which case—what is the question? What good is Kant? If
That's what you want to know—
If you haven't triumphed and you have busted
Your ass trying, trying—remember this:
When does raising ever end?
She says that and leaves the curb by the Arena,
Now thick with dealers and pimps.

Strangers

Deep inside the trail where the gravel
Tapers into the wild when I hear voices
I think: must be the girls sharing joints.
Turns out, some stranger, grieving
Over a landscape of dead nasturtiums.
She looks up at me as though she knows
I would come searching.

It's the end of day, and we search
For the half-moon upon the river,
Thick with detritus and still vacillating
Blond and brunette; rippled skin
Around her eyes forming into mounds
Before gleaming into tears.

Fish, we think we can see them
Streaked and striped in the afterlight
As if they had done all the crying
And are ready to sleep, when I ask
If she can hear the madroves singing
To which she shakes her head
That's thunderclap.

Things You Do Racing a Storm

A blizzard is heading your way,
Hailstones, big as golf balls have wrecked homes, cars
North of Dayton, in Columbus.
The radio crackles. Go Home!

Mind is racing storm—to Madrid—twenty years ago.
An evening of bullfighting after a day in museums.
The bugle! Toreros—costumed in gold,
Ambling into arena, the bull's majestic walk,
Gallop of the picador, glint of the lance
Seconds before it stabs the little muscle mound
Behind the bull-neck—
First draw of blood.

Cars gone. The road's empty.
Maggots feed on a deer carcass by the shoulder.
Last week it was moose hunting in Clarenville.
Now cutting through the wind
Cutting on lanes unclaimed by summer construction.
The economy has tanked.
The storm is coming. Go home!

The best thing about Madrid—
Past Mezcal, bars, whores, tomatoes.
Oh! Halved tomatoes will tell you of truths you only half know
—Way she said it—bulge of purple tongue,
Lips pursed to the climb of vowels,
Breath oaked with Merlot—
Before vinegar and gall and crucifixion. Oh!

Even in deceit,
In death she must have been stylish;
Ahead of the dashboard: textured floppy hat—
Gold-striped and callow on the polished casket.
Oh death:
Your earlobes remind me of a place I long forgot—
Quires bailar conmigo?

Outside, clouds are coming in rugged and silver
As if they were made of steel wool and slough.
A wafery blue moon on late April Ohio skies,
Heading north—a hummingbird
Flying backwards over wrens locked in love.

Cows, carry on grazing.
Never stopping to look what's passing.
Their bells ring as they shuffle.
The bells ring and fade into Billie Holliday.
Go Home! The radio crackles again.
Storm's coming.

Katie McGarry

Puberty

is a bitch and deep
down I still smell

what my friends
must have before

the come-to-Jesus hygiene
speech I got in the armpit

of Sheppard subway station
circa 1998.

Gym days were the worst—
no way could I rinse

the sweat from every crevice
in the five minute gap

before four flights
to French class. Finally,

at Grade Eight Graduation, swimming
in layers of every possible ocean-

scented Body Shop product,
Richard Mills said I smelled

nice. Twenty years later, I Ziploc
Birkenstocks in the freezer and long

to cake myself daily with clinical-
strength deodorant, but fear

it would eventually lose
its potency and, I guess,

cancer, so save it
for special occasions,

special body parts
only.

I Couldn't Help But Wonder

The kids I'm babysitting are asleep.
My house has one TV & a hospital bed

in the living room. This house has a skylight
& HBO. Carrie's in a pickle. Big

is moving somewhere like
Paris without her.

I'm a Charlotte
but broke & fat

& fifteen. I'm dating this guy
who's like Aidan except

he doesn't exist. Carrie asks Samantha:
Don't you want to judge me, just a little bit?

Samantha winks. *Not my style.*
A girl could build a home

in that wink. Live in it
her entire single life.

State of Affairs

I forgot to get a savings account and now my friends are buying houses without me so I tell myself they just got husbands who already had them and think *I could do that* but I've been trying for years and the closest I got was three dates with a man who drives a Tesla on the bright side I got my licence at 28 got my very own 1999 Toyota Camry but never change the tires with the seasons instead let snow treads hit summer tarmac and it might be the death of me so I eat Kraft Dinner out of the pot and spend hours plucking ingrown hairs from my inner thighs while sending obscene texts to current lovers besides my iPhone is caked in grime from too much Tinder swiping but they all have a girl hotter than me in their profile pictures so I can't swipe right only left worrying about my sister who hasn't had babies yet who's even older than I am who had the gall to get sad when Dad died get a PHD get a traumatic brain injury get a puppy and maybe her eggs will never forgive her meanwhile I'm coddling mine with grease and coffee but feel virtuous because I've never smoked a joint (in small print you read I've never been offered one either) but I was in love once and was loved and lost my

virginity the night before a morning after pill
on the walk to the pharmacy with red leaves
and amber breeze holding hands and I didn't
know my love would destroy me now I'm 31
and I like being alone until someone mentions
her husband picked up groceries on the way
home

Sarah Mostaghel

little rebellions

persian heritage praised for providing
thick dark hair on my head, brows, lashes
yet everywhere else deemed disgusting

gazing into magnifying mirrors searching for coarse
unruly subjects, I am a queen surveying her domain
if not for close attention, I will be overthrown, overgrown

the smell of burning hair, sting of chemical creams
taste of sugar lulling me into sweet contentment
broken by the sound of a strip being ripped from my upper lip

today a long hair in the middle of my forehead taunts me

how many people have seen this?
how long has it been there?
why haven't I noticed it before?

no tweezers in sight, I pinch the hair with my fingers and pull,
I dig my nails together in futile attempt to remove the offender
finally throwing my hands up in the air, a frustrated defeat

finally defiantly deciding to let this strand be
I shall see it as the humble beginnings
of my very own majestic unicorn horn

Tub Thoughts

how much water does a bathtub hold?
how many times has it been filled?

turn on the taps, light a few candles
pour in some epsom salts, not too much

open the drawer to pick an effervescent sphere
from the christmas stash of four or five

a favourite one smells like blackberries,
fizzing while it turns the water purple

slip into a warm enveloping hug,
anxious thoughts drifting away on the steam

heat dissipating slowly until the cold is surprising
leaving space for the guilt to creep in

precious pure water, polluted by bombs
exploding glitter, colours and scent

how much water has been used
for such selfish purposes?

months later, a house with no pretty polluters,
shame won over such pointless pleasure

no purple ring around my tub.

never-ending job search in a small city

Create profile after profile on 7 different websites. Fill out details of your history over and over. Why even bother making a resume? Because you must! Write 15 cover letters with slightly different wording. Apply for jobs you want, jobs you don't want, and jobs just because you need the money. Answer questions by saying you are passionate about customer service, passionate about retail, passionate about operations. Are you passionate about lies? Or is it just that you're passionate about housing, food, and paying bills. Be whatever you think they want you to be. Be a pleasant agreeable chameleon that is a team player. Apply for jobs you're overqualified for. Apply for jobs you're underqualified for. Rethink your life choices. Ruminate on your career trajectory. Use words like efficient, proficient, and effective. Try to be everything, and therefore nothing special. Wait for an email, or the phone to ring. Hope they choose you, acknowledging untapped potential for sorting mail, selling products, or stocking inventory. Every job posted requires a 1 or 2 year certificate. Think about taking that lab assistant certificate, or one for an office administrator, or a legal assistant. Dream about working in a library. Look up a master's degree in library science. People will tell you there are no jobs available and that libraries are dying. Look into a master's degree in speech pathology ... again. Confirm that acceptance rates are still less than 10% in Canada. Take a medical terminology course so you can work in a hospital. Take a securities course so you can work in a bank. Take a yoga teacher certification so you can chill out and not lose your damn mind. Look at your credit card bill. Question your life goals.

How a video of Nicki Minaj and Miley Cyrus caused a fight

"I'm watching this" you snap with
annoyance, my presence in the room
offending you, interrupting your
stupid clickbait video
of vital importance

I was there to ask you a
question, so instead
I shut myself in the office
to block the distant echo
of our raised voices

you enter the room
I pause my video to listen
our digital tendencies
betraying our priorities
people used to look at us
and smile

so obvious
          was our love

rainfall reflections

sitting on a wooden bench
fingers tracing cracks and splinters
as the rain falls down around me
a peaceful drizzle
the green grass gets slicker
the dirt path turns to mud
watching people's feet as they
stride past
sandals slipping with no traction
boots made of fabric
fashion and comfort
over function
I turn my face upwards
to see the murky grey sky
droplets of water
splatter my face and drip
down my coat, soaking my legs
people hurry past to get indoors
I inhale the cool, clear fog
and it tastes like freedom
I see their strange looks
wondering at this
seemingly sad girl
but I am calm and love
the rain

it's just a bit of water

Megan Frazer

Mended

I

Locked in the fluorescent-lit change room
in my underwear and fresh pressed shirt
I wait for the mini-mall tailor to hem my pants

I peek at my forty-year-old backside
below dappled thighs
pale and adipose pocked
my calves a map of blue veins

my grandmother's legs

II

In the care home, my grandmother squinted
trying to see the present
          and asked:
                    Who are you with now?

Someone new. You met him once … remember?
He's going to be a lawyer, I reassured

Her eyes widened
she touched the collar of my intentionally crinkled shirt
          and hissed:
                    You'll have to invest in an iron
                    if you're going to be a lawyer's wife.

Never mind a few years back, I caught her
past midnight eating raw weiners from the fridge
hunched above the vegetable keeper
wearing a stained bra and underwear

Never mind that in the Kerrisdale store
          she had raged:
                    You   just   want   my   money
oblivious she was naked
beside the open change room door

III

She always blamed our mother
for sending us on the Greyhound
without proper clothes.
On summer visits, she rummaged through our duffel bags
   to decry:
      What on earth will you wear to church?

She matched her shoes with her bags
but blamed her bunions
on the second-hand oxfords she wore to school
walking miles on the Alberta prairie
newspapers crammed in the toes

      There's always some way done,
she would encourage or berate
dragging us through the only uptown
department store's mishmash
of fishing tackle
polyester pant suits, baby shoes

We never found anything suitable for church
I wore clogs and knee socks in '79
black vinyl pointy flats in the '80s.
My brother always
disappointing in sneakers

Once she painted his nylon Nikes
with granddad's white leather polish.
When she handed them back
he shrieked: *I can't wear those!*
There were streaks across the scuffs
globs of white smushed onto the frayed toes.
She planned to stitch them too
but she'd run out of time

And you! she turned
to see my fuchsia shaker knit sweater
matching lipstick and shadow,
All that grease makes you look cheap
like the Mona Lisa
with paint splatters on it.

IV

I have my grandmother's wide forehead
not just her legs

while I wait for my pants
I inspect my makeup
wishing I hadn't over-plucked my eyebrows in the '90s

pick hair off my shirt and picture her scalp
poking through her once a week
pink rinse and set

when the tailor knocks I tell her
she's a lifesaver

it's an hour before the fundraiser
I attend as lawyer's wife

happens all the time, she says
hem is fine in the morning, wrecked in the afternoon

Lorne Daniel

A Run on Flowers

Spring running everywhere, pooling
so briefly, the air
light and lifting. A run on
flowers at the shop.
Nothing's up yet. The selection thin,
a few stems he takes
to her. When she asks
after their names he will pretend
to have forgotten.
Quilted to her bed, she
should be up, out walking, the south face
of each cracked and storied Grandview sidewalk
now free of snow. Melt
spilling off the lip
of gutters, his car idling in the drive.

She reached out to catch a falling sister, them both
failing, the wheelchair rolling aside, she says. *Stupid.*
Shouldn't have been so
stupid. Her back out good
now. He waves the tinted pastel
petals and she raises a weak backhand,
gesturing to the bedside table. A magazine folded
open. *You should read about Margaret Laurence.*
She lived quite the ordinary life.

She smooths the quilt, her torso and legs such
soft furrows. An eroding landscape.
It's such a short season, she says.
That's all. *Yes*, he says. *Well,*
I have to run. Later, he will wonder
if he left without remembering to put the flowers
in water.

Night Vision

The moon, when it's not there
is still

there, his daughter says, eyes
turned up to the night

sky, shining. And how better
might anyone

define the way
vision works, how

light slips through.

Witness

Where the animals come down
to these autumn shallows,
thirst and passage are written
into eroding clay
banks. An osprey high
in the circle of sky plummets,
strikes water and thrusts back up.
Stirs the blue silence.
Drops,
climbs once more, falls
free, strikes again and turns
to spiral up, claws empty
in the dry air. Time and again.

On a gravel island a man
stands amid driftwood, looking up
and downstream for clues to ancestors,
their plain pasture, two summers they lived
somewhere near here.
Gone now
a full century. No accounting. Maybe a dozen
times the bird falls and fails.
Light slips.
Shadows slide
down the banks, darken
water. The raptor works on,
silver in the sky, disappearing

into black pools. The man stands,
growing hungry. Each dive brings the hunt
downstream, closer. A splash and quick flash, imagined
capture and escape. Still the man stands
watch, mere witness
to what slips by, the ripples.

Razielle Aigen

Mountains

We try and think of all the homonyms we can think of

a prayer

spell-wording a wish to stave off confusion keeping

a vigil of meaning

so the demons don't mess with your raft

on this border-crossing
your passage
your passing

your ascent

You're going to where we can't
So when you get there just wait
don't freeze us out

At a loss for words we count on all the ways
a word can
mean a thing
all the
ways a thing can be said
just in case

this can be taken differently or better still be
undone

fingertips trace letters

in a film
a thick coating
this dusty cloak of an icebox

you've left us in impervious to the cold

I've been hit by a typewriter he says

We're dying

to know what this
means

To be
hit by a typewriter

we want to believe

means something
along the lines of

i n s p i r e d b y m a n y w o r d s a l l a t o n c e

Or maybe

a state
of emergency

a five-minutes-to-midnight-type-thing

in which there is no choice
but to hack away
spinning words
destroying

worlds

We imagine this to be as good a way to go as any

The language of loss defies reason

In a
backwards
attempt at
proving it wrong

we try try to

put the inky letters back on their keys

push the heavy boulder of it back up over &
over crimson & moreover

try to dig it into a logical fallacy by adhering
to the face

of the mountain

Reaching the apex we reduce
it to sand

its hardness undone
one silken brush stroke at a time

rendering

consonants and syllables to granules
fractals
of what they once meant

when unified

a kalpa's passing

By relevance through omission   by deductive reasoning

we turn lick & leaf
every page for inference

It bugs us that we can't make out

the meaning of this
criss-crossed
web
Hiding
under its confusing gauze
We pretend

no one can see us
under

the surface
grammar

Waiting silently in the strands of magical thinking

for a monkey theorem to validate

something

we know we know
but don't want to
believe

We bank on timescales
being infinitely slow
and the probability

of meaning
generated by a simian
at a typewriter
to be infinitesimal

slim to none
read very very small

This stratagem makes us feel clever and not afraid

We ask ourselves what's the worst thing that could happen?

And then it does

like a mountain

Erin Brown-John

Matthew

I

It was hard in Saskatchewan.
First there was no water, then the wind
claimed the soil.

With neither
he was an empty mouth to feed.
So he left, went west,
followed the CPR to the Rockies,
walking.

At Revelstoke he met a works crew; begged for a job
they said *come back Monday*.

He was hungry and eager.
When they asked his name he said *Matthew*.

He never went hungry again.

II

He stocked up.

Weekends he'd take the Interurban to Woodwards
and come home with bags bulging
with shirts and ties, tins of food, tools, linens.

He stacked them neatly along the wall.

The pile grew and grew
until he couldn't
use the room.

Never heated the house.

Turned the water off in the winter
so the pipes wouldn't freeze

Then, had to use
the toilet down the street in the pub.

Never bathed.

More unused items stacked up
just in case.

One by one,
rooms lost
to clutter.

III

It's not like he didn't try—

Subscribed to *Western Heart*,
the *Dominion Friendship Club*,
awaiting their arrival each month
to pore over lists of women looking for love.

He wrote thoughtful notes
to postboxes of
honest Protestant ladies.

Met them sometimes
in Victory Square.

Afterwards they'd write back to say
he was nice but ...

IV

Approaching sixty-five he got his first letter from HR.
He ignored it. They sent another.

But he couldn't retire—risk
losing it all.

If he collected his pension
they might discover
that Matthew was a lie:

So many people he'd met
had lost fathers to the Huns.
It wasn't the time
to have a name like Adolf.

The letters kept coming.

He arrived at work
and worked as if damned,
convinced he would starve if he didn't.

Finally two strong lads escorted him out
and locked the door.

With over forty years of service
his pension was generous.

V

The paperboy came every day
with *The Columbian* rolled up with twine.
Matthew stacked them unread against the wall
floor to ceiling, layer after layer
until the hallway was impassable.

He kept paying the kid
so he'd keep coming.

Some days
the kid was the only person
he'd talk to.

Speculative and Young Adult Fiction

Brook Warner Jensen

Baking with Betsy

A long marriage is a happy marriage, my grandmother used to say. It's a comforting sentiment, one I find myself coming back to each morning I wake up in this concrete bunker tucked beneath the rubble of our once beautiful suburban home. Bronze swords clatter outside the small window as an army of feral ratmen lay siege to a mire of venus flytraps the size of street lights, and I begin my morning chores.

Stretching, dressing, purifying a stored gallon of putrid water I need to get me through the day. One finds solace in these simple tasks. My father would always complain that a housewife has it easy. But try waking from cryogenic slumber every hundred years to a brand new uncaring hellscape and improvising new ways to cook, clean, and scrounge, while still making time to chat with your frozen, slowly dying husband, and tell me that's easy! Now, my father did invent the nuclear fusion generator in 1965, but I've been married to the same man for ten thousand years. Plus, given that the cities of man outside are now buried beneath the ruins of four or five fallen empires, I think it's plain to see which of our accomplishments proved to be the most enduring.

Mornings are the trickiest part of this new life. A ratman is chomped in two and tossed like a salad before being devoured in front of his fleeing comrades. I struggle to take tea without fresh milk. This sort of destitution in a home once beaming with middle-class affluence can be demoralizing. Outside, invertebrates have evolved to melt the minds of their enemies with their very thoughts, and I still have to live with the same tattered rugs! But it's only for one day in every century, and thoughts of David keep me going. We were frozen the day before the illness would have taken him, and he hasn't left his chamber since. Although his cells still move, immeasurably, the freezing turns the seconds into decades.

Oh Dave, I know you would share in this terrible toil with me if you could. I know you would wrestle with the venomous vines in the alley behind the old bodega for sustenance if I asked. But you have to rest. Sleep, dear husband, sleep. Enjoy this hat I've woven for you from the silk of those metal-eating spiders, and sleep.

Speaking of insects, those tenacious beetles have sacked the grain stores again. On today of all days. Thankfully, I don't need much. Near the beetles I sprinkle some greywater and the last of my dehydrated flesh-eating worms. The bee who sold them to me boasted in a buzzing drawl that they would expire on their own once the unwanted pests were devoured, but I swear I saw one the other century, engaged in something licentious with the rusted remains of my lamp. The salesbee's great-great-grandson chided me, insisting it was my wild, ape-brained imagination. Apparently their language has mutated too much to read the warranty on the old package, or so this scion of a salesbee dynasty claimed.

Vermin and interlopers aren't the only things keeping me busy. Batteries need to be tested for charge, wires for gnaw marks, and all kinds of culinary experiments to be done on whatever flora now dominate the biome outside. Some centuries I wake up to are more arduous, like the one where I had to cater the armistice between the shattered fragments of a marmot hive mind. Most times, though, I do what is needed to keep this place running for the next hundred years. I eat, I think, I sleep. I fashion a chair from debris, wipe the perpersation from the glass on David's chamber, and say how I feel.

Do you want to hear my dreams, Davey? Quietly, though. A creature is laying much-needed eggs outside.

The slumber between each century is lucid. I find myself floating through a cerulean, crystalline expanse, drifting above an amber pit of glowing hot nails. Ice sheathes me like a tucked blanket, and memories real and imagined pass through me like sand sifting through a sieve. It doesn't feel like I am whipped from disparate moment to moment, sliced by an unfelt century. I am unmoored, soaring faster than the others who live only in their moment, their movement, their crisis, their war. Whatever the stakes are, whatever it is to be prevented or protected, it's nothing to me. Nothing that matters to me changes. It's like going to sleep while a friend is in crisis. For you, the night is a minute, a dream. For her, hours. Time has always been like this, I think. Only now I don't feel so guilty.

What beautiful eggs you've laid out there, strange bird. Excuse me, Dave, while I retrieve them from outside.

Was it difficult for me to wake up the first time to a vacant cul de sac, only a hundred years after we'd both entered our cozy chambers? Was it alarming to see that instead of a more advanced, more affluent society with the means and willingness to cure my husband, I had found nothing but desertion and ruin? I like to think not. I like to think I didn't crunch into a limp bundle on the street and claw at my arms till they bled. I like to think I didn't starve myself for days, believing that if I was hungry enough, desperate enough, imperilled enough, someone would have to come and save me, because someone has always come to save me. Someone has always come.

Apparently something came during the last century. Our storage closet is coated in a thick green paste with handprints as long as spatulas, but the only thing missing is the black pawns from my glass chess set. Goodness. The propane tank is still here, but will it still work? It's so heavy.

But no, as I drag the tank toward the oven, I am sure my first morning after the fall was not like that at all. No. I wasn't so weak, so feeble, so distastefully pathetic. No. I was a strong woman. A strong woman who lifted her bruised body off the pavement even though her legs were trembling too terribly to stand. A strong woman who soaked a handful of dried beans even though her arms were shaking and her sliced skin stung in the murky water. A strong woman who forced them down her throat even though they tasted like dirt, and who gorged on the tumour-lined lemons in her yard as she watered them with her broken tears. She sowed the seeds for her future, without even the faintest clue as to what would grow. Then she reset her machine, kissed the icy glass enclosure around her very slowly dying, handsome husband, and climbed into hers. The freeze took her like a swift embrace, wrapping around her belly and nuzzling against her neck. She sank into those peaceful depths. She rolled the die.

The afternoon is almost up. I grab one of the carnivorous worms, with a fear-stricken beetle half crunched in its maw. A whiff of its butt makes me wheeze. Acrid gas is better than none. They're too slimy to escape once collected in a bowl. Flour sticks to their slick bodies, and they try to wriggle away. Not yet, my friends, not yet. Enjoy some fresh water. This bake will take time.

And all I have is time. Dave's got time. I've got time. We've all got time. The cryogenic process only slows down the disease so much, but who could get anxious at the eons and eons it gave for something to come my way, some break that was more than finding food and heat and safety for a few hours. Millennia: an amount of time you can't really conceive of, can't even really imagine. You can't imagine living it. You can't imagine expending it! Can't truly internalize that fifty years from today will be how long 24 hours is for Dave, for his cells, for his virus, and for his bristling stubble. Fifty years and there's a cure, or there's none. He'll be alive somehow, someway, or done.

But there's so much left to do. So many important things to do! I'll decorate the archway with that calico algae teeming in the pond outside. I'll smear the counters in that fluorescent ooze gurgling in our pipes and spell his name in the blood of those pantry raiders! To all these improbable marvels, my father would have said: impossible. Wouldn't believe it if he read it in his books. Wouldn't believe it if he saw it with his own eyes!

Impossible. Impossible! Impossible, like the doctors said about my husband, said about a cure. As impossible as a nomadic tribe of trader bees? Ha! Insanity is the new logic now. Flour, centuries old, plus propane and water, plus eggs from a creature which feeds on light, and gas from these worms instead of yeast, and it blossoms in my oven like a velvet flower. Not sure why it's velvet, but it's festive! Impossible, they would say, but here it is! Anything can be done.

I set the chamber for fifty years instead of a hundred. These things can freeze people, why not cuisine? I climb inside and raise the match perkily above the makeshift candles. Steam erupts from the chamber's turbines and the glass sheath spins into place. Ice freezes from air on the curved window and I take my breath, my last breath for the next fifty years, and ready myself to burst into song.

Delightful, collected, committed—that's what I want his first healthy thoughts of me to be. Happy birthday, Dave. I hope you love your cake!

Benjamin Thiede

Stay Out of the Tall Grass

PERSONAL LOG ENTRY: CAPT. MARINA DAWSON
DAY 1135
LOCATION: PRAEGRESSUS

Step one when being charged at by a pissed-off five-ton herbivorous dinosaur: make yourself appear as non-threatening as possible and freeze. Alone and minding my own business in a shallow depression between soft rolling hills in an idyllic countryside, I contemplated this ludicrous advice while an enraged scaly monster fifty times my weight crashed through the tree line and bore down at me full tilt.

The sun—or least the celestial body we habitually call the sun on this planet—had yet to break free from the horizon. Still, I couldn't shake that nagging feeling that my Tuesday was shaping up to be one of those damned days again. You know, one of those forgetful clunkers where first you stub your toe on the bedpost while blindly feeling your way around all the mysterious objects underneath your bed in search of the missing itinerant slipper, then coffee spills all over your uniform while you're rushing out the door fifteen minutes late, and lastly, to top it off, within a few minutes of being on the clock, you're being bull rushed by an ornery megaton dinosaur who's decided to unleash what appears to be a lifetime of pent-up fury and rage solely at you.

Yeah, one of those days.

Before getting any further, I must pause to weed out my unintended audience. If you're an agent, employee, or summoned demon lord of the Alpha Horizon Corporation, my official logs can be found in my tablet.

My notes and entries were dutifully recorded every day throughout my three-year contract. I can't promise, however, that the tablet's password hasn't been hacked and changed to something about Randall Jones being an excrement spore.

Just for kicks, let's say, reader, that you do happen to be an AHC representative who's slithered through the interdimensional portal to our chummy little home-away-from-home mesozoic-like planet. For one thing, what the heck took you so long? Seriously, if I'd known I was going to be abandoned in another multiverse this long, I would've brought my cat. And lots more Hot Pockets. Sigh. My cat sitter's bill is going to be enormous.

Let's just say that you recovered my tablet and—here's the big *if*—it's still *operational*. (But let's not kid ourselves. Since when does any techno gadget ever have a lifespan longer than a hamster's? It's one of the immutable laws of technology. Stuff breaks on non-Earth planets just as fast, if not faster, as it does back home).

If for nothing else than to play out this series of increasingly unlikely events, let's just assume that you happen to encounter issues logging in to the miraculously still-functioning tablet. Heaven knows what you'll need the files for. I have no delusions that I'll be long gone by the time these hypotheticals ever play out; the records would hardly be useful intel by then. In any event, here's a little tidbit: to secure access, it may be worth trying combinations of our CEO's name with as many synonyms of fecal enterics that you can think of.

Phew. I'm happy to get that uncomfortable little bit of housekeeping out of the way. For everyone else, those who may have been duped into coming to Praegressus, or those who may have mounted an independent rescue mission to try and save us, I've written these journal entries for you. Who knows how long our society will survive, left to its own devices and cut off from the world. Or cut off from the world with shopping malls, health spas, and community centres, to be exact. Our world, as you'll notice, doesn't have many creature comforts. Just *creatures*. Scaly, leathery, feathery, and prehistoric-y. There needs to be a record of what our lives were like here in dino-land. Or at least what mine was like. We now return to our regularly scheduled programming.

Thankfully, all border rangers are fully equipped with the concise second edition of Edwin Marsh's *Dinosaurian Survival Guide*, which is where I came across that sparkling advice that, on its face, amounted to little more than doing nothing. The antithesis of the old Nike advertising slogan from back on Earth. *Just Do Nothing.*

It's a strange and unnerving feeling when your subconscious flips a binary switch to completely reroute all of your biological hard-wiring in a split second. One moment you're your normal self: cool, calm, moderately good-looking, and rational. *Hey, those sharp notes over in that elm sound like a distressed songbird. Maybe I should investigate what's giving it trouble to see if there's some bigger threat looming nearby?* The next moment, your body puts all its chips on the fight-or-flight response. *Oh. My. God. I've somehow taken a wrong turn at the Pamplona Cathedral and am now in the middle of the running of the five-ton bulls! Move, legs! Now! Faster!*

In retrospect, it was amid this confusing internal chaos that Marsh's advice filtered into my brain. *Do nothing?* I couldn't do *nothing.* I found it hard to accept that the advice applicable in situations where an inebriated ex-boyfriend sends you taunting text messages at 2:00 a.m. should *also* just happen to be the same for dealing with a faceoff with a cantankerous prehistoric monster.

Do nothing?

I can bite my tongue at sophomoric, puerile jibes when all that's at stake is honour, dignity, and the reality of what really went down in the hot tub at that after-wedding party four years ago, but I draw the line when my life is on the line. With grit and determination, I rifled through *Dinosauria* in a frantic search for some other tip better suited to my fancy, as if the book were more of a choose-your-own-adventure novel than a survival guide. I just wanted something that offered the chance to be proactive. That's my style—I'm a woman of action!

It was hopeless and I knew it, but I thumbed through at a breakneck speed anyway, almost as if the thing was a damned flip book. I had no practical or second-hand experience to draw on, so I hoped Marsh's guide would offer something more useful. After all, if everything I had to go on amounted to doing practically nothing, then there wasn't much to lose by quickly scanning through the book. I knew already that I was pretty darn good at doing nothing—I could hang with the best. I just wasn't sold on the idea that for once in my life it was actually the recommended course of action.

I'm flipping through. Yes, there is still a monster barrelling at me—that situation hasn't changed—and it dawns on me that I have my nose in a book. If I'm a goner, I'll be going out the nerdiest way possible. They'll discover my crumpled body and deduce that I must've treasured this fine dinosaur literature so much that I'll probably be buried with it. "She couldn't part with it in life," they'll solemnly state in my eulogy, "so she shan't part with it in death." My makeshift coffin will be lowered six feet into the ground. My right hand will be staged over my heart, while my left will be clutching this presumably prized copy of *Dinosauria*, which I inexplicably couldn't peel my eyes away from in the face of impending demise. Just like with the Egyptians, the book will be left open at a supposedly interesting page, so that I can read my treasured book throughout eternity. My luck, it'll be something on the *Compsognathus*.

Oh, the abject horror. *Compsognathus* are such annoying little shits.

Arms pumping and legs churning, the bulky dinosaur crested the hill and descended in my direction, a scant two hundred yards away. With gravity-enhanced momentum now powering its top-end speed, the bipedal dinosaur careened toward me on a direct collision course that my comparatively lithe frame stood little chance of withstanding. Streams of spittle sprayed from its mouth and nostrils, lathering its face in a frothy slime that gave it the appearance of a rabid, crazed beast. *Twelve feet tall, ten thousand pounds or so of rippling muscles … and it looks bat-shit crazy*, I thought. *A combination as terrifying as a* Tyrannosaurus.

Check that. *As terrifying as a preadolescent* Tyrannosaurus … *maybe.* Fully grown adult Tyrannos, while exceedingly rare—I'd only ever seen two—could leave lifelong scars from the encounter alone. Mental scars, to be precise. I hadn't come across any victims of violent interactions who'd survived long enough for their torn appendages or shredded flesh wounds to form actual scars.

Sure, there were always going to be handfuls of thrill-seeking adrenaline junkies, peer-pressured youths, data-collecting scientists—or, more commonly, their unwitting assistants—and street gang initiates from the neighbouring Sonatrian colony who combed the Hateg Forests hoping to flush a live one out. But for every one of those nutjobs, there were hundreds of sane colonists who prayed to God that their daily routines would be free of one of the land's most feared predators. Scrambled eggs for breakfast; short commute to work, which in a walled city was mostly a given; and no bloodthirsty Tyrannos on the way home.

The great Praegressus dream.

D. R. Spicer

Application Reboot

AN EXCERPT

PROLOGUE

Recipe for a Spy
1 cup bravado
2 cups stupidity
3 ½ cups intelligence
1 tablespoon psychopath
½ teaspoon sociopath
1 pinch of love
a dash of death

MAYHEM IN MOROCCO

His eyes blurred, just when he needed them to be clear. The rough pavement and speed of his racing-edition Citroën DS3 weren't helping. The vibration in the car worsened as he accelerated, but he was finally getting close to his target. His quarry was on a motorbike and easily slipped through the narrow passages of the medina.

"Come in, Tick. Do you have eyes on the asset?" The words buzzed in his earpiece.

"For now, but it's tough to keep up," Tick answered.

"I'm almost at the next gate. I'll join you inside the walls."

"We've got to corner him."

Nigel and Tick needed to finish this never-ending dance with the biker. It seemed like one of a thousand minuets they'd done over the last two years. Chasing bad guys together seemed to be their fate, at least until headquarters changed its mind.

The modern roads outside the medina were crowded, but the mayhem inside its walls was far worse. At least on the outside they could borrow a sidewalk if needed. Tick hated to think of the mess they were making, but this guy needed to be alive long enough to tell his tale.

"I'm coming in." Tick could almost hear Nigel's neatly trimmed mustache bristle over the roar of his engine.

Deep inside the market, piles of spices suddenly blurred past Tick, creating a kaleidoscope of colour through the windows of his car. He veered to the left, narrowly missing the merchant and a barrel piled high with a deep red powder, but rammed an oversized canister of rosy-orange spice. The powder coated the right side of the windscreen, and he hoped it wasn't getting sucked into the cabin. Having his eyes and lungs on fire seemed like too great a punishment. He glanced back at a reddish-gold cloud, the colour of his hair, and a screaming merchant who was chasing him between painful, burning coughs.

The biker disappeared, but Tick kept going. There was only one way he could have gone. Momentarily, the telltale sign of another angry merchant with fists raised signalled his path ahead.

"It may be our luckiest day ever," Tick said, hoping the chase was over.

"What?"

"The biker, he got himself wrapped up in a rug."

As the narrow passage opened, the biker swerved to miss invisible targets. He had one hand on the handlebars and the other was fighting with an orange Berber rug that was draped over him. He was struggling to wrestle it off his helmet.

"I'm almost at the gate," Nigel announced.

"Promises, promises." Tick knew that a little sarcasm went a long way with Nigel.

An instant later the target was free, and he forcefully sped up. The rug flew into the air and brushed some of the spice off Tick's car before crumpling on the ground behind him. Tick saw the next gate and raced toward it, struggling to keep up with the bike. "Hurry, you need to block the gate. He's heading right for it."

As the words escaped Tick's mouth, a gleaming green Jaguar with eight cylinders and a wealth of chrome all ablaze burst through the archway. In this earthy context, it looked like it had landed from another planet.

Out of options, the rider reared his bike up like a horse and leapt over the Jaguar as if he were showjumping at Olympia in London. The biker was free of the walls of the old city.

"Dammit, that tosser's escaped, hasn't he?" roared Nigel.

"I'm still in pursuit," said Tick, as he veered around the rear of Nigel's car and raced through the crowded gateway. The thickness of the wall startled him. As he tore off the passenger-side mirror, he knew that one more inch to the right and he'd be dead. "He's following the outside of the wall."

"Keep on him," said Nigel. "He wasn't heading into the medina just to lose us. He's got unfinished business in there."

"I'll force him to stay close to the wall out here. We'll try again at the next gate."

It didn't work, and moments later the biker was back inside. He wove his way through crowded stalls, taunting Tick on the left momentarily and then spreading his cheer in front of Nigel, until he broke for another gate and escaped the medina.

Nigel followed. Tick screeched to a halt, narrowly missing two children who had freed themselves from their mother's attention. The look of horror in their eyes and anger in their mother's made time stop. Thoughts about why he was doing this for a living crowded Tick's head, until he swept them away with the gear shift and continued his chase.

Their dance was now a sad comedy. They were continuing the same pursuit but, once again, on opposite sides of the wall. To make matters worse, Tick heard sirens behind him. The local police had joined in the chase, and he suspected they weren't after the biker.

So far Tick only saw one on his tail. "Police engaged. He's gonna get away!" he yelled.

"There's another gate ahead. Get there!"

Tick downshifted and sliced through the crowds. The roar of his engine and the sirens behind him helped part the sea of pedestrians, cyclists, and donkeys. As he approached the gate, he stopped, and the police whizzed past him. The biker blasted through the gate. Nigel and his great green wonder pounced on him, knocking him through the air and onto the bonnet of Tick's car.

"Bollocks, Nigel, he better be alive." Tick almost vomited.

Nigel leapt out of his car and Tick wobbled out of his. With guns raised, they approached the biker. He was still moving. Nigel reached over and opened the helmet's dark visor. The biker focused on Tick and smiled, just before his mouth started to ooze blood. His head rolled to the side; his eyes were now frozen. He was gone.

They heard clicking behind them and knew they were surrounded by police who were cocking their guns.

Slowly Tick stood and raised his hands above his head. Nigel followed in a surprisingly reluctant way. Tick could tell he was thinking he could take them on, or better yet, escape. Instantly they were frisked and stripped of their mobiles, ID badges, and guns, before they were pushed down to their knees.

With a sense of relief, Tick saw others from their team, including Noelle, arrive and begin to work with the police. "Cleanup on aisle seven," he joked. "We made a mess. Time to tidy up."

"Not helpful, Atticus," declared Noelle. Atticus Cecil Ward was his full name. Everyone just called him Tick, except strangers, and Noelle when she was upset.

Wendy Naava Smolash

The Institute

AN EXCERPT

On Tuesday, Gwen meets Doran at the dining hall for lunch. He slips a codex onto her tray. "Thanks," he says.

Gwen smiles over her spaghetti and pockets the business-card-sized paper-thin screen. "I'll get it to him tomorrow," she says. "I'm crossing over for the morning meeting."

"Tomorrow," he says. "Okay."

She laughs at him. "That hard to wait?"

Doran blushes, goofy grin breaking out on his broad, handsome face. He ducks his head in the graceful gesture she by now finds endearing in her friend.

She cuffs him on his broad shoulder. "You two are sweet. I'll get it to him."

Getting to her morning meeting in the Tech side of the Institute entails checking in at the central security hub for permission to transfer sides from Martha, the security manager. She greets Martha with a polite nod, friendly as always, and slides her belongings through the hole in the plexiglass. She tries not to look at the ear insert or the grasping hands as Martha slides the metal tray into its inner slot to receive Gwen's things for inspection.

Martha works alone in a hexagonal white office at the centre of the Institute, at the hub where the Institute's sections join. Her office is a small, efficient hub of plexiglass windows with slots for receiving objects. Trays slide objects from one window to the other, subject to Martha's determination: which are appropriate, which can be shunted along to other Institute area windows.

She is the only person with direct access to all points outward—and downward and upward—from the security centre. Not even Klamm has the access that Martha does. She can put a line straight up to Command if need be. Martha approves all package transfers, all messaging between areas, all shipments, all phone calls across security areas. Much of the actual delivery is automated—the continual quiet movement of porters—but Martha's plexiglass office is the crosspoint through which all communication across Institute areas must be approved. She keeps meticulous records.

Once she approves Gwen's purse, wallet, keys, pens, and tablet, and logs the time of transfer, Martha slides the tray containing Gwen's possessions over to the Tech window and nods her through the electronically sealed grey security door. "Meeting with Tech today?" she inquires with a tight smile, though Gwen knows perfectly well that Martha's calendar clocks every meeting.

Gwen gives back a polite nod as Martha clicks her tray into place in the slot on the Tech side. From the other side of the security door, the window into Martha's office looks exactly the same: a slot for the tray near the bottom, a plexiglass window through which Martha in her white hexagonal room of other plexiglass windows faces other Institute areas. Gwen wonders how she doesn't go mad in her plexiglass room with its many small holes in many windows, like the eye of a bee.

"Just the weekly update between Tech and Creative," Gwen murmurs as she retrieves her things, including Doran's codex, stashed between cards in her wallet.

Gwen spots Anders after her meeting. He's in the Tech Work Hall, absorbed in his workstation. His lithe, strong body is hunched over the screen, his dark head nearly tucked into the workstation.

She catches his eye, and he breaks into a grin that lights up his face. "Lunch?" she asks. "I have an hour before I have to be back."

He glances over his shoulder at the Supervisor, a skinny man with the standard earcoil, under a table fixing wires. "Okay." Anders shrugs. "It's only ten minutes till my break anyway. Let's eat."

In the Tech cafeteria they talk lightly of nothing much: work, deadlines, his projects, her meeting. Anders's glowing eyes are expectant.

"Hey, have you seen my new business card?" Gwen asks, still in that light tone. "Doran helped me with it. You remember Doran, right? From the orientation tour?" She grins.

"Hm. Oh, maybe. Tall guy, yeah?" Anders's hands shake, but his voice stays level.

She holds out the codex and he palms it casually in his large hand. "That's right. He worked on the design for me. Let me know what you think."

He taps the paper-thin screen and reads for a moment, then his head and his broad shoulders tip back and he laughs. At Gwen's curious expression, he tilts the device her way.

In typical Doran obscurity, all that appears on the thin digital sheet is a single number, an elegant 7 in black Garamond on the white screen background.

Gwen looks up at Anders's laughing face and wrinkles her nose. She whispers, "Honestly. You're both so strange. You deserve each other." She smirks.

In reply, Anders feigns a serious face and taps the screen. The 7 rotates, blurs as it spins, slows, and stops upside down. His grin breaks across his face.

Gwen, though puzzled, is used to her friends' strange shared humour by now. "Geeks." They both laugh.

Although there are no Supervisors in the dining hall, someone at the next table glances over, annoyed at the sound of their laughter, and Gwen stiffens. "I should head home," she mumbles, her voice lower.

Anders is too happy to be cautious. "Okay, okay, one second. I've got some suggestions for your business card. See if you and Doran like this." He pulls up the coding page, taps through a few screens, and enters some simple code, then taps the codex off and passes it back. She takes it loyally, shaking her head at Doran and Anders's mysterious shared humour.

They stand and hug. Gwen shoots him a reassuring glance, hoping the people around them don't notice. "I'll see what Doran thinks," she says casually. "See you next week?"

When Gwen returns the codex to Doran that afternoon—easier, on their own side, to find a moment alone—he breaks into a similar open laugh as he reads, his head tipped back, large Adam's apple bared in his broad throat.

At Gwen's curious face, he tips the screen toward her, though all she sees are three dots in a triangle. He taps the screen and the three dots spin, become the digit 3, which slowly rotates to become ω.

She shrugs. Doran laughs again, his head back. "What are you doing tonight at seven?" he asks her.

"You tell me—what am I doing tonight at seven?"

"I believe that you want to play hockey at the exercise centre at seven, and you want to bring me along," he says through his surreptitious smile.

"Oh," she says, nodding. "Bring the boobs, is that it?" They both laugh, then stifle the laughter, but their eyes keep laughing.

"Help us out?"

Gwen nods, still holding back her grin, a note of fear in her eyes. "Of course, don't be silly."

Regular exercise is encouraged, and thus the exercise centre can be accessed through Martha's office from any other Institute area. Normally people play sports with friends from their own area; occasionally, teams formally arrange competitions between areas, managed through Martha's scheduling regimen.

Luckily, Martha seems to have taken to Doran. She actually smiles at them as they cross over into the exercise centre. As the grey door clicks behind them, Gwen murmers, "Did she just smile at you?"

Doran grins his usual trickster grin. "I hear she has a nephew, back in one of the outpost towns. Apparently I look like him."

"Handy," she replies pensively.

This night it will be just a coincidence that both Doran and Anders will be bringing friends from their own areas to play a practice game at the same time. And it may be a coincidence that only Gwen and the Tech friend will actually end up on the gym floor, clashing metal sticks, as their friends disappear to find a quiet place.

Time clocks on like this for weeks and then months. Flashes of doing her work, meetings with colleagues, careful passed messages. Several times she almost confides in Isaacs, but her confusion keeps her quiet.

As Gwen goes about her days at the Institute, writing, producing research, submitting to distribution, she finds she is often distracted. What before was deeply fulfilling work now can barely keep her attention.

The tension is beginning to wear on Gwen's friends. And on her.

Spencer Miller

Forever in Warfare My Heart Is

I was alone in darkness. Breathing still air, standing upon nothingness. Naked in that absence of wind or temperature, like a sensory deprivation chamber. I felt the cool metal and inert rubber housing of the console in my hand, the only light its laser-white readout and alphanumeric keypad. I was in super space, as empty as they said it would be. I had a lot of work ahead of me.

Where to begin? I was standing normally, not floating; gravity and other physical laws we take for granted were default settings in there. They could be adjusted later if desired. I wasn't suffocating either, inhaling a close approximation of Earth's atmospheric mixture of gases.

I glanced at the console, and the technical readouts were gibberish to me. Fearing the gizmo would interfere with my sense of immersion, I decided my first priority was to transmute it into something more flavourful. "Console, reconfigure anthropomorphically," I said. I was holding it up close to my face to talk, which was probably unnecessary. "I will give directions verbally, but I want you to capture the images and textures directly from my visual cortex. I'm going to imagine you …"

He winked into being before me: a wizened old man with a robotic monocle and a big billowing cape draped over matte-black armour. And he was floating just a couple of inches off the ground, bobbing gently in the void like a helium balloon.

"It is done," he said, his voice a deep baritone with synthesized edges, reverberating like an oak barrel rolled slowly over bundled steel cable.

"Hello, consul. I'm going to name you Zur." I waved an arm at the surrounding vacuum. "Welcome! I'm going to create a whole world, perhaps a series of worlds, side by side or in some other configuration, and I want you to help me. Do you understand?"

"Yes, master." Zur's monocle pulsated green light.

"Man, don't say 'Yes, master.' It makes me sound like a fuckin' vampire. Just call me by my name: Barbarossa … X. BX for short, if you like. Let's get started. First, our pantheon. Aloft on a cloud, stone pillars and carved seats, translucent crystal floors, and a central dais where we can cast our gaze upon the mortals dwelling down below."

Zur mumbled magic words and red runes appeared to issue from his mouth and then fade, like afterimages when you close your eyes against the sun. And just like that, the structure was there around us, exactly as I had pictured it: the polished marble pillars with fluffy white tufts beyond, the dais surmounted by a little pool of water like a birdbath.

"Okay, how big can our land mass be?" I asked Zur.

"Typically, super-space environments range from anywhere between one and a thousand square miles."

"Okay, but what's the maximum?"

"I can generate a world with a mass of up to 7000×10^{21} kilograms."

"Is that bigger than Earth?"

"No, Barbarossa. It's a little smaller than the moon." Did I detect a tone of condescension in Zur's modulating timbre?

"Okay, fine. Well, let's start small, anyway. Our continent should be the size of, like, Lichtenstein. I want it just floating in space, like a flat Earth. Let's get those mountains growing. Beyond the mountains, golden and green valleys and plains, stretching out to meet a distant ocean."

"As you wish." Zur raised his arms and twirled his fingers around a bit, probably more for my benefit than anything else. Down through the crystal floor, an island of icy peaks, bright slopes, and blue canyons dilated out of nothing. I watched the landscape coalesce outward from the mountain range. Like a Catan game board, the continent bloomed in colorful hexagons of forest and prairie and desert.

I strode to the edge of the pantheon and looked out at the newborn horizon. Was that a silver blade of ocean, far beyond the contoured vista of hills and plains, below the depthless black infinity? "Nice, consul. The sky needs some work. Geosynchronize our sun's journey with Earth time, as if we were in, say, California."

"Pacific time, then." That was definitely sarcastic. More magic words and finger twirling from the mage, and shadows pivoted, slanting deeply.

"Mimic the visual attributes of the Earth's atmosphere," I told him. The void bluened like it was wired to a dimmer switch. "And exaggerate the magic hour. I like my sunsets." Then we were bathed in magenta. "Beautiful. Now, let's go down and take a stroll around."

Zur floated and I stood in the wide mouth of a mountain pass, and I looked down upon the bowl of the valley, a wide expanse of seemingly endless meadows. The thick honeyed smell of grass and blooming flowers rose, tinged with sea salt. I stooped and dragged my fingernails through the earth, rubbing the moist dirt between my fingers. It felt perfectly real.

I then had Zur animate a thousand minions, golems, in a myriad of colors and models. Over the course of the day, they lay the foundations for the citadel and surrounding convolutions of an aqueduct, perched in solitude among treacherous precipices and overlooking the abyssal void. We sent one legion of golems into the valley to construct a maze of faux ruins, where my war games would be staged, and another to terraform vast tracts of land for the cultivation of agricultural crops. We sent winged emissaries—golems with a skeletal framework of feather-light joints, hollow like birds' bones—soaring to the snow-crowned mountain peaks, with instructions to build trails and monasteries and strongholds. We sent armies of excavators to dig for metals and the stuff of elemental and alchemical potency with which our golems could procreate, and to fortify and expand the Byzantine architecture of the newborn realms. The kernel of the super world was sprouting before our eyes.

I spent that first night in my nascent castle, which was otherwise vacant, on a bed hand-built by golems, swathed in bedding woven hurriedly of fibres from our already copious supply of hemp.

I had been afraid of sleeping in super space, unsure of which world I might awaken to. I worried that, already inhabiting what seemed like a dreamworld, I would descend progressively into a doubly subliminal realm of super dreams, and finding myself returned to the initial emptiness, be doomed to recreate an endless procession of shadow realms.

Instead I dreamt of the old world, my first life. The fringes of a fairground, with friends, surrounded by swirls of low-wattage light strings. Balmy summer twilight, sitting near a basketball court in some suburbia, as the windows darkened one by one in houses lining the high verge of a retaining wall. A girl in an antiquated light blue dress clasped me by the shoulders and kissed my cheek in greeting, gave me a soft fleeting kiss upon the lips.

I was roused by the violent shaking of the bed as it danced across the stone floor. The room tilted and sank. Dim light from the low fire cast weird shadows on the unfamiliar walls. Zur appeared, grabbed me by the shoulder, and started shaking me.

"Get the hell off me, I'm awake! What's going on?"

"The golems have gone silent."

"Gone silent, what do you mean? Which ones?"

"They suddenly stopped reporting back to me. All of them."

"What about the earthquake, man!"

"Yes, that too."

The disconcerting smell of woodsmoke assaulted my nostrils. I went to the window to survey the nightscape. Far off beyond the valley there were fires burning. Immediately below the castle spire, the citadel grounds were cast in an eerie shifting moonlight. I looked up at a firmament streaked with bands of purple gas, thick with stars, teeming with accelerated moons that cruised along as though part of an orrery spun carelessly by a curious child. Everything was wonky. "Zur! What's with these moons ...?"

"Barbarossa, I have detected a malignant force growing in the furthest reaches of the realm."

"A malignant force? We've created everything there is. What are you talking about?"

"It appears that when you empowered, uh, myself to synthesize your mental function, a stray fragment of your subconscious mind was erroneously manifested, somewhere very distant, in human form. This fragment grew into a separate entity: an embodiment of your deep subconscious, a kind of doppelgänger."

"Whoa. Okay. But what's the problem?"

"As it is derived from the divine material of yourself, master, the doppelgänger possesses an equal command of the super-space realm. It is likely to be adept in the manipulation of super space. There is a great possibility that it has also conjured into being a counterpart of myself, and begun to assemble its own army. Based on the primacy of the survival instincts nested in your human psyche ... the doppelgänger will seek to destroy you. In time, its army will arrive here with the intention of conquering our realm."

"Excellent!"

Yuki Abovearth

Chariot

AN EXCERPT FROM "THE FORTUNETELLER'S FATE," A YOUNG ADULT SPECULATIVE FICTION NOVEL

"I present to you … the second revision of the Anthroporium design."

Gasps echoed through the speakers.

In the back of the room, Nazareth's assistant, Quinn, monitored her boss's vitals, ready to assist if he were to have a panic attack. Nazareth knew without looking that his heartbeat was a steady green line punctuated by small, regularly spaced peaks. It had been Quinn's call to make the entire meeting a virtual reality experience, removing any risk that a Star Cult member could infiltrate and set off another bomb.

The Anthroporium had been drastically changed in design since that last disaster. Now, it was a sparkling multi-level structure, reminiscent of the glittering Saudi shopping malls often shown in historical films. The ground level was a bright, clean tiled open area. Glass elevators, walkways, and escalators connected the different parts of the building. The new Anthroporium hummed with symmetry and order. The living spaces were spacious and luxurious, while the larger spaces on each floor were dedicated to food and water procurement stations, entertainment theatres, and medical clinics.

Using their VR glasses, viewers wandered through the halls exploring. Some pointed with childlike excitement at the vast rectangular strips and square blocks in the walls and ceilings. Like glass windows, they reflected a soothing landscape of blue skies, billowing white clouds, and evergreen trees on mountains.

Sunlight didn't exist in this world either, but the area was bathed in a soothing soft white.

"Well, this is ... a *lot* better looking than the previous design," the President of K3 murmured in Mandarin. A slow, twitching smile spread across Nazareth's face as he understood without waiting for the translation to kick in.

But the President had more to say. "The one thing that worries me, as an engineer, is that this space seems to fit a lot fewer people than the last design. Will there be room for everyone?"

Nazareth sucked in a breath. *Here it comes*, he thought. "Right," he said. "There's been ... an adjustment to those initial plans."

"So ... you still haven't told us," Bezel said.

Emile looked up. "About what?"

Bezel and Emile huddled on the floor of the apartment early that morning, untangling power cords and cables that Bezel had scavenged en masse from a dumpster. She was going to sell them to her friend Selveraj on the black market. She tossed her red bangs out of her eyes and squinted out the window, where early risers were getting ready for the day. Even though their clothes were ragged and the ground was covered in rats and garbage, the sun outlined everything in soft gold light, making this hellish illegal camp seem momentarily like heaven.

"What brought you here, anyway? Don't you have a fortunetelling gig to go back to?"

"Oh. That." Emile shrugged. "Well. It's all right. I'm just one of a whole school of young fortunetellers. My school is filled with a lot of street kids or poor children whose parents can't feed them anymore. Most of them have no psychic gifts, but they're trained to give readings that fit with their clients' needs."

"But you're supposed to be the real deal, right?"

"Yes," Emile said simply. "I was the original."

Bezel gulped as her hands sifted through the cables. She sensed she was treading in deep waters here. Emile had never talked this openly about his past before. "Wouldn't your school be worried about about losing its star fortuneteller?"

"Not necessarily," he said quietly.

"What about your friends? Don't they miss you?"

Emile stiffened. He touched the scars across his bony cheek, the ones that Bezel thought had been carved out with a chisel. "I have no 'friends,' " he said.

She frowned. "Wouldn't management come looking?"

"Well, no, they can't. The ones who were with me are gone now."

"Oh? They left?"

"No … How do I say this? They're all dead."

Bezel's hands stopped. She looked up warily.

Emile met her eyes and flinched at the accusation written across her face. "No, no, no!" He put his hands up in front of his face defensively. "It wasn't me! I had nothing to do with it!"

"Well, what the heck happened, then?"

His face crumpled, and he covered his eyes with both hands. "I'm sorry!" he groaned. "I shouldn't have told …"

"*Yes, you should have!*" she yelled. "Right from the start! Stop bullshitting and tell me the truth. What happened?"

Emile's hands slowly detached from his face. "It was … a client. I'd told him his wife was going to leave him, after years of his abusing her." He exhaled deeply. "I'm sure you can take a guess what happened next …"

"No, I'm not psychic. Spell it out."

He gulped. "The client—the man—raced back home as fast as he could and caught his wife packing. He strangled her. Then he came back with a gun and sprayed my school with bullets, as expected. I was the only one who survived."

Bezel sucked in a breath. She saw something like a hint of madness beneath Emile's soft-spoken veneer.

"It happens a lot," he continued. "The clients who can afford to have me tell the future are the same ones who can't handle the truth when I reveal it to them."

"Wait. Back up," she cut in. "You said 'as expected.'"

Emile blinked, his expression blank. "Yes?"

"You *knew* the guy was going to shoot up your school. And you didn't warn them?"

He blinked a few more times, uncomprehending. He looked disoriented, as if stumped by a puzzle. Finally, after a long pause, he opened his mouth and said in a warbling voice, "Why would I?"

Alarm flooded Bezel's grey eyes. She abruptly stood up and staggered away from him as if she'd been burned.

"W-wait!" he called after her.

She was reaching for the door. He stood up to chase her. "Stop! Please!"

"You fucking *knew* people were going to die and you didn't say anything?" she seethed, a look of pure disgust in her eyes. "What's *wrong* with you? Oh my fucking God! Get out! Get out right now!"

He reached out and caught the end of her sleeve. "No, wait, please! Please let me explain—"

"*Don't touch me!*"

She pushed him away, hard, sending him crashing to the floor. Panting, she balled up her fist and lunged forward to punch him, but halted as her eyes caught a glimpse of the scars—deep red grooves like wires around his ankle. He'd had them since he arrived in the refugee zone. It was the leg he'd constantly been limping around on. She froze and stared at his disfigurement.

Emile raised his hands defensively, as if expecting to be hit, but didn't drop his gaze away from her face. "Well, what ... what was I supposed to do?" he whispered, panting. "The school rescued me but always had me captive. They always tortured me when my readings didn't fit what they wanted. They hit me when I didn't tell them. They never let me leave. It made me feel so helpless ... I just wanted to escape, even if it had to be like that."

Lula García

Patos

AN EXCERPT FROM A NOVEL SET IN RURAL MEXICO IN THE LATE 1960S

The powerful noon sun shines over a small dirt plain where a huge *pirul* tree grows in the middle of a few huts. A group of small children are playing.

Anita covers her eyes as she stands against a wall of double air bricks, next to the open steel door of her house. "Ten, nine, eight ... one!" she shouts.

The rest of the children scatter to find a place to hide. Justino hides behind the washboards, huddled under a large tub. Angelina, a chubby girl wearing a faded blue and yellow dress, hides behind the tree. Half her body shows from behind it. Laura and Dante, the youngest of the group, hide in a small chicken coop made of old wood, with an aluminum fence and a worn-down door. Two white ducks sleep, huddled, in a corner of the chicken coop. Dante gently caresses their white, soft plumage.

Anita looks around, scratches her full, thick brown hair. Spotting Angelina's yellow dress poking out from behind the wide trunk of the tree, she races back toward the steel door, yelling, "I see Angelina hiding behind the *pirul* tree!"

Angelina walks out of her hiding place with a long face. Anita continues her search, walking farther away from the steel door. As she approaches the tree, Justino bursts out from underneath his steel tub, which bangs loudly as he tosses it aside. Anita turns and races toward the steel door, but Justino gets there first. His freckled face, red from the heat and the effort, has a big smile. "Ollie ollie oxen free!" he yells.

Laura and Dante come yelling out of their hiding place, "Ollie ollie oxen free!" They're followed by the ducks, quacking and waddling, who seem to have joined the game too.

The children restart the game. Anita is still "it," and now she has to start counting again.

In the afternoon, the children sit on a concrete bridge by the side of the road. They stare up the road to where an old yellow passenger bus is approaching. The sign on the front of the bus reads *Indios Verdes*. As the bus stops, the children crouch to look under it, at the feet of the people who step off on the other side. The people walk away and the bus drives down the road.

Rain falls and the children continue to wait. Another bus stops. This time they count the people getting off. A lady with plastic shoes steps down, the mud sticking to her shoes like a second sole, followed by a man with leather boots that have big buckles and steel points on the toes. Cold raindrops slide down the children's faces like tears. Another bus stops. The legs of a woman, covered in sheer light-grey pantyhose with black high-heeled shoes, step off the bus. Her shoes smear with mud. When the children see the high heels, they run toward the house and close the door behind them.

The next day, Anita walks out of her house holding a fistfull of corn kernels. She drops them a few at a time as she steps away from the house. The white ducks follow her, eating the kernels on the ground. Anita stops dropping the corn. The ducks stop next to her and stand very still, looking like two puppies in training.

Alba, Anita's mother, walks out of the house wearing the same high heels and yells, "Feed the ducks in the chicken coop! They're not your pets, Anita."

In the afternoon, Alba and her neighbour weave, sitting in chairs outside her house. Their children play by the *pirul*, tossing small pebbles and peach pits covered in coloured chalk.

"My cousin is coming on Saturday," Alba says.

"That's good. What are you cooking for her?"

Anita, searching for small pebbles that she gathers inside her dress pocket, walks by the door.

"I'm going to make duck stew," Alba says.

Anita's eyes open wide in shock and, speechless, she turns to her mother.

"Sounds delicious," replies the neighbour. "Save some for me."

Later that evening, Alba chops vegetables on a wooden cutting board over the kitchen table. Anita stands on a chair next to the stove. She stares attentively at the milk heating in a metal pot on the stove. The rest of the children swing in a hammock that hangs from the tiled roof in front of the kitchen.

"Who's coming over on Saturday, Mom?"

"Your Aunt Licha from Veracruz."

"Mom, Aunty Licha doesn't like duck."

Alba keeps chopping the vegetables and does not look at Anita. The milk begins to boil, rising toward the edge of the pot. Thick cream begins to form on its surface. Anita blows on the milk and tries to turn the gas off, but she can't, and the milk spills over the edge of the pot onto the stove.

At the sound of hissing, her mother turns toward her. "You're such a clumsy child. I told you to take care of the milk!" she says.

At sunset, Alba lies in bed in her bedroom, trying to take a nap. Anita sits over her on the bed, stroking her mother's hair and head with her fingers. "Mommy, please don't cook the ducks," she pleads.

Half-asleep, Alba pays no attention to her daughter.

"Mom, please don't cook the ducks!" Anita yells.

Alba jumps, startled. "Shut up and let me sleep. Keep massaging my head!"

Anita continues rubbing her mother's head. Tears roll down her cheeks.

The next morning, Alba readies herself to leave the house, carrying several empty grocery bags. "Justino, we're going to the market!" she says. They leave the house. The rest of the children stay at home.

Anita waits for them leave, then turns to her siblings. "Mom is going to kill the ducks."

Angelina, Laura, and Dante yell at the same time, "No!"

"We need a plan. Come on," says Anita.

Angelina carries one of the ducks as the children exit the house; Anita carries the other one. Angelina warns Laura, "Bring a knife, in case we run into snakes." Laura takes a dull butter knife from the drawer. The children have filled their pockets with corn kernels. They cross the street and begin walking toward a hill nearby.

They climb up the hill, walking until they reach a low fence made of two barbed wires. Anita pushes down one wire with her foot and lifts the other with her hand so her siblings can cross. Angelina holds the barbed wire fence open from the other side as Anita crosses last. They walk slowly and carefully through the hard, thorny rosettes of an agave plantation. They keep climbing. On a plain near the edge of the hillside, three black bulls moo and stir as they see the children. The children run away until they lose sight of the bulls. The landscape has changed now—several trees, a small brook, and grass at the top of the hill.

"Here," Anita says.

She ties a red wool thread around the leg of each duck and ties them both to a tree next to the brook. The children take out the corn that each of them brought and put it in small piles near the ducks. The ducks eat earnestly. Dante bends down and kisses both of them.

"Goodbye. We love you," says Angelina.

When they return home, Alba has changed the drapes for new blue ones that go well with the blue and white tablecloth in the dining room. On top of the table sits a new flower vase filled with white chrysanthemums.

Alba sings as she cooks in the kitchen. "*Bésame, bésame mucho ...*" Inside a pot, chopped white onion fries with ground garlic. She adds finely chopped red tomato and some laurel leaves, sliced mushrooms, pepper, cumin, and pieces of white meat. She begins to stir, basting the meat with the sauce. The aroma spreads all over the kitchen.

Anita enters. "Mom, where are the ducks?"

Alba smiles. "Don't worry. I've cooked some chicken. I remembered your Aunty Licha doesn't like duck."

Kimber Anderson

Mystery of the Jack of Diamonds

AN EXCERPT

Kip sat at the dinner table with his family. Derek told a long story about his class gerbil going missing. Dad talked about how a friend of his was in the shop today and had coffee with him. "He said that Hendrickson the Second is bad-mouthing me all over town and saying that I'm a terrible body man."

"That's ridiculous," Mom said. "Why would he do that?"

"I assume because his dad and my dad were enemies," Dad said. "It's not like anyone will listen to him anyway."

"Hendrickson the Third is no better," Kip said.

"Is he giving you a hard time at school?" asked Dad.

"Not really, just told me to stay away from his sister." Kip pushed his peas around his plate with his fork. There were the butterflies again. "I only helped her with her science lab questions."

"Kip's got a girrrrlfrieeeeend," Derek dragged out. Kip threw his roll at him across the table.

"If that guy gives you any trouble, you make sure to talk to a teacher," said Dad.

They ate in silence for a minute and then Mom said, "Oh, I almost forgot, I'm going for an interview for a part-time job at the library tomorrow morning, but Derek has a swimming lesson at ten. Can you take him, Hank?"

"I may be able to sneak away from the shop, but I have to have a car out by noon."

"I'll take him," Kip offered. It was a great excuse to get to the rec centre to check out the locker.

Mom and Dad exchanged a confused glance. "Really?" Mom asked.

"Yeah," said Kip. "If you get a job at the library, I'll have an inside track on when all the new books arrive." He smiled. *That was quick thinking.*

Mom and Dad both laughed. "I guess you will," Mom said. "And thanks."

The next morning Kip and Derek walked to the rec centre. There was definitely a fall chill in the air. Mom had privately asked Kip to stay where Derek could see him so that he would know someone was watching him swim.

Kip sat on a bench not far from the pool, but he was preoccupied with thoughts of getting to the lockers. *What if this key is old and they've cut off the lock?* His stomach turned at the thought. He would never find out what his grandpa was trying to tell him then. He turned the key with its bright yellow fob over in his hand, and then it was gone.

Kip sprang to his feet and grabbed an arm as big around as a tree branch.

"Whoa, take it easy, Chip," Bob said.

"Give me that!" Kip grabbed for the key, but Bob held it up too high for him to reach.

"Got something special in the locker? Your favourite pair of superhero swim trunks?" Bob laughed like he was the funniest guy in the world.

Kip looked behind Bob and said, "Is that your sister?"

"Where?" Bob turned his head and Kip snatched the key back. Bob might be big, but Kip was fast.

Kip glanced at the pool and saw Derek was watching the exchange.

"Those must be some special trunks, loser." Bob gave Kip a shove, but not hard enough to knock him off balance. Kip thrust the key into his jeans pocket and sat down. He managed a smile in Derek's direction to let him know everything was fine.

When Derek got out of the pool, Kip took him his towel.

"Who was that big guy?" Derek wrapped himself up.

"He's that jerk from school," Kip said. "Don't worry about it, everything's fine."

"Didn't look fine."

"He's not as scary as he thinks he is," Kip said. "Go get changed and I'll meet you out front. Make sure to dry your hair, it's cold out." Mom had told him to say that.

As soon as Derek disappeared through the door to the change room, Kip took off to the bank of lockers close to the lobby. He found locker number seventy-two and got the key out of his pocket. He looked in both directions and behind him to make sure there was no sign of Bob. His hand shook a bit, and he had to take a deep breath and focus to get the key in the lock. He turned the key, the lock clicked, and he pulled the door open.

For a moment he just stood and looked in the locker. At the bottom there lay a playing card, the Jack of diamonds, and a blue poker chip. He picked up both items and shoved them in his jacket pocket before Derek or Bob showed up.

Kip turned toward the door to the pool just in time to see Derek come running through it.

"Ruuuun!" Derek yelled, and kept going straight to the exit. In his arms he had a pile of black fabric. Kip couldn't tell what it was, but he ran after his little brother.

Derek seemed to be running as fast as his short legs could carry him, a long piece of fabric whipping out behind him like an aviator's scarf. Kip caught up and jogged along beside him. Derek finally slowed down to a brisk walk. He was breathing heavily and looking back over his shoulder.

"What's going on? What is all that?" asked Kip.

"It's the big jerk guy's clothes," Derek panted.

"What?"

"He was in the shower. I peeked around the corner and he had his eyes closed and was singing into his shampoo bottle. I saw the clothes on the bench and grabbed them and ran." Derek tucked himself behind a big tree and stopped. "These stink." He dropped the clothes on the ground and leaned over with his hands on his knees. "Phew, that was fun."

"He didn't see you?" Kip asked.

"No."

"Did anybody?"

"I don't think so."

Kip started to laugh. He laughed until tears poured down his face. And Derek laughed, too.

"Put your hood up," Kip said. "Your hair's not dry." He felt an odd surge of pride in the parasite that he had never felt before. "That was stellar." He gave the top of Derek's hooded head a rub.

"Look at all the apples on the ground," Derek said.

Kip looked at the apples, and then looked up. "Hey, I think this is that big tree Dad was talking about."

"Can we take some of the apples home?"

"Yeah. I mean, I guess so," Kip said. "But not off the ground. Give me your backpack and I'll get a few out of the tree."

Kip took Derek's backpack and easily climbed up into the tree. When a car drove by, he kind of accidentally (but not really) happened to toss an apple with a little bit of force, never expecting it to connect with the passing car's trunk.

"What are you doing?" Derek asked.

Kip whipped his head around and saw Derek in the tree behind him.

"Shhh," Kip said. They both sat very still and stayed very quiet. The car slowed down almost to a stop and then drove off.

"Did you throw that apple at that car?" Derek asked.

"No, it just slipped out of my hand." Kip winked at Derek. "Dad got one job before from this tree, but I don't think that one hit very hard. Don't you dare tell Mom or Dad."

They left the pile of Bob's clothes right there by the tree and walked home. Kip really wished he could have seen the look on Bob's face when he got out of the shower.

Zahida Rahemtulla

Julio's House

AN EXCERPT FROM A CHILDREN'S NOVEL

Julio is our best friend and neighbour. He lives with his mum, dad, and new baby brother who just came to his house when we went to Grade 4. Julio says we shouldn't talk about the new baby that much, though, because it's not such a big deal, and he's not that cute anyways, and stuff like that. Julio's grandma also lives in the room beside him.

The best thing about Julio is that we don't feel embarrassed when he comes to our house and sees Nani watching the new channel. That's because his grandma has the exact same one, except hers is in Spanish! We made a deal with Julio that we wouldn't tell anyone at school about his grandma's channel if he didn't tell people about ours. So far it's top secret. Julio is really good at keeping secrets, and we have lots. That's why he's our best friend.

We found out about Julio last year when Mum couldn't take us to school anymore, after she started working at the hospital. Now we take the breakfast she leaves on the table for us and we eat it on the way to Julio's house, which is the last one on our street. We always have to wait for Julio and his dad while we stand in the hallway of Julio's house. From there, we can see his mum carrying around the new baby in the kitchen and his dad running around them, yelling, "*Where are my keys? Where are my keys? Jesus Christ! What a mess!*"

Julio's grandma is the only one sitting in the living room, looking at us real happy from the couch because she doesn't know how to say a lot of things. Sometimes it takes a really long time before Julio's dad says, "*Aha! Aha! In the same place!*" and that's a long time to be smiling at Julio's grandma.

One time we accidentally got the rollies when we were standing there. The rollies are when you can't control your laughing, and the more you try to stop, the worse it becomes. We tried really hard to make our rollies very quiet, but then Sirish turned to me and his face went like it does when he has a question he doesn't want anyone except me to hear, and he asked me, "Where are her tee—?" And then I noticed that Julio's grandma didn't have any teeth on, and we got the rollies even more.

When Julio finished his breakfast and saw what we were talking about, he got them too. That's why Julio's dad asked us, "What did you eat for breakfast to make you go out of your minds, ah?"

But we couldn't answer, because just then we noticed his grandma was looking at us *and* laughing with her mouth *all the way open*. So we followed Julio's dad to the car and the rollies didn't stop until we put on our seatbelts and we couldn't see her anymore.

Julio's dad loves to play old music. Whenever we drive to school, he plays songs of people singing about peace and tells us about something called the Resistance, which is why he had to leave Chile. I love those songs and the rock 'n' roll he plays. Usually when Nani and Sirish are watching TV, I go to the internet so I can hear them again. On the day we had the rollies, Julio's dad was playing my favourite CD, which has all girls singing on it. The only problem was that Julio's dad sings along with them, and on the morning we had the rollies, the main part of the song went like this:

When I'm with you …

I feel …

I feel …

I feel like a …

Beautiful woman!

Sirish, me, and Julio tried not to look at each other because we knew what would happen if we did. But after a while, the same part of the song played again and Julio's dad sang it *even louder.*

"When I'm with you …

"I feel ...

"I feel ...

"I feel like a ...

"Beautiful *woman!*"

And when he said "*woman!*" we got so embarrassed, the rollies *really* took over us.

Then Julio's dad looked at us in the rearview mirror, surprised, and said, "What's the matter, ah?" And then I guess he figured it out, because he stopped singing, and he didn't play any music when he picked us up on the way back from school. After that I felt bad for Julio's dad and tried not to laugh in the car again, because grown-ups don't always say when you hurt their feelings.

Miraya Engelage

The Crescent

AN EXCERPT

After Ariana, her best friend Sophia, and her dog Duke are thrown into an unknown world in search of her father, Ariana is separated from her travelling companions and brought to the castle in the capital

Ariana swallowed nervously as she followed the guard into what looked to be a throne room. It was mostly empty, save for an intimidating-looking throne at the far end and two armed guards on either side. Intricate tapestries adorned the stone walls, creating a garish look when put together with the red and green stained-glass windows. The guard glanced back at her, and Ariana stopped gaping and followed him the rest of the way.

"Wait here," he commanded without even turning around. Ariana watched him slip behind the stone wall and out of sight. Tapping her foot, she studied her surroundings. For all its reported splendour, the castle looked more workmanlike than anything. It was also completely silent. All she could think of was her dog, Duke, waiting for her down at the gate, and she wished she had been allowed to bring him in with her. She wouldn't even be in this situation if she hadn't been separated from Sophia and Jon, or if Doran had showed up at their meeting place the night before.

The sound of a door creaking open punctured the silence, and the same guard from earlier emerged from behind one of the less hideous tapestries. He strode purposefully toward Ariana and halted directly in front of her. "Remember to kneel," he said neutrally. She nodded, confused, and watched him exit. Really? Kneel for their monarch? She internally rolled her eyes. How old-fashioned.

Ariana may have been waiting expectantly, but their queen or king, or whoever was supposed to greet her, was clearly in no rush. While not a particularly fidgety person, she could not help but continually tap her boot against the stone floor and fix her ponytail multiple times. After what felt like an age, but was likely only ten minutes, she perked up at the sound of the unseen door creaking open.

Eager to see this elusive royal, she did her best not to bounce on the balls of her feet in anticipation. Just before the person emerged, both guards dropped to one knee and bent their heads in reverence. Ariana followed suit, feeling temporarily thwarted, but did her best to peek at the figure moving toward her. All she could see was the swishing of a shimmering blue skirt, with what looked like silver slippers emerging with each step. The slippers came to a stop in front of her, and she felt her nerves peak.

"You may look at me," said a slightly amused voice above her head.

Ariana slowly raised her head, her eyes travelling over the intricately detailed and voluptuous skirt, to the diamonds glittering around a pale neck, and finally to the woman's face. The most startling thing was not the pin-straight silver hair with blackened ends, or the pale and sharp birdlike face, but her eyes. They were silver, almost white, and made her look like she had just stepped out of a fairy tale. Her blood-red lips were quirked in a half smile, but Ariana didn't feel comforted by the expression. "Are you the Queen?" she asked, her voice practically breaking with nerves.

"What gave it away?" mocked the Queen, gesturing to the room. In any other situation, Ariana would've sassed her right back, but she felt too on edge. "Tell me, what brings you here?" The Queen bent at the waist, and Ariana felt rather than saw a sharp-edged fingernail underneath her chin. The Queen tilted Ariana's head up, her unsettling silver eyes examining her. "You look too soft to be from my kingdom."

"I'm not soft," Ariana couldn't help but reply indignantly. She had been through far more than she had ever imagined since falling into this world. Soft she most definitely was not.

"Of course not, dear." The Queen's lips quirked upward again, and Ariana felt all the condescension seeping through that one small action.

Taking a deep breath, she schooled her temper as best she could. "I'm looking for my friends," she started, relieved when the Queen let her hand drop and stepped back. Ariana was not one for sharing her personal space, after all. "I lost them in the city. Their names are Jon and Sophia."

"And why would I know where they are?" the Queen asked, her skirts swirling as she turned and sauntered toward her throne. She sat down daintily, as though the seat were not made of iron. "And your name is?"

"My name is Ariana."

"Hmm, can't say I know any Arianas in my kingdom. Nor any Sophias, nor Jons." She tapped her lip thoughtfully. "Something tells me that's not quite what you're after."

"They're exactly what I'm after." Ariana cleared her throat uncomfortably. Doran had forbidden her from mentioning his name, and it took all of her willpower not to take a gamble and ask about him anyway. "I'm also looking for my father, Finn Allard."

"Finn Allard?" asked the Queen, her face impassive. "He's been quite troublesome in the past. Why are you looking for him?"

"He's my father." Ariana tipped her chin up defiantly. "I think that's reason enough."

"Oh, certainly." The Queen stood quickly, smoothing her skirt almost absentmindedly before descending the two steps and walking back toward Ariana. She still had not released her from her uncomfortable kneeling position. "And what do you want to do with that traitor? I could kill him, you know, and I certainly should."

"You most certainly should not!" Ariana's words came out in a strangled shout. Kill her father? For what? He was a university professor, not a terrorist. "He's the best man I know. He could never be a traitor!"

"Oh, it's very sweet that you think so." The Queen was circling her now, occasionally reaching out to card a hand through her curls.

Ariana shivered in disgust, growing more uncomfortable and disheartened the longer she knelt on the unforgiving stone. Even if she wanted to get up and leave, she was pretty sure her leg had fallen asleep, so it would not be a graceful or smooth escape.

"Although, I never knew Finn had a daughter. Remarried after all, did he?"

"No." Ariana hated being needled like this, and the already tenuous hold she had on her temper slipped its leash. "I have no mother," she couldn't help adding in a vicious tone. She didn't need a mother to be whole—her father was plenty, thank you very much. Now if she could just find him, she'd be happy.

"Interesting."

"Hardly," Ariana scoffed. The Queen's smirking face reappeared in her line of sight, and she cringed when the cold fingers took her jaw in a firm grip. The mocking look on the Queen's face only served to anger her even further.

"Were you not good enough for your dear mother?" crooned the Queen. "Or was your father too weak to fight for her?"

"Only a coward leaves their kid," Ariana spat angrily. She held the Queen's gaze unflinchingly, even though her jaw was beginning to smart. How had their simple plan gone so far awry?

"Is that really what you think?" Lowering her hand, the Queen leaned in and regarded Ariana carefully.

"Yes," she snapped. "What does this have to do with my friends? Or my father?"

"More than you know." The Queen seemed utterly calm, gazing at her without blinking. "Although, my love, you should be more careful. Blood is thicker than water and all that."

"What are you talking about?" Ariana's stomach dropped to her boots, her mind racing to connect the dots. "I want nothing to do with you!"

"Tsk, tsk. That's no way to speak to your mother, now, is it?" The Queen's lips curved into a satisfied smirk, and Ariana stared at her in shocked silence. This was definitely not part of her plan.

Elise Thiessen

Green Eyes

AN EXCERPT FROM "FOREST," A FANTASY NOVEL

The arms that held her were thick and strong, and her cheek was pressed against a firm chest. A canopy of trees waved overhead, filtering the fading daylight between shadows. Nym was moving—swaying—but not of her own volition. Someone carried her, and their breaths were harsh and loud in her ears. Her clothes were damp and smelled musty, as though she'd taken a swim without undressing. Her front was stained with blood, but it was faded and pink, as though washed.

Fear struck, drumming up her heartbeat and heightening her senses all at once—the feeling of the arms trapping her, the smell of damp clothes, the scent of pine on a stranger's breath. When she looked up, green eyes scowled down at her from under a low brow and a head of dark hair, still damp and curling at the ends.

"You're awake," he said. His voice was unfamiliar to her. The only voice she knew was the Master's, and his had grown thin and stretched with age. This man had a low timbre that she felt in her very bones. She couldn't speak for fear. Who was he? What would he do to her?

Her heart stuttered in her chest. Where was she? What had happened to her Master?

The man stopped walking. "I'm going to set you down. You might be a bit unsteady."

Her bare feet hit damp earth and her knees almost gave way. The stranger steadied her by grasping her arm. His grip had the potential to break her bone. She tried not to cringe at his touch. She ought to push him away. She ought to run.

She was tied to this stranger by a rope at her waist.

"Who are you?" She didn't look at his face when she asked. She barely managed to speak.

"It doesn't matter."

"Where is Master?"

A hoarse bark escaped him—something like a laugh, full of derision, the way the Master laughed at her when she did something stupid. He tugged at her arm to make her start walking, and she had to rush her feet to keep up. "Shouldn't you be thanking me?" he asked, as though he didn't mean to say it out loud at all.

Her eyes scanned the ground, frantic. A tree root reached up and tripped her, but the man dragged her on. The Master had done the unthinkable, but he couldn't have meant it. He must have had a reason—he would have explained it to her if this man hadn't interrupted their lives.

"Thanking you for what?" she breathed. Her heartbeat rose, and her breaths came faster. Shallower.

"If I hadn't come when I did, you might have been killed."

He knew she wouldn't have died. He had to know. Did he not see she was healed already?

"You left him to die!" she whispered.

"Your master stabbed you with a knife. He was trying to kill you!" His grip on her arm tightened, and she resisted, planting her feet and pulling away. The man stopped in his tracks. His green eyes turned and stabbed at her with his dark glower, daring her to try anything to free herself.

"He was good to me," she gasped. The Master was alone, and cold, in their small house. The sun would have moved on from their clearing. Who was going to wrap him in blankets and stoke the fire this night?

"I suppose the knife to your chest was just an accident?" His words cut just as sharp.

"What do you want?" Nym demanded.

He dismissed her with a click of his tongue. Then he laughed. "It's all your kind deserves anyhow."

"At least tell me why you took me?"

He let out an angry breath. "Like you don't know."

He wasn't going to give her anything with this hatred between them. Nym swallowed against the tightness in her throat. She didn't want to cry. She would only be humiliated if she cried.

She tried again in a fluttering voice. "Where we're going . . . ?"

"That's enough questions."

"Please, just —"

He jerked on the rope and she stumbled and fell hard on her knees. "Stop. Talking."

His touch was almost gentle when he set her back on her feet. They trudged on, step by step, over the soft forest floor. The man brushed at bugs flying around his ears and eyes. They were near water—a river or a stream somewhere. The Master had taught her how the damp drew insects and insects drew bats. She looked up to search the dark spaces between trees for the rapid flap of wings. When her feet sank into the ground, she almost fell.

She looked down. They were up to their ankles in a thick forest swamp. They were soon both soaked past their knees.

They were halfway to the opposite shore when he pulled up short and tugged on the rope. She stumbled, her feet sloshing and sinking into mud and mulch. She opened her mouth to protest, but he clamped a hand over her lips and shot her a steely glare in the fading light. His fingers smelled of steel, and words shouted at her from his eyes: Quiet. Danger. Keep close.

His hand clutched her jaw tight enough to cause her pain, but she didn't dare move lest her feet disturb the water. That was when she heard the leaves rustle out of rhythm—so quiet, so brief, like a whisper—and the slow crack of a twig underfoot.

Her breath caught. His grip tightened. Something—someone—was out there. And not far off.

His eyes warned her to hold her tongue before he pulled his hand away from her lips—and chaos erupted. Something hulking burst out from the bushes ahead of them and flew forward in an ambush, to which the green-eyed man reacted most unpleasantly: he grabbed Nym by the back of her head and threw her face-first to the ground.

The swampy, water-logged, and mulch-filled ground.

She struggled her way up out of the water, spluttering and coughing bile and mud. The rope burned on her skin, even through her wool tunic. She struggled—desperately—to find a way to her feet, up from the marsh, so that she could breathe, while feet and bodies sloshed water and mud around her from all sides and the rope yanked her back and forth with no warning.

"*Down!*" The command came from the only voice she now knew, and she obeyed.

Spluttering. Coughing. Sloshing. Thuds and grunts and a wild howl of pain, followed by a heavy splash. Nym floundered, trying to right herself. A strong hand gripped her forearm and dragged her to her feet, ushering her forwards before she could steady herself or even think of understanding what was happening.

"Run!" Her green-eyed captor. He had her still. Was that relief she felt?

They splashed to shore, with his grip threatening to rip her arm from her shoulder while her feet flailed in an effort to keep up with him. She could make out nothing but shadows and dark obstacles that could be trees or something more sinister. She couldn't tell. She was still hacking water and mire from her lungs—drowning as she ran—and she was soaked from head to toe, dripping with wet and mud. She shivered under a wash of cold evening air. Tree branches and leaves lashed at her face, her neck, her arms. Tree roots crawled up to trip her every step and branches clawed at her back, trying to hold her in place. The green-eyed man dragged her relentlessly on, offering no sound or sign of tiring.

"Wh-who?" The word came out in a gasp, but he shushed her. The exertion—she could hardly breathe. He suddenly yanked her toward him and, before she even had time to think of resisting, swung her over his shoulder like she weighed nothing. He held her down with an arm and wove his way through the trees, away from the sounds of pursuit.

Shivering in his grasp, she finally found the time to cough up her lungful of water and replace it with cold, fresh air.

"Not far now," the green-eyed man breathed as he ran. She wondered if he was talking to himself. "If we don't make it soon … we'll be overrun."

Samara Malkin

Porcelain

AN EXCERPT FROM A NOVEL ABOUT A BALLERINA WHO SUCCUMBS TO THE HAUNTING PRESSURES OF HER CAREER

Pippa locked herself in the bathroom, her hip throbbing. She hobbled toward the mirror. The lilting notes of her childhood music box spun up in her mind, the little porcelain ballerina perfectly undulating in its pirouette. Pippa closed her eyes, blotted out the mocking image. She would never be as perfect as porcelain. Not if things like this kept happening. Pain shot through her mind and her eyes flew open again.

Drawing closer to the mirror, she pulled up her tutu, struggling against the mass of crinoline, and pulled down her tights. She traced her finger around the blossoming bruise that spread out from the red petal-like puncture where the corner of the set piece had pierced her hip in the fall.

She scowled. He'd dropped her, she thought. It wasn't her fault, she didn't make mistakes like that. He messed up the lift and he dropped her. Tears as hot as embers pricked her eyes and her throat constricted. Another tremor, like the one that had just happened on stage moments before she fell, seized her leg muscles, shaking her thigh, and she stumbled sideways off the leg. No, no, she thought, squeezing her eyes shut again. This was his fault, not hers. There was nothing wrong with her.

Pippa angled closer to the mirror, squinting. The wound wept the same clear runny fluid that burst out of her blistered toes after hours of rehearsal. A drop of the fluid, mixed with blood, dribbled down her leg. She swiped it up with her finger and frowned at the stickiness. She grabbed a handful of paper towels and pressed them against her glistening hip, wincing at the pressure.

When she tried to pull the paper away, it resisted. She tugged. Up came the paper towel, and up ripped Pippa's skin with it, the welt cracking open wider. She shrieked.

Blood bubbled from the torn flesh, streaming down her leg. Something white stuck out from inside her hip. A piece of paper towel, she thought. More sticky blood dribbled down her leg.

Whimpering, she wiped at the welt, trying to clean the mess. The more she wiped, the more clearly she saw the white object. Her thoughts jumped, scattered. It wasn't paper towel, she could see that now. Her mind ticked through the options. Surely it wasn't deep enough to be bone. But if not bone ... With a moan, she began to wipe more frantically, trying to get the wretched thing out.

She grabbed another wad of paper towel and scavenged into her hip, brushing and brushing away the smearing of red that frothed out. She had to get the thing out before it dug into her further, but the blood wouldn't stop and she couldn't see it anymore. Already the muscles in her leg were stiffening, adapting to it. The thing was growing larger, becoming her. She could feel it, clinging to her skin with its sharp, nasty edges.

She threw the last clump of paper towel to the floor. There—yes—now she was certain. A small white shard of smooth porcelain glinted back at her. It was nestled in her hip, fused deep into the muscle. She blinked, shook her head. The porcelain remained. She brought a shaking finger to it, tapped it with her fingernail. It sank a little deeper, tightening its grip.

Gritting her teeth, she dug into her hip with her fingernail until she found the edge of the porcelain. Her vision wavered in and out. She tried to focus on her panting breath. The searing pain mixed with waves of nausea, and an acidic slime crept up her throat. The porcelain didn't want to leave. She gasped as she dug further in, squeezing the porcelain between thumb and index finger and tugging. It resisted, as though she were trying to pull a barnacle from a rock. The porcelain burrowed itself further in; it had made itself a cozy home within her.

She tightened her grip on the piece, pulled harder. Choking on a scream, she separated the shard from her hip with a suctioning squelch. Still breathing hard, she held it up and eyed the mocking porcelain. She tossed the piece into the wastebasket, where it fell without a sound, and rubbed her eye, her head throbbing. She held her breath, but her chest continued to flutter, and tears dribbled from her chin.

The music box's melody danced up inside her mind again and she straightened, her spine cracking, eyes darting around the empty bathroom. The ballerina spun toward her, its once demure mouth forced upwards in a broken smile. The corners of the mouth cracked up into the cheeks like miniature lightning bolts. A malicious glint flashed in its porcelain eye.

Pippa's skin goosepimpled, the pressure building behind her own eye. Hesitantly, she peered into the trash can. Her skin crawled and she straightened roughly, her spine cracking again. The was no piece of porcelain in the trash.

She rubbed her eye again.

The music box grew louder, throbbing in her head, a cranking whine that split her mind apart. The ballerina's mouth cracked open fully, the deathly shrieking music vomiting out from within her.

Pippa lifted her gaze to the mirror, looked with trepidation at the gangly woman hunched before her. She leaned closer, eyes wide. It bulged behind her eye, she was sure of it—a shiny white piece of porcelain, clinging to her eye socket, pressing through the skin.

The ballerina raised a shaking hand up to her eye, fingernails curling in.

K. J. Kwon

The Bully

AN EXCERPT OF AN HORROR NOVELLA

I feared morning would come too soon and take away my imaginary self, to replace it with the insignificant, pathetic me.

Lying on my sweat-covered bed, I blankly looked at the ceiling and questioned myself.

Have I done anything wrong?

I closed my eyes, but I couldn't sleep. Beside me, the square black mobile phone kept on vibrating, as if it was enticing me to reach for it. From afar it looked innocent, harmless, but I knew once I got near it, it would bite me with its colourful texts and rhythmic sound. I knew to stay away from it, but it kept luring me, as if I were an insect attracted to light.

I wanted to switch it off, but to do so, I had to take the bait.

I reached for the phone and immediately blamed myself. It rattled and spilled out notifications of unread messages. Its vibration shook my heart, and now ringtones pierced through my ears. Somehow, Han Dabin had found a way to encroach upon my already disturbed evening and pull me into harsh reality. She had bombarded me with new assignments overnight, like a hunter waiting for me to step right into the trap she had set up. She had assigned two more fresh projects with impossible deadlines after I had innocently left the office earlier tonight.

The digital texts brimmed over the screen, rearranged their shapes, and formed themselves into a long, thorny vine. Dripping black digital ink, it crawled out of my phone and curled around me. I writhed in agony, but I couldn't break loose. The harder I squirmed, the more strongly the digital vine pulled me close and forced my eyes open. Before I realized what I was doing, I had finished reading all the messages Dabin had sent me.

I sank onto the bed and closed my eyes. My eyelids fluttered, perhaps from exhaustion or from anger. So I pictured the scene—the long stretch of green horizon and a group of sheep, some encrusted in mud, standing afar, chewing on grass, silently. Birds whistled as they flew over my head. The serenity soothed me as I began counting sheep.

One, two, three, four...

I stopped counting when a high-pitched wind whispered in my ears. I held my breath. Right next to the fifth sheep, I spotted a figure standing in a long white dress. Her black hair stretched long, touching the ground. She stared at me from where she stood in the middle of the herd, motionless. Slowly she lifted her arms and pointed at me. I wheezed for air.

In the blink of an eye, darkness enveloped the entire field. In another blink, the woman stood right in front of me. With her cloggy hair, her soulless eyes, and her mouth ajar, she looked too familiar. I was sure she was Dabin.

Her mouth gaped wide, like she was about to feast on me. And in the time it took me to take a breath, she was upon me.

Something shook me and I sprang out of bed. It was the alarm clock.

This nightmare irked me, and my patience ran out. My boss had not promoted me, and I needed to talk some sense into her.

The high-rise I worked in looked nothing like it had on my first day of work. Now it was a venue of torture, blighted by lies and conspiracies against me. The clear glass entrance to the office felt like a gateway to hell, and my soft-spoken boss appeared more villainous than the devil itself. She was constantly on the lookout for vengeance.

Today this would change, once and for all. Today was my chance to send her the clear message that I refused to be exploited and that I demanded rightful compensation.

I sat down at my desk, located right in front of my boss's. Through the glass door I saw her entering the office, wearing earphones. Our eyes met. I nodded at her and mouthed "good morning," but she kept staring at me as she walked past, her Prada coat fluttering like the devil's cape. Her perfume stung my nose like sulfur and the sound of her heels clicking stabbed my ears.

She sat at her desk in front of me. "Aren't you even going to say 'good morning'?"

"I did when you walked in."

"No. I didn't hear you say it."

"Ma'am, I nodded."

"I'm not a dog, you know? If you see your boss walk in, you get up and say, 'Hi.' And why are you talking back to me? This doesn't have to be this difficult. All you need to do is apologize and say, 'Hi.' What is wrong with you today?"

"I'm sorry. Hi."

"See how easy that was? By the way, did you submit our marketing strategy to Lucky? I just received an email from them."

"No, ma'am. I was waiting for your approval."

"Do you have any idea how important they are to us? You know it would be tens of thousands of dollars if we lost them as a client."

"Ma'am, I sent you the proposal last week and I was waiting for you to respond."

"You know I was off last week, right? You need to focus and act professionally. If I'm not present, you need to make your own decisions for once, I beg you. I'm not your babysitter. You need to get your act together."

"Ma'am, last time I sent a proposal to Lucky without your approval, you insisted that I needed to wait until you signed off."

"I can't believe I'm having this conversation with you again. That was a totally different situation. When you submitted the report last time, I was sitting right here. It was as though you were saying to my face that you didn't have a boss and you would do whatever you felt like."

"Ma'am. That was not how it happened. You were on holiday. I was waiting for you to approve—"

She cut me off. "Are you talking back to me? Why are you talking to me like that? What is wrong with you?"

"I'm sorry, ma'am."

"Listen, you're not a kid. You've been working for this company for more than five years. I need you to grow up and make your own decisions from time to time. Sometimes it's harder talking to you than my ten-year-old daughter." As she stared at me, her pupils expanded, then disappeared. Her face paled, and her mouth twitched and began spitting out an incomprehensible sound like a squeaky faucet.

I blinked in surprise. The figure slowly changed back to my boss. She seemed to be mumbling inaudible words. Then she spoke again. "Are you spacing out or something?" she said quietly, flicking my forehead. "I'll be back after the 9:00 a.m. meeting. Submit the proposal to Lucky before I return."

"Miss Han, I need to speak to you."

"Speak."

"In private, please?"

"Gosh, what is wrong with you today? Why can't you leave me alone for one second? Okay. Let's go out. I need a smoke."

Smoke from her cigarette swirled past my face as I carefully assembled my thoughts and chose my words.

Not a single muscle on her pale white face moved, and her eyes were fixed on mine as if she was telling me she knew exactly what I was about to say, as if she was warning me against saying anything.

I blew out the toxic air that had filled my lungs and said, "I saw the promotion notice yesterday, boss."

Koreen Heaver

Grounded

AN EXCERPT FROM A NOVEL

Emma takes desperate measures to free Luke from a deadly curse

Emma had spent the early evening gathering everything she could think of that was grounded and solid. With deft hands she moved about the kitchen. She scrubbed clean the white roots and placed them on a sheet to roast in the oven. She hoped it would bring out some sweetness in the ghostly pieces.

She scrubbed the lemon-sized stones in the kitchen sink. They shone in her hands under the cool running water. On the small stove behind her, a large pot of broth simmered. Placing the freshly washed stones on the cutting board, she began to ready the moss, shaking out into a bucket the beetles that had travelled unknowingly so far from their homes. Later, she would find a place to set them free. Stirring her hands through a small bowl of warm water to dissolve the salt, she laid the moss in it to soak. She set it aside, careful not to spill. The brine would tenderize the green moss and heighten its weighty flavour.

The rich soil from the cotton sack flowed easily as she jostled it through a fine sifter, removing any lumps and small, unnecessary pebbles. *They might not soften in the broth*, she thought, *and they would be hard to chew*. She sprinkled the fine soil into the mortar and pestle, placed a few of the roasted roots on top, and ground it into a tawny paste. The earthy scent filled the kitchen, and she snuck a peek at Luke.

He was still sitting in the overstuffed recliner in the dim living room. His shoulders drooped, and his head hung low. The peppery scent of the ground earth reached him and he shifted in his chair. Emma took that as a sign that she was on the right path.

She stirred the paste into the simmering broth, then finely chopped the rest of the roots and added them to the brewing pot. She took the freshly washed stones and grated them into the broth. She cringed and clenched her teeth against the hollow, dense sound that echoed in the kitchen as the hard stone scraped against the metal teeth of the grater. *They will be much easier to digest grated*, she thought. Stirring the soup, she leaned over the pot and drew the scent to her nose with a quick wave of her hand. She smiled; the pungent soil broth had a kick to it. Just the soup to keep you grounded.

As the soup simmered away, she set the table, humming a little. She hoped this earthy stew would cure Luke's floating curse once and for all. He was succumbing to the illness; already he looked less dense than he had this morning. This stew could give him the grounding anchor he needed. She allowed herself a fleeting moment of triumph. *Yes*, she thought, *this was very clever.*

She set a spoon on the table; a chill washed over her. Deep down, she knew they were in over their heads.

The last ingredient was the moss, which she had patted and rolled into perfect small French dumplings and slipped into the pot. She dished up the soup into a mismatched pair of china bowls and gently placed the tiny moss boulettes so they did not separate. She had rolled them so carefully that the small specks of the moss's golden capsules still protruded on thin stalks above its leafy surface. She sprinkled a few clips of the green summer grass on top.

Emma sat by the bed and watched as Luke's laboured breath drove him deeper into sleep. She waited until the earthy soup took ahold of him and grounded him deep into the bed. His limbs lay heavy, immobile.

Reaching both hands under the bed, she dragged out a large stone.

She struggled to bring it up to the bed's surface, where she paused, all the while keeping her eyes on Luke. He murmured in his sleep, and she waited until he was still again before she placed the heavy stone on his stomach. She was not going to let him float away tonight.

Emma dreamed that night. She had a sharp scalpel and sliced expertly through Luke's olive skin. Like a true surgeon, stoic and calculating, she folded back the layers of his chest to reveal the ribcage. Through the bars on the cage she could see his heart beating. It thumped slow and weak, *lub-lubb, lub-lubb*. It seemed to have a coating on it. She cracked open the rib cage and swung it wide to get a closer look.

She adjusted the mask covering her mouth. It was actually a folded and creased map of Paris, an origami version of a surgeon's mask. There were marks, placeholders, showing where they had been. The map was sepia-stained and much older than the one they had been using. The wishing tree was crudely drawn on it at Madelaine Square. Rue Lepic was marked with a bold red line. It traced along the curve in the street just where they had climbed to Sacré-Coeur.

In her hand was a pair of tweezers. She started to nudge the coating on his heart, gently scraping and tugging at it. Feathers. A layer of small, fine feathers was covering his heart.

She angled the tweezers to grasp the first feather. It was pale grey and wet. A clear slime pasted it to the softly beating heart. She carefully lifted the first barb and separated it from its translucent vane. The tip of the tiny barb was pronged and sharp; it caught and deeply embedded itself into his beating heart.

She tugged at the barb. It suctioned loose with a wet pop, and his heart started bleeding. She tried to put it back exactly where she had lifted it from, but as she laid it back down, blood bubbled through the separated barbs. She patted down the feathers, deeper into the slime covering his heart, but it was no use. Blood seeped between each wet feather.

There was too much blood. It filled the cavity and flowed over the rungs of his ribcage. She jabbed the tweezers into the feathers, trying to stop up the small gashes. The tweezers only plunged into the soupy blood and did not make contact with the heart below. She cast them aside and pressed her hands against his ribs until the blood ran over those too. Helpless, she watched as the blood ran down his chest and filled the operating table. She shivered as his life oozed out of him.

Lorraine Erickson

The Night

You were an only child. You did not know your mother, so you were raised by your auntie. From the time of your birth, she told you fantastical tales of the night. Eventually, she led you out in the night and slowly introduced you to its beauty and magic. First only from the doorway, and then a few steps out but shielded by the low dipping branches of the oak tree, and finally out and into the circle, where you were welcomed.

You didn't know you were different. You thought everyone could see it, the light that blew in from the west at night—the light that held the magic. You spent your days in harmony, blissful and content, waiting for the night to arrive again. When the others told you that the night held only terror for them, you could not understand. There were no whirling dervishes in your night, no screaming banshees, no black hole of nothingness that swallowed the rest of them whole. No, for you the night exploded with brilliance, full of shifters that came clothed in luminescence and danced and laughed and held you close.

You lived in a small hut, a tent, really, with just enough posts to give the illusion of walls. You were happy there. On the night your auntie passed, she asked to be taken outside one last time. You took her beyond the oak tree, and you held her, and you eased her way. You knew you would see her again, in the night. The shifters came, garbed in even more brilliance than you had become used to, and they took her with them, passing her into the next place. Their soulful call-and-response chanting kept the settlement up for hours, and you joined in with them, knowing the songs from your heart.

While the settlement was inclusive and loving, they did not want you with them or their children at night. So, though you were only ten, they let you live alone, your strangeness worn like an apron. You spent your daylight hours with the others. You ate your meals with them and played in the forest with them, but at dusk you went back to the hut and squatted in the door, waiting.

In the morning, you would often sleep late, worn and exhausted from the night. Sometimes your feet would be raw and bleeding, the dancing having gone on for hours. On those days you stayed in your hut and the others brought food to your door.

Some nights, the shifters lifted you, carrying you high above the settlement, and took you out and over the land. You saw great wonders there: a land filled with pink water, where immense sea creatures swam and played; a land that was only trees, so thick you could not see through them; and a land that was a sheer wall of marble that stretched beyond the heavens, and where the people lived in holes dug into the cliff face.

On the mornings after these trips, you would be full to bursting with what you had seen. Early on, you learned that the only one you could talk to about this was the old man. The old man alone would let you speak of the things that the others did not want to hear about. But even his patience was small, and so you kept your stories to things that could be talked about in the daylight.

The years passed for you, the days full in the growing settlement. You reached adulthood, but marriage was not for you. Though your face was handsome and your body compelling, no other wanted to be with you in the night. You did not think you had been robbed. You would not have given up the night for any of them. So you gravitated to the very ill and to the dying. Sometimes, when the dying had no one to spend that last night with but you, you would take them out into the night and let them witness the magic as you saw it, and you would let the shifters take them. The others did not like this practice. Some spoke of it as a sacrifice, that you were practising blacker magic than was allowed.

When someone died amidst family, they did not pass to the other place but stayed and lingered on. The others preferred this, having houses full of ghosts. But you did not like it, for you knew these ghosts were sad. They asked you to take them with you at night, and sometimes you would slip one out. But after, the price would be high. You would be banished to your hut until a crisis, until an illness so great that only you could sit with it. Then the others would have you back into their homes, and the ghosts would sigh and look at you in longing, and you would nod and promise that one night you would take them out too.

The shifters taught you about grace, showed you ways that would help the suffering of the others. Amidst the feasting and the dancing and the travelling, they would stop and tell you stories, and you would ask them questions. Their answers, like their stories, were slippery, though, and sometimes they fooled you. You learned their language, their way of being, and sometimes you even thought you were one with them. But you were not. Not yet.

Sometimes you would have visitors during the day, wanting more from you than stories and healing, wanting you. But you were not interested. Not at first. But then you realized that you wanted a child, one of your own to share the night, so you carefully chose one of the others and visited with him often, until you were sure of your condition, and then you ended it. He was not happy to be spurned, and the settlement was not happy with your condition. But you birthed the child, alone in the night, encircled by the shifters. You bore the child into the shimmering light, and the magic entered her and it shone from her eyes.

Your child was beautiful, and she craved the night even more than you. The shifters would take the child and pass her amongst them, laughing with her, enraptured by her huge eyes and chubby fingers. The others loved the child too. They also wanted her near, and when she could walk, you let her visit the houses of those who had fed you as a child. Your child grew, but she was too wild for school, and she spent her days following you and learning your arts. She spent her nights also following you, and then leading you, as she embraced the magic.

The nights were full, so full that the settlement moved you into a new hut, farther away, where your nighttime revelries would not disturb them. They heard only the howling of the wind and the screeching of metal against metal, and it kept them up. They were tired and wanted more sleep.

You grew old, much older than the others, though you did not look it. The magic clothed you and kept you magnificent. But you were old and you were tired. Your child, now grown, had taken over your work with the old and the newly arrived, and you slept all day, waking only to go out in the night. The shifters were gentle with you, coaxing you to stay with them, to follow them when night passed to morning. Your child watched, curious but silent.

One night you did not want to see morning—not that morning or any other morning—and you turned to your child to say goodbye. You did not ask her to come; you knew she would find her own way at the time that was right for her. But you, your time was now, and you turned and took the hands of the shifters before you, and as the sun rose behind you, you entered the never-ending night. Your clothes fell off, and luminescence dripped from your fingertips. You could fly on your own now, your body made of only light and luminescence.

You came back sometimes to your settlement, drawn to see your child and to dance with her in the light. You sometimes helped the others enter the night with you when they were sick and ready to pass, and those were good nights for all. And some nights, the most beautiful of nights, you were the howling banshee, the metal-on-metal screeching that kept the others inside.

Rory Andrew Stevens

Fission

The drive home was so bad, I just left my car on the road and ran the rest of the way. I wasn't going to die in traffic. I wanted to see you again, so we could go blind under a mushroom cloud together and melt into each other, become a two-headed shadow against a wall that maybe an alien would see.

But the crowds on the Fourth Street Bridge were as bad as the gridlock. People were screaming that the missiles were coming. Somebody said to get down under the street. He had a flushed red face. I couldn't imagine where I would have hidden, though. The missiles that hit the East Coast melted the rock and boiled the ocean. Instead, I thought of you and how you must have cried when the emergency tone cut into your favourite TV show.

You always loved this world and hated to be alone. It would be the last cruelty of this terrible earth if you died alone, soaking tears into apartment shag. So, I ran for you, like I did when you blacked out in the tub or told me this life was more than you could do, from some dead-end road near the sea. I shoved upstream against the downstream of shoulders in a madhouse rush of terrified humans. None knew where to go or what to do, but I had spent thirty years in this human suit: I knew what it could and couldn't do. It couldn't take a bright white fireball that drank the soil and spit it back as radioactive dust at a bent-over city with glass beaches. But it could soften the worst days with an embrace that lingered. I knew a human could make personal magic that the universe—and its terrors—would never understand.

We were eight blocks apart when the first flash opened the clouds. I tried to cover my eyes, but they went black in an instant. We were seven blocks apart when the heat melted me away. There was pain and I thought of how you must have screamed. I apologized before it melted my brain.

I never thought I would think again, but I came alive in a sea, as some slick and limbless minnow that wriggled out of an egg, reborn as something far removed from the human I had been. Free of the egg—which was now just a tissue clinging to the reef—I was carried into a current that pulled me out into the waves. The swells split the orange light of the sky like a rose window, hidden from everything above the tide. The current grew hotter as I pulled wildly from side to side. I was small fry and my flippers were feathers in a hurricane.

Ahead of me the water was pulled up by the atom bomb. Its tower was a siphon that grasped at the sea with a grimacing fireball eye. I'm not sure if it's a thing minnows do, but I saw another silver streak far behind me that I knew was you. I knew our souls had been thrown again into the same soup. I was certain it was you. No minnow would escape that boiling tower of atomic heat, but I struggled against its current—and back toward you—because how many can say goodbye once they've once died?

The scales were peeling off my back and rolling over my eyes in a jet stream of sequin flesh as I began to boil to death. I couldn't scream, but I tried. You were a foot away, but a foot in a current that turbulent was like a league or a thousand miles above the sky. You were scared, and I could see that in the frantic twists of your tailfin. You dodged the crumbling flesh of raining chum that was drawn up into the nuclear spout, boiled, and rained back out, only to cycle through again. But my efforts were not a loss because—before my small minnow strength gave out—your tail brushed my nose like you used to do when you teased me that you'd stolen it then ran from our couch. *You got my nose*, I thought, then let the hateful fire pull me up.

I had wondered—when I was a mammal—how much fish feel, and I can say it is quite a lot. Water runs rough as sand when you have no skin and you are bursting in a flash boil of salt water. I thought of that lobster you wouldn't boil, and knew you were right, but you still ate it with me, and I guess karma knew too, because up we went to the crest of the mushroom cap. We died close, but not close enough for me to apologize for melting in the street and leaving you to cry alone. Then my little minnow head popped and I died again.

But, again, I awoke. This time I could hear the rumble through a thin blue shell that was glowing with a gloomy light across the egg's dome. At once, I felt suffocated and itched for the air. I pushed my hard beak against the shell until it split its jigsaw piece free and let in the fire's light. My vision was sharper than that first day after Lasik—the Lasik you bought me, but could you remember why? Do the dead remember giving a gift, even after I insisted I would never celebrate my birthday again? From my nest, I saw the fading flash that had melted and boiled those other me's away. A flash that was maybe two miles from the island I was being born on.

I flexed my sticky wings to crack the egg, then I was free in my weak and wet bird body, which clung with its feathers ten storeys above a smoldering jungle. The heat of the burning underbrush was shrinking the green palm leaves into crooked black fingers, curling as a fist over the climbing fire. My nest of twigs was already smoking, perhaps from the radiation shower. It must have been spreading along a mile of upwind gust from the collapsing mushroom cloud. But maybe I could fly? I wanted to try when I decided you must be nearby. Twice we had landed together in the swirling smoke of experienced time. *Some rhythms must be constant*, my bird brain surmised. I knew somewhere you were nearby and afraid to die.

The smoke and heat burned my wide eyes but dried my wings and gave me confidence to dive. I leapt from the bound basket of branches that held one other blue egg, which I had been sitting with on the cliff-side. I leapt and—as gravity took hold—I heard that last egg crack, then saw your beak emerge. My bird thoughts were richer than a fish's, but only formed once I was hurtling down: *Oh no, you were right beside me!* I flipped and writhed in the blackening air, trying to fight my way back to you, but those bent arms barely moved. So, the wind roared against my regrets. *I could have left early and been by your side, but instead I insistently lied and finished out the day because I thought the alerts were surely untrue.* Then I struck a branch and was Kentucky fried.

I couldn't hear or see, but I bumped against crowding forms in some soup. The fading static of a lightning blast permeated through my cell and then I multiplied. Then I polymerized. I had no thoughts and no sense of time, but somehow I knew that with this saline I would find legs—and somewhere ahead something like me would find something like you, and then you would never again die alone.

Contributors

FOREWORD

Carleigh Baker is an *âpihtawikosisâniskwêw*/Icelandic writer who lives as a guest on the unceded territories of the xʷməθkʷəy̓əm, Skwxwu7mesh, and Tsleil-Waututh peoples. Her work has appeared in *Best Canadian Essays, The Short Story Advent Calendar*, and *The Journey Prize* anthology. She also writes reviews for the *Globe and Mail* and the *Literary Review of Canada*. Her debut story collection, *Bad Endings* (Anvil, 2017), was a finalist for the Rogers Writers' Trust Award, the Emerging Indigenous Voices Award for fiction, and the BC Book Prize Bill Duthie Booksellers' Choice Award, and won the City of Vancouver Book Award.

AUTHORS

Yuki Abovearth is a writer, Japanese-English translator, and comic illustrator. She enjoys speculative fiction stories and ancient myths from around the world. She is a fan of Japanese and French literature and graphic novels.

Razielle Aigen is a Montreal-born writer whose poems and essays have appeared in both print and online publications, including *California Quarterly, Synapse, écho!*, the *Halifax Review*, and *Hinge*. Razielle works as a naturotherapist, focusing primarily on trauma resolution therapy. She holds a BA in history and contemporary studies from Dalhousie University/University of King's College in Halifax, she is an alumna of the Writer's Studio at Simon Fraser University, and she will begin a master's degree in bioethics at Université de Montréal in the fall of 2018.

Brad Akeroyd is a fourth-generation Canadian whose poetry and prose focuses on his experiences as a *hafu*: a term pertaining to a person of mixed Japanese heritage and some other ethnicity—in his case, British. Brad has had the privilege of making friends and meeting students and teachers from a diversity of cultures and social backgrounds. He uses what he has learned, and his studies of Canadian history, to tell the tales of those whose stories remain a mystery to most. Growing up in Canada as a visible minority was difficult, but writing about those experiences has become a blessing in disguise. All My Relations.

Kimber Anderson has been writing for, and working with, children for almost twenty years. Her experiences with children from preschool to high school, as both a preschool teacher and a special-needs education assistant, have helped her to create unique voices in her middle-grade novels and picture books. Through various writing courses and workshops—including the prestigious SFU creative writing program, the Writer's Studio—Kimber has been able to develop a style that kids love to read.

Nadia Ashley has been a professional actress with BBC Radio Drama. She has also directed several high school drama and theatre programs in both England and Canada. She has written plays with youth theatres and acted at the Edinburgh Fringe, as well as here in Vancouver with United Players. She had her own company, Anima Women's Theatre Company, in London in the 1980s. She has a BA (hons.) in theatre and literature from the University of East Anglia, Norwich, and a master's in education from UBC. Her poetry has been published in *English Quarterly* and performed in England as part of Poetry in a Pub.

Debbie Bateman is drawn to overlooked lives and problems we think we understand: Alzheimer's, anorexia, binge-eating, anxiety, lack of sexual desire, infidelity, and addiction. She looks for the hidden narratives. Her latest short stories focus on a group of women at midlife and their struggles with their bodies. Her personal essay "Amongst the Unseen and Unheard" was included in *Shy: An Anthology* (University of Alberta Press, 2013). Debbie makes her living as a writer and editor of learning materials and other content.

Joanna Baxter is a native Vancouverite. She has a BA in French literature and political science from the University of Victoria. She has planted trees, delivered sailboats, ski patrolled, and travelled extensively in Europe and Asia. She taught drama and art, and has owned her own design businesses since 1999. She ran twice as a candidate for city council. She is married and has two young children.

Jonathan M. Bessette lives and works in Vancouver, B.C., on the unceded Coast Salish territories of the Musquem, Tseleil-Waututh, and Squamish peoples. Here he writes poetry, short fiction, novels, and screenplays. He has published poetry in the *New Orphic Review*, fiction in *TAR magazine*, and non-fiction in *Adbusters*. He is currently working on a sci-fi novel and a poetry manuscript. For more information visit his website, www.jonathanmbessette.com.

Avalon Bourne is a writer of fiction, and is currently working on her first novel. She has a Certificate in Professional Writing and Business Communication from SFU, as well as a BA in English literature from UBC. She has spent much of her career immersed in business and corporate writing, including proposals, reports, and operational and strategic plans, but her real love is writing fiction.

Matt Brandenburg is a horror fiction writer from Kalamazoo, Michigan. He has been writing for the last couple of years, exploring broken people and haunted things. He has had pieces published in the *Sirens Call* e-zine and The Horror Tree's *Trembling With Fear*. He also writes book reviews for *Gingernuts of Horror* and *Storgy* online. During the day he works as a digital project manager for a medical device company. You can usually find him in a record store or bookstore, or frequenting one of Kalamazoo's many breweries.

Erin Brown-John is a poet based in Vancouver who works in digital marketing and engagement. She studied at The Poetry School in London, UK, with mentors Roddy Lumsden and Clare Pollard, and is currently working on a full-length collection exploring themes of family, identity, belonging, and the lack thereof.

What can we say of Ms. **Dianne Carruthers** Wood? She applied to TWS so she could write more good! With her many ideas and elaborate plans, her first lesson was to not write by the seat of her pants. With a wonderful mentor, cohort, and group, she learned to front-crawl through prosaic soup. In case you are worried, don't be confused by her diction; she may not be a poet, but she really likes fiction! If only she could, she would do it again, and if you are thinking of applying, we need some more men!

Lorne Daniel is a Canadian of Scottish and American ancestry. His poetry and non-fiction have been published in dozens of literary journals, most recently *Earthlines* (UK), *Soundings*, *Red Wheelbarrow*, *Cirque*, and *Terrain* (all U.S.). Author of four poetry collections and past winner of the Jon Whyte Memorial Essay Prize, Lorne left the literary world for many years. He has recently found his way back to the practice of writing. Lorne lives in Victoria, B.C.

Stewart Dickson writes as he cooks: he does not follow a recipe, and he produces content that looks strange and lacks nutrition, and that sometimes—surprisingly—is delicious. Stewart writes because his wife likes him to, and he draws inspiration to apply himself from her, his two rambunctious boys, and his murderous cat. Stewart is a first responder who has enjoyed a myriad of professions through travel in over forty countries: from gravedigger in England to facilitator in Saudi Arabia. Stewart currently lives in northern B.C. and enjoys embarrassing himself in pursuit of outdoor activities.

Sareh Donaher was born in Tehran, Iran, in 1978, the year of the Iranian Revolution. Sareh's family fled Iran in 1980 and lived in Europe for a year before immigrating to Canada in 1981. She is currently writing a book of poems recounting her family's escape from Iran and life in Canada. Sareh holds two bachelor's degrees from UBC, in international relations and education. Sareh's poems have been published in the the *Teachers of English Language Arts Writing Journal* (1994–95), *Elephant Journal*, and *Grilled Cheese Magazine*. She lives in Vancouver with her husband and two children.

Marian Dodds's childhood in Canada's Arctic nurtured her passion for learning across cultures. She has taught at public schools and universities, coordinated union social justice programs, designed curricula, edited teacher publications, and volunteered in Africa and Central America. She recently spent three years working in Ethiopia where, to avoid deportation from a country famous for jailing journalists, she became adept at self-censorship while blogging at *Spider Webs Unite.* The Writer's Studio is her opportunity to freely investigate the existential underbelly of her experiences within the context of colonialism, feminism, and cultural learning.

Alex Duncan is a poet, actor, and director—depending on the day. Born and raised in Vancouver, she received a BA with honours in fine arts and theatre from Bishop's University before journeying to New York to study at Circle in the Square Theatre School. She has published a children's book—*An Army of Hearts*—which she recently adapted into an award-winning short film, and is currently working on the final revisions of her first feature film script.

Maureen Duteau is an outdoors enthusiast with a penchant for writing. She grew up in a small coastal town but spent her early adult life living in Japan, where she learned to observe the world through a different lens. An avid reader and literary buff, she put her love of words to the page when she joined the Writer's Studio in 2017. Maureen has published several non-fiction articles for local publications and is currently working on a young adult graphic novel.

Rowan EB is an Egyptian Canadian writer and performer. Her work in poetry and other genres uses the power of asking (gently and bluntly) to explore winding experiences of gender, resistance, and migration. When she is not posing questions in poetry, she can be found seeking answers through social science research and grassroots community-building.

Miraya Engelage is an aspiring writer living in beautiful Langley, B.C., with her husband and their two rescue dogs. Miraya has always enjoyed writing stories in her free time, as well as reading whatever she can get her hands on. When she's not working for the family business or planning her next travel adventure, Miraya can be found at the barn with her two horses and competing at local show-jumping events.

Lorraine Erickson is a writer and artist living in Victoria. She writes short stories, non-fiction, and lyrical prose, and is currently spending all of her time exploring speculative fiction. She graduated from SFU with a BA in history. Lorraine is taking this year to pursue her writing practice in a more structured way, and to see where that leads.

Kate Flannery is a writer and attorney who lives and practises in the small college town of Claremont in Southern California. Her work in a wide range of practice areas of the law has informed her writing in many respects. Her flash fiction and poetry have been published in *Literary Alchemy*, and one of her short stories, "The Odds," will be published in a forthcoming volume of the *Chiron Review.*

Megan Frazer is a poet and memoirist who sees language as a cathartic conduit connecting her inner worries to the outside world. She completed her undergrad at UBC, majoring in history, and fed her love of writing by working at the university bookstore selling expensive pens she could not afford. Today, she is a student of the Writer's Studio at SFU, in the poetry group under the mentorship of Betsy Warland. Her writing has appeared in *The Writers Caravan* (Otter Press). She lives in Vancouver with her husband and two children, who she no longer posts about on Facebook.

Lula García was born in Mexico. She loves literature. To earn a living, she has worked in the film industry, starting as a production assistant and becoming the owner of her own film production company. She has produced five feature films; one of them is currently on Netflix. Seven years ago, she decided to embark on a new challenge in her life and moved with her family to Canada. She is working on a novel, where she is portraying ordinary characters who move in a specific time, place, and environment, showing the universal archetypes of society.

Julie Gordon is a writer and communications consultant. Originally from Toronto, she now lives in the Pacific Northwest region that is the traditional home of the Coast Salish peoples. She likes to share stories about people and place, and the abiding relationship between the two.

Averill Groeneveld-Meijer grew up in New York and The Hague, Netherlands, and spent summers in New Brunswick. She moved to Vancouver to attend UBC, where she completed a BA in human geography—to figure out where she is—and an MA in historical geography—to clarify when. Averill's current approach to time and space involves writing creative non-fiction, along with the occasional snippet of fiction thrown in for clarity.

Evie Gold is a non-fiction essay writer whose personal stories have appeared in *Thought Catalog* and *Brevity*. She has climbed the Himalayas, survived living in a tent in the Amazon rainforest, and actively avoided cult recruitment. She and her husband share a nomadic lifestyle and try to move every couple of years, so home is more of a mindset than a physical space. To learn more and sign up for her newsletter, visit eviegold.com.

Deborah Harford is a lifelong poet, nature lover, and proud single mother of one large son. A published non-fiction writer, Deborah is co-author of *The Columbia River Treaty: A Primer* and one of the voices in *Global Chorus: 365 Voices on the Future of the Planet*. She co-founded and runs a think tank on climate change at SFU and is a vocal advocate for ecologically friendly solutions to humanity's challenges. Amid all that seriousness, Deborah's heart beats fastest for poetry and its potential to reconnect people with nature—and maybe save the planet—through humour and the heart.

Koreen Heaver is a writer of speculative fiction, children's picture books, and poetry. She has a passion for visual storytelling. One of her greatest strengths lies in her ability to take the unbelievable and whimsically transform it into the plausible—while deftly entangling her readers along the way. She resides on the edge of the ocean, nestled in the urban rainforest of Vancouver, B.C. She is looking forward to publishing her first novel.

Erica Hiroko is a Chinese and Japanese Canadian writer raised on the unceded territories of the Musqueam, Squamish, and Tsleil-Waututh nations. Her work invokes queer diasporic imagination through fiction, poetry, and narrative non-fiction. Her writing has appeared in *Poetry Is Dead*, *EFNIKS*, *Schema Magazine*, and a variety of community-based publications and DIY zines.

Sriram Iyer is a British physician who is acutely aware of his Indian ancestral origins and the tangible life-and-death element of his profession. His written work is eclectic, focusing on his upbringing in a middle-class family in South India and his experience of dealing with people when they are at their most vulnerable. Dr. Iyer brings his physicianly wisdom to his stories. His forthcoming collection of linked short stories, "Broken Shards," will regale, uplift, and enrich. There is regret, but also hope in a malleable future: a high school boy embarks on a quixotic journey to meet his first crush; two ordinary men plot to kill a man they hate, but . . .; a cocky medical graduate faces harsh reality.

Brook Warner Jensen is a writer and game developer living in Vancouver. His prose is mostly a pastime, but his games can be found online at www.studio.brwarner.net. His latest game, *It's You: A Breakup Story*, is set to be released in August 2018.

Nicole Jess is an Australian of the world. Having travelled and studied extensively, she extracts her stories from lived experiences and journeys taken both locally and abroad. As a healthcare clinician, Nicole revels in the unique intimacy that is evoked by human vulnerability. She is deeply intrigued by the intersection of perceived, assumed, and projected reality. Her writing is an exploration of the kaleidoscope of thoughts, emotions, perceptions, and projections that cause us to think, act, and believe as we do: an analysis of the recipe of life.

Tamara Jong is a Montreal-born mixed-race writer of Chinese and European ancestry. Her work has appeared in *Ricepaper, Room*, and the *New Quarterly.* She is a graduate of the Writer's Studio at SFU.

Kathleen Kerwin is an emerging writer learning to straddle her professional and authorial worlds. "San Domenico" is her first published short story.

Karla Kosowan is a proud helicopter parent by day and writer by night. She loves miracles, subtext, and carbs. A longtime Vancouver resident, she doesn't think she will ever run out of stories she wants to tell.

K. J. Kwon is a South Korean storyteller obsessed with all forms of content that make him sit on the edge of his seat. In his previous news jobs, he travelled across the world to observe and record different lives and current affairs. His deep interest in untold stories and, of course, the supernatural stems from these experiences. He is currently working on a horror novella that exposes lingering concerns of greed, grudge, and exploitation in the modern day workplace. He spent nearly half of his life in China and considers Beijing his second home.

DeeDee LeGrand-Hart has discovered fiction's potency for truth-telling—although until recently she wrote exclusively non-fiction, published in national media such as *Inc.* and *Wired.* Hart earned a BA in journalism from the University of South Carolina. She earned a Certificate in Creative Writing from SFU to support her transition to fiction. Her novel in progress, "Dancing in Water," is a social satire on the identity makeovers required to endure culture shifts of the last few decades. Also in progress, her series of fictional short stories, "Out Last," reveals our intimate relationship with history, as characters witness the very last moments of a dying era.

April Lewis wrote her first poem when she was nine. Her teen years were filled with more angsty poetry, until she transitioned into writing the kind of stories she loved to read, including fantasy and science fiction. From a career as a massage therapist to an account executive, she is now ready to take the leap into sharing her novels with the public as a professional writer. Will a publisher catch her if she falls?

Shane Leydon is a writer, actor, and director from Flin Flon, Manitoba. He currently tries to score work in the city as an actor and has appeared on a few TV shows. His favourite project is the Canadian Screen Award–nominated *Hello Destroyer*, on which he worked with friends. He has a day job, too. He serves vulnerable persons in the Lower Mainland who struggle with addiction, mental illness, incarceration, and homelessness, with the John Howard Society. Here he won an award for his kindness and generosity.

Dayna Mahannah has been writing in journals since she was six years old. Her resume includes, but is not exclusive to, the following: traveller, actor (*Vulgar Drifter Girl*), blogger, journalist, and agony aunt (but not necessarily in that order). Though most of her work is based in non-fiction, she tries really hard to make stuff up from time to time. Dayna has been published in *Adbusters* magazine and *Got a Girl Crush* magazine, among others. On a recent excursion through her old diaries, she deemed the author unknown.

Samara Malkin is a fiction writer who often enjoys dabbling in the bizarre. Never one for happy endings (except in real life), her characters are bound for an adventure of misfortune. She loves to play with unreliable narrators and to mess with the minds of both her characters and readers. When she's not writing, you'll likely find her nosing through a bookstore or baking with her friends.

Vicki McLeod is a writer, poet, and columnist. She is the author of *#Untrending: A Field Guide to Social Media That Matters: How to Post, Tweet, and Like Your Way to a More Meaningful Life* (First Choice Books, 2016) and the founder of Main Street Communications, an award-winning consultancy. Currently co-authoring *The Digital Legacy Plan: A Guide to the Personal and Practical Elements of Your Digital Life Before Death* (Self-Counsel Press, March 2019) and writing a manuscript based on coming of age in the 1960s, she can be found in her home on the banks of the Fraser River, in pajamas, making something.

Katie McGarry lives in Waterloo, where she works as a mathematics laboratory coordinator at Wilfrid Laurier University. Her writing has recently appeared in the *Humber Literary Review*, *filling Station*, and *GUSH: Menstrual Manifestos for Our Time* (Frontenac House). She was a first-place winner in *Room*'s Winter 2017–18 Short Forms Contest.

Spencer Miller was born in Vancouver and grew up in idyllic Deep Cove, North Vancouver. He studied film production at Concordia University in Montreal over the span of a decade or so. Present-day Spencer teaches English at multifarious international colleges and enjoys an unreasonable amount of support from his family and his partner Claire in support of his desire to write. In his spare time he enjoys mountain sports, soccer, and playing the guitar as a devotee of heavy metal.

Carolyne Montgomery is an emerging writer recovering from a career in medicine. She has boxes of journals from the last fifty years, filled with observations about people, places, and situations. Marriage and motherhood also helped shape some of her ideas. The Writer's Studio experience is helping her to organize a variety of these thoughts into small fiction and occasional non-fiction works. Her best ideas come while she is riding her bike up steep hills, or swimming in salt water anywhere. She still thinks recipes are poetry. Her two cats unreservedly support her.

Sarah Mostaghel is a writer living in Kamloops with her loving partner and two dogs. From the diagnosis of a chronic illness at age eleven to battling depression to wondering what life path to take, poetry became a therapeutic act of self-expression, self-preservation, and sometimes self-flagellation. Upon winning a contest in April 2018, her poem was published in the *Kamloops This Week* newspaper. She is currently working on her first book of poetry.

Sabyasachi Nag is the author of two books of poetry: *Bloodlines* (Writers Workshop, 2006) and *Could You Please, Please Stop Singing* (Mosaic Press, 2015). His work has appeared or is forthcoming in several anthologies and publications, including *Grain Magazine, Contemporary Verse 2, Perihelion, R.kv.r.y Quarterly*, the *Squaw Valley Review*, the *Rising Phoenix Review*, *Void*, and the *VLQ*. A native of Calcutta, India, Sachi lives in Mississauga, Ontario, with his wife and son. He works in human resources and education.

Joseph Onodi is of Cree and Austrian ancestry; he was raised in the South Peace Region and moved to the Lower Mainland in 1989. He was awarded the 2014 Canada Council for the Arts Grants to Aboriginal Peoples: Creation Grant for Writers and Storytellers for his manuscript "Woodland Creetures." Joseph continues to refine his own style of storytelling and unique take on traditional knowledge. Visit his website, starblanketstoryteller.ca, to see more.

Spencer Lucas Oakes is a Vancouver-based Canadian writer. His work has appeared in *PRISM International, Daily Hive, Occulum Journal, Soft Cartel*, and elsewhere. His story "Melt" won second place in *PRISM*'s 2018 Short Forms contest. While working for the Vancouver Whitecaps he created and edited *MAJOR*, a free periodical focused on Canada's soccer subculture. Spencer is currently enrolled in Simon Fraser University's 2018 Writer's Studio. He also works as a copywriter.

Zahida Rahemtulla is an emerging writer of fiction and theatre. She studied literature and Middle Eastern studies at New York University in New York and Abu Dhabi. She currently works in the immigrant and refugee non-profit sector. She also serves as the local coordinator at The Shoe Project Canada, a program in which newcomer women to Canada author stories of their arrival with the support of established Canadian novelists and theatre professionals.

Tamar Rubin is a physician and poet living in Winnipeg. Her work can be found in both medical and literary journals, including *JAMA, Canadian Medical Association Journal, Hippocrates Medical Poetry Anthology, Prairie Fire*, the *New Quarterly, Vallum*, and others. She is currently at work on her first manuscript.

Lynn J. Salmon is currently working on her first-ever novel, "Loss of the *Sea Dragon*," set in Prince Rupert, B.C. Her varied work experiences include archaeology, museum curating, and shore-based coast guard radio work. She has written marine-themed articles for the web-based Nauticapedia Project and *Western Mariner* magazine, received honourable mention for short fiction in the 2017 Cedric Literary Awards, and placed second in the 2018 LitFest New West short story competition. She enjoys life—and writing—on Vancouver Island with her husband.

Emi Sasagawa is an award-winning journalist whose work has been published by the *Washington Post*, *Al Jazeera America*, and the *Tyee*. Recently, she started dabbling in creative non-fiction. She writes about her experiences being a queer woman of colour.

Wendy Naava Smolash holds a PhD in English literature from SFU, focused on nationalism and race theory. Her essay "The Opposite of Rape Culture Is Nurturance Culture" is used in counselling centres and university classrooms worldwide. Her writing appears in academic and popular publications, including *Studies in Canadian Literature*, *West Coast Line*, *Briarpatch*, and the *University of Toronto Quarterly*'s special issue *Discourses of Security, Peacekeeping Narratives, and the Cultural Imagination in Canada*. Current projects include a book on nurturance culture and a speculative fiction novella entitled "Cipher." She teaches in the English department at Douglas College and lives half-time in Montreal.

D. R. Spicer is a Vancouver-based fiction writer who loves to weave the magic of technology into human stories. He chooses to tell his tales through quirky and courageous characters. He has been an adviser to tech companies for over twenty years and brings this unique perspective to his books. While science and technology will be featured in his writing, music and cake may make appearances as well. He has completed a manuscript for a young adult novel highlighting a future that is frighteningly close to our current reality. He is also working on a spy thriller.

Isabel Spiegel is a writer living in Los Angeles. Her poetry and prose have been published in *Corium* and *No Ink.*

Rory Andrew Stevens was born, raised, and will likely die in Greater Vancouver's suburbs, probably while eating, climbing, or cooking. He knows this because he met his many iterations in the multiverse and they were all writers in Vancouver. This fact has given him the distinction of being the most consistent complexity ever found in quantum theory (S. Odin, Physocks *487*, 279–89). He just hopes to be in the only multiverse iteration where he doesn't starve.

Ann Svendsen is a sociologist by profession and a writer by choice. She is fascinated by the dynamics of relationships. Her first book, *The Stakeholder Strategy: Profiting from Collaborative Business Relationships* (Berrett Koehler, 1998), spawned an international university teaching career. She has also written non-fiction articles for numerous magazines and newspapers, including *Western Living* and the *Globe and Mail.* Ann is currently working on a novel about spiritual awakening and the vicissitudes of love. She lives on the Sunshine Coast.

Georgia Swayze has dabbled in writing for years but only recently decided that it's something she might like to pursue professionally. One day while at her soul-sucking day job, she came across a brochure for the Writer's Studio and decided to apply to the program. Her goal is to blend the darker elements of life with the comedic, and hopefully publish a book someday.

Griffin Tedeschini is a fiction writer and poet who has performed both poetry and story on numerous provincial and national stages. In 2015, they were on the Calgary Slam Poetry Team that participated in the national spoken word festival. The past three years have seen them explore both the Calgary and Vancouver poetry scenes, as well as the Vancouver story slam events. They were a featured poet on Vancouver Co-Op Radio's *Wax Poetic*, as well as a featured storyteller in their series *Terminal City Tales*. Griffin was invited to perform as a storyteller at the 2018 Verses Festival.

Benjamin Thiede has explored nature at the molecular and cellular level through many fancy high-powered microscopes in life-science research labs around the United States. Now a recovering scientist, he spends his time in business development in biotech during the day and writing speculative fiction stories by night. He lives in Vancouver with his wife and son.

Elise Thiessen grew up travelling the world on the heels of missionary parents and developed an early fascination with cultures and languages different from her own. Raised on Narnia, *The Lord of the Rings*, *Eragon*, and Harry Potter, she makes it her goal to always be reading a book in the speculative genre, to grow and refine her own storytelling skills. Elise blends the magical prose and made-up worlds of fairytales like *Graceling* by Kristin Cashore and *The Goose Girl* by Shannon Hale with the pounding, gory pace of a thriller or a fight scene from Brandon Sanderson's Stormlight Archive.

Gillian Tregidgo is continually interested in, and surprised by, the human psyche. She has worked in both physical medicine and psychiatry as an occupational therapist for the last thirty years. She has found her career to be a rich source of inspiration for her short stories and films. Her favourite moments in life occur when the unexpected comes out of the blue to excite her imagination to build stories and create a new vision. Gillian attended UBC, where she studied film production. While there, she made two short films, one of which toured North America and won several awards. Gillian is now focused on dedicating her life to writing in mixed genres.

Paula Wellings is an emerging writer and a design strategist who usually writes near-future fiction, when not obsessing over her fish tank. Her current fascination in fiction writing is exploring how small and oftentimes frivolous changes in our tools, devices, and entertainments stretch, tear, and reconstruct large swathes of a social fabric intended to hold us together.

Ann Wilson hails from rural southwestern Ontario and has lived and worked on the unceded traditional territories of Coast Salish peoples since 1980. A passionate activist for social justice, Ann has pioneered cross-sector responses to the complex issues of homelessness, addiction, unemployment, and poverty in Surrey, B.C., for the past twenty-five years. Ann sees writing as a form of inquiry and a way of knowing, which led her to pursue a master's and doctoral degree in education and to enter SFU's Writer's Studio, where she is writing in the creative non-fiction genre.

Felix Wong has lived half of his life in Vancouver and half in Hong Kong. Thanks to his upbringing, he is ninety-eight percent sure he has an advantage when it comes to writing stories that can captivate both Western and Eastern audiences. His feature film script, "One Day, Three Autumns," placed as a quarter-finalist in two competitions—which in his opinion is kind of like a backhanded compliment. He is currently working on "After Simone," a coming-of-age novel about a young man's search for a lost love in Hong Kong.

Maura Wong is a native of Hong Kong and currently still lives there.

Production Credits

Publisher
Andrew Chesham

Managing Editor
Emily Stringer

Editorial Team

Section Editors
Rebecca A. Coates – Speculative and YA Fiction Editor
Zoë Dagneault – Poetry and Lyric Prose Editor
Nikki Hillman – Non-fiction Editor
Alessia Yaworsky – Fiction Editor

Copy Editors
Brad Akeroyd
Sareh Donaher
Averill Groeneveld-Meijer
Dayna Mahannah
Spencer Lucas Oakes
Ann Wilson
Felix Wong

Production Team
Reese Kim Carrozzini – Production Editor
Joanna Baxter
Zahida Rahemtulla
Taylor Reynolds

Acknowledgments

The students of the Writer's Studio would like to thank their mentors for the guidance and insight they have provided. We would also like to extend special thanks to the mentor apprentices for their support throughout the year.

We extend our gratitude to Cottage Bistro (4770 Main Street) for graciously hosting our monthly reading series.

Joanne Betzler and Grant Smith's continued support of our program and the anthology has allowed us to make the *emerge* book launch a fun and lively event. As well, Grant's Spring session on business and tax planning for writers has helped prepare our community for the business of writing.

We would all like to thank Vancouver's local independent bookstores for selling *emerge*. We urge our readers to support the booksellers that support local writers.

We thank Jordan Abel for his mentorship of the poetry group in the Writer's Studio Online, 2017–2018.

We would like to thank John Whatley for his keynote talk at the Writer's Studio 2018 Graduation and Reunion. As well, we thank John and SFU Publications for co-publishing *emerge*. Once again, their generous support has enabled our alumni and students to work together on the production of this book.

Finally, to Betsy Warland, who planted a seed called TWS and nurtured it with great care over many years. Thank you for placing pens in our hands so firmly, empowering us as writers, and recognizing how much we need the company of other writers in our solitary craft.

Artist's statement

Kitty Widjaja

The art of this year's *emerge* cover was inspired by the connection between the mineral rejuvenating aspect of an onsen (a Japanese hot spring), emerging anew from these waters, and the emerging writers in the publication. The artwork was conceived in Vancouver, drafted using paper and pen, then completed on a laptop while travelling across Japan via the Shinkansen (bullet train). Each train stop provided a new element for the final image. The tree, which sprouts from the typewriter, reflects the growth and confidence TWS graduates take away from the program. While the typewriter is an iconic symbol for writing, turning it into a environmental setting illustrates how writing is not merely words on paper, but an experience—writing borrows from life, and influences it too. The story is a space that writers populate with characters, and that readers and/or viewers give meaning to—each will have a different interpretation; it is a place open to many states and emotions. This piece highlights the meditative, healing, exploratory, and at times magical aspects of writing.

Kitty Widjaja is a graphic designer and illustrator of multicultural descent, and a TWS graduate, 2016. Kitty's illustrative style takes inspiration from graphic novels as a form of storytelling through image.

Elzevir A*a* Q*q* R*r*

The interior of *emerge* is set in DTL Elzevir. Originally created in the 1660s, Elzevir is a baroque typeface, cut by Christoffel van Dijck in Amsterdam. As noted in Robert Bringhurst's *The Elements of Typographic Style*, baroque typography thrived in the seventeenth century and is known for its axis variations from one letter to the next. During this time, typographers started mixing roman and *italic on the same line*. The Dutch Type Library created a digital version in 1993 called DTL Elzevir. It retains some of the weight that Monotype Van Dijck, an earlier digital version, possessed in metal but had lost in its digital translation.

The interior of *emerge* is printed on Rolland paper, produced by Rolland Inc, Canada. The cover for *emerge* uses Kalima C1S paper, made by Tembec Inc, Canada. Both papers are Forestry Stewardship Council (FSC) and Sustainable Forestry Initiative (SFI) Certified, and are acid free/elemental chlorine free.